"A promising first mystery
of particular interest to readers of Native
American mysteries."

Booklist

"Nifty, X-Fileish without the alien tint, this novel
slyly pulls you in and under, immersing you in an
intricately woven plot…All the delightful
intricacies of this book blend with Native
American culture and form into a delicious romp
of a juicy read. Taste it for yourselves."

Buzz Review News

"Exciting and fast-paced from the very first
pages, When the Dead Speak grabs hold of
readers, thrusting them into a story filled with
intrigue, plot twists, humor, a bit of romance, and
Native American mysticism."

ForeWord Magazine

"The book opens with a bang, literally…It looks
like Tooley has a winner on her first novel and I
look forward to her next, Nothing Else Matters."

Mystery News

"…an action-packed mystery that will garner
much attention from fans who enjoy a police
procedural with a twist."

Harriet Klausen, The Midwest Book Review

Also by S.D. Tooley

Nothing Else Matters
The Second Sam Casey Mystery

....

Written as Lee Driver

The Good Die Twice
The First Chase Dagger Mystery

Coming in October 2000
Full Moon-Bloody Moon
The Second Chase Dagger Mystery

The author is a native of the Chicago south suburbs. Her *Sam Casey* series is set in a fictional suburb of Chicago. The *Chase Dagger* series is set in a fictional suburb of Northwest Indiana.

Available from most wholesalers or call:

BookMasters Distribution
1-800-247-6553

WHEN THE DEAD SPEAK

A Sam Casey Mystery

S.D. TOOLEY

Full Moon Publishing

Full Moon Publishing
P.O. Box 408
Schererville, IN 46375

www.mysterypublishers.com

Library of Congress Catalog Number 98-96463

ISBN 0-9666021-3-7

Hardcover edition / January 1999
Paperback edition / June 2000

Printed in Canada

10 9 8 7 6 5 4 3 2 1

<u>ACKNOWLEDGEMENTS</u>

Many thanks to:

George J. Behnle, Jr., retired chief investigator for the Cook County medical examiner, for his vast knowledge and unlimited resource material in the area of forensics.

William Sherlock of the Illinois State Police Forensic Science Center in Chicago, for taking time out of his busy schedule on numerous occasions to let me pick his brain and for pointing me in the right direction.

Indian Country Today newspaper for opening my eyes to the issues facing Native Americans today.

Chris Roerden for making sure I crossed my t's.

Connie Goddard for her professional advice and friendship.

My husband, Bill. Without his knowledge and expertise, this project might never have been completed.

*"It only takes a few
words to speak the truth"*

Chief Seattle

WHEN THE
DEAD SPEAK

Prologue

Legend says that overcast skies are nature's way of hiding evil, protecting the gods from seeing sinister deeds. So the clouds hovered, suspended by some unseen cosmic force. Even the Chicago winds weren't able to blow the thick clouds away. The sun had tried to make a showing, desperately seeking a flaw in the haze. But it finally gave up as dusk bullied its way in, permitting the sun one brief shining moment before sinking below the horizon.

Like a string of dominos, expressway lights clicked on in succession along the Bishop Ford Freeway. A thunderous crash filled the air. Billows of smoke drifted up, spewing grainey dust in front of headlights, pitting windshields.

In an attempt to avoid another vehicle, a semi had swerved onto the median plowing headlong into the center support pillar of the overpass. The collision had sent the back of the semi fish-tailing into a jackknife. Tires screeched and rubber burned as cars and trucks slammed on their brakes. Loud, shrill horns replaced the sound of the disintegrating column. Chunks of concrete pelted the cab of the semi sending the driver running for cover.

Above the cab wedged under the overpass, the concrete pillar began to change. As if flicking a pesty insect, another piece of concrete dropped away followed by others, pounding out a musical tune on the cab.

A portion of the pillar was taking form, a recognizable shape as it seemed to shrug out of its concrete tomb. Little by little, more of its tomb crumbled away revealing a town's long-kept secret. Fingers clenched tightly, a mouth silently screamed freedom. Eyes wide in terror reflected the victim's last fatal seconds.

Harvey Wilson had a story to tell. And only one person would be able to hear him.

1

Most deals were made in back rooms of cornerstone restaurants after a *Closed* sign had been hung in the window, or behind closed doors in city council chambers away from the public and press. But in the living room of State Representative Preston Hilliard's home, there was more than deals to be made—there was money.

The air was as thick as the wainscoting on the walls and the decor as rich-looking as the socially elite that graced the rooms of the oldest mansion in Chasen Heights, a suburb fifteen miles south of Chicago. One hundred of the most influential businessmen and women had been invited for cocktails and a buffet dinner of entrees which included Maine lobster, crab legs, and filet mignon.

"What's your name, Sweetheart?" A billow of foul-smelling cigar smoke drifted toward Sam's line of vision. She had been inhaling the stench and forcing a smile for the last two hours.

"Enise," Sam replied, pronouncing it *E-NUSS*. She passed the six decks of cards to the distinguished man at third base, the last seat to her right. He winked at her and slid the yellow cut card one knuckle's width from the end.

"You sure do have the prettiest blue eyes," said an elderly man sitting next to the card cutter. His drooping eyes skimmed the length of her white satin cropped top.

The heavyset cigar smoker seated to her left leaned

11

over to view the length of Sam's frame where she stood behind the waist-high blackjack table.

"You think she looks great from the front, you should see her from the back." His laugh came from deep within his water-soaked lungs ending in a coughing spasm.

"Stick your tongue back in your mouth, Judge. We're here to win some money. Deal those cards, Honey." The man front and center hadn't cracked a smile all night, deadpan, with eyes that seemed to cross-examine everyone's movement for a motive. She didn't have to be a brain surgeon to determine his occupation since he had been spewing legalese since he had arrived.

The players had been coming and going throughout the night depending on how long their money lasted. All wearing tuxedos, they congregated around the bar or sat on the floral sofa and love seat. Some wore their tuxedos quite nicely. Some looked as if they had to be squeezed through a steam roller first. They were from all types of businesses and looking forward to making some money. But the odds were against them the moment they walked through the oak-paneled door.

"Well, Enise," the banker said. "Let's see a few blackjacks." Square bifocals rested on the banker's nose. Sam spread out his one-hundred-dollar bills, and expertly clicked out two thousand dollars in black chips from the bankroll. The metal tray in front of her divided the chips by color in their respective denominations—red for five-dollar chips, green for twenty-five-dollar chips, black for one-hundred-dollar chips, and lavender for five-hundred-dollar chips.

"Good luck," Sam told him as she slid the stack of black chips across the green felt. Another belch of foul smoke spouted from the judge at first base. He had spilled more drinks tonight than he had consumed. Sam kept hoping he'd lose his money and leave but he had a royal horseshoe up his butt. The cards were all falling his way. And he was doing stupid things like splitting tens and doubling down on a hard twelve. He seemed to get a blackjack every third hand. And he just got another one.

"YEH!" the doughboy screamed. "Way to go, Anus."

"That's ENISE," Sam said between clenched teeth. *I knew I should have picked a simpler name.* "E-NUSS." Sam clicked out seven hundred and fifty dollars in chips from the bankroll and set them by doughboy's five-hundred-dollar bet. "And you won't get another blackjack tonight if you don't pronounce my name right."

He clamped his teeth over his cigar and in his gravelly voice said, "Okay, Anus." Another phlegmy cough erupted from his throat as his chubby hands grabbed for his chips.

This night will be worth it, Sam kept repeating in her head. Her eyes swept the room looking for the host. He wasn't hard to miss. His eyes were as cold as gun metal with well-defined lines etching a frame around them. Standing ramrod straight, he surveyed the room as though assessing if everyone was worthy of his presence. He had thick silver hair and had been working the room, going in and out, shaking hands, practically campaigning.

Sam couldn't help but notice the Remington statues, and the huge stone fireplace one could almost stand in. She wondered exactly how much money was too much and doubted the words *too much* were part of Preston's vocabulary.

"Hey, Murphy." The attorney waved toward the doorway where a familiar-looking man stood. "Come pull up a chair." Voices and laughter spilled in through the opened door.

Sam couldn't match a name with the well-tanned face, plastic-looking hair, and expensive jewelry. The man ran a hand through his too-perfect shade of brown hair and strolled over.

"You know everyone, don't you, Dennis?" the judge asked.

Dennis, Sam thought. *Dennis Murphy.* The name sounded oh so familiar. She tried to focus on the cards she was dealing as her mind flipped through the filing system in her head.

It was the attorney's voice again. "You all know Captain Dennis Murphy."

"Dealer busts," Sam announced in a voice she hoped sounded steady. She avoided Murphy's eyes as she paid the players. Instead, she was searching for Jackie. Sam had never met Murphy, only seen his pictures, saw his name on several documents at the office. Still, she half expected him to do a double-take and say, "Aren't you Sergeant Samantha Casey?" Of all places for Murphy to show up. But why not? What's a friendly illegal blackjack game among the powers of Chasen Heights.

Sam was somewhat confident Murphy couldn't recognize her. He had never met her, she was wearing a red wig styled in a pixie, and had enough make-up on to camouflage an elephant.

The host moved toward the table. It was more like slithering, Sam thought, his tongue darting in and out, his eyes never blinking as if he were afraid of missing something important.

"Please, join the party, Dennis." Preston pumped Murphy's hand and pulled him toward the table.

"Don't mind if I do." Murphy placed two hundred dollars on the table.

Jackie slid up beside Sam. "Hey, Enise, aren't you about due for a break?" Jackie pulled on the bangs of her short, curly wig.

"You are a lifesaver," Sam whispered, struggling to get her heels back on. Turning to the men, Sam said,

"Monique is taking over. Behave yourselves now."

"Little warm in here, boys." Jackie unbuttoned her jacket and tossed it on a chair. With that one motion, Jackie turned the temperature in the room up another twenty degrees. Talking ceased, heads turned from the bar and sofa. Jackie's cream-colored halter top revealed the largest breasts these men had probably ever seen, except in a centerfold.

Slowly, she tugged on the gold chain around her neck and withdrew a two-inch long gold pendant from her massive caramel-colored cleavage. The pendant was in the shape of a man, like a miniature Oscar statue, if you looked close. But from where the men sat, it looked more like a miniature replica of the male organ.

Jackie flashed her Whitney Houston smile revealing full lips over gleaming white teeth. She kissed the pendant and said, "My good luck piece." With deliberation, she slipped the pendant head first back down her cleavage, using one long talon to tuck it slow and deep.

The banker's bifocals slid down the bridge of his nose while the somber-faced attorney dribbled a scotch and water down his chin. Preston gripped the back of Murphy's chair. The doughboy's jaw slacked. The cigar the size of a tree trunk hung precariously from his lower lip until the weight alone sent it careening down onto the green felt table.

"Let's not burn the table, Sugar." Jackie grabbed a towel from under the table, set the cigar in the ashtray, and rubbed the ashes off the felt, taking her time while her massive breasts swayed heavily from side to side. No one noticed that Sam had left. No one cared. That was the plan.

2

Guests sat at circular tables placed randomly in the ballroom. Some stood near the buffet table snatching bits of paté and caviar or grabbing glasses of champagne from the trays offered by roving waiters.

Wandering through the crowded ballroom, Jake Mitchell and Frank Travis studied the artwork lining the walls, the heavy burgundy drapes framing the windows, and the marble floor glistening under crystal chandeliers. Preston had hired Jake as a security guard for the reception. Jake had asked Frank to tag along.

"They could fit ten precincts in this place," Frank said, his deep, soft-spoken voice resembling a television evangelist's pulpit tone.

"I doubt he loses any sleep worrying about where his next meal is coming from," Jake said. He eyed the guests in their expensive dresses, tuxes, jewelry. The women gave him more than a passing glance back and tried to give Frank their empty glasses as if he were the butler.

"See. Bring a black man to a party and they immediately want you to clean up," Frank quipped. "And this is the best I could do on a Saturday night?"

"What the hell does Preston have here? A harem? I've seen very few men."

Frank studied the portraits hanging like a family tree. "What's the story on Preston?"

"From what I've heard, old man Byron was the CEO

of a rather lucrative import/export company. Byron was going to be the next Howard Hughes. But a boating accident brought those plans to a screeching halt."

"Wife, too?"

Jake nodded, adding, "And there were no other living relatives."

They made their way into the foyer with its cathedral-type ceiling painted with a scene of plump, winged angels. The staircase was wide and winding.

Frank struggled with the top button on his shirt. "I would have never agreed to this if I had known I'd have to wear a tux. I haven't been in one of these since my wedding."

"It becomes you, Frank. You look like one of the Four Tops."

They stepped outside the front entrance for a breath of fresh air. A valet had just pulled up in a black Lexus. Two guests were making an early departure.

The night air was cool for June and dew was already forming on the grass. They watched the tail lights as the Lexus headed down the long driveway.

Jake lit a cigarette. Behind the glow of the match, his thick eyebrows furrowed. The soft wind riffled through his short hair revealing a two-inch long scar near the scalp.

Twisting the cap off a bottle of spring water, Frank said, "I thought you gave those up."

Jake blew the smoke out slowly. "I love giving them up so much, I do it every day. Besides, I only have two cigarettes a day."

Jake peered past Frank's shoulder, watching the security guard inside the door. A man of about thirty in blue jeans and a sportscoat was slipping something to the guard, who then nodded for him to pass.

"Hold it," Jake said through the screen door,

motioning for both the guard and the guest to step outside.

"He's okay. I checked him out." The guard's uniform was strained around his midsection.

Jake flipped open the guest's sportscoat to reveal a camera. "Give him his money back," he said to the guard. Reluctantly, the guard handed the folded money back to the reporter.

"First Amendment rights," the reporter muttered under his breath as he walked away.

"By invitation only," Jake yelled at the reporter's back.

"You've got eyes like a hawk," Frank said.

"Who else did you let buy themselves in?" Jake asked the guard.

"Nobody. He's the only one."

"He better be. Or this is the last security job you'll ever work."

Sam inched her way into the study on the second floor. She had been in Preston's house one other time when he had conducted a secret meeting with local politicians. She had posed as a bartender but spent most of her time snooping. The study had two entrances. One from the hallway, and the other from the master bedroom. Sam had entered from the master bedroom.

Moving past a wall of bookcases, Sam peered around the corner toward the conference table and bar. Just as she had hoped, she was alone. Self-conscious, she pulled on the short white skirt Jackie had forced her to wear. All night she had felt a draft in places not normally exposed to air in public.

She unscrewed the mouthpiece on Preston's desk phone and pressed a tiny receiver inside with the tip of a pen. She stood back from the desk and scanned the bookcases, the credenza against the side wall, the pictures on the wall.

"Okay," she said aloud, "where would I put a safe?" To the left of the mahogany desk hung a large picture of Byron Hilliard. Sam smiled. Feeling the edges, she peered around the side and pulled gently. The picture swung away from the wall on a hinge, revealing a wall safe.

"Just like in the movies."

Thin white gloves protected the surfaces she touched from fingerprints. The digital sensor did its magic and in seconds Sam was pulling out papers and placing them on the desk. Preston also had cash, all one-hundred-dollar bills banded in three separate bundles.

Along with the money and papers were a brown envelope with the word *Capetti* across the front, a large book that looked like an accounting ledger, and a smaller envelope with *A.M.* printed on it. She zeroed in on the small envelope, pulling out the contents. Smiling and breathing a sigh of relief, she quickly fanned through the pictures to make sure these were the ones. Satisfied, she shoved the pictures into her purse and inserted replacement pictures in the envelope. She quickly took pictures of the items from the safe.

When she gave the safe one last check, a gleaming object caught her attention. She reached in and picked up a lapel pin, about an inch-and-a-half wide, three-quarters-of-an-inch high. It was heavy for its size, gold or gold-plated, and shaped like a lightning bolt.

She caught a faint whiff of something unfamiliar, an odor that was musty, indistinguishable. She wrapped her hand tightly around the pin. *Lightning strike.* The words echoed in her head but meant nothing to her. For a brief moment she had a vision of dirt darkened with blood, the smell of gun powder, a flash of body parts. It was the body parts that made her gasp and drop the pin.

Muffled voices came from the hallway outside the door. She quickly placed everything back in the safe and retreated to the closet just as the door to the study opened.

Carefully, she edged the closet door open. Feet padded across the carpet and a button was pushed on the phone.

"Sorry to put you on hold, Av. I didn't want to take the call downstairs," Preston said. "Where are you? The party's almost over."

"Sorry. My meeting in Springfield took longer than I expected. I couldn't get away." The caller's voice drifted from the speaker phone.

"That's not good. I wanted you to make the announcement tonight at my reception. Are you backing out on our deal?"

"I don't care to talk..."

"My phone in the study is secured and there's no one in the room with me."

Sam could hear the caller inhale deeply. Worse yet, she recognized his voice. She could see a portion of Preston through the partially-opened closet door. He was sitting at his desk, an arrogant smile plastered on his face.

"It's bad enough you're pressuring me into this. The least you can do is let me pick the time and place."

"All right," Preston said. He turned the pages on his calendar. "Pick it now."

"Come on..."

"Pick it now." Preston's voice was even, sharp. "And this time it better be kept."

Sam could hear the caller's shallow breathing, the sound of pages being turned. "July nineteenth. Take it or leave it," the caller said.

Preston threw his pen across the room. "July?" Preston forced a laugh. "I don't think you're in a position to bargain."

"I'll be in town next week. If you're available, I'll stop by to discuss it further. I can't talk right now."

"Fine." Preston hung up, leaned back in his chair and gazed out the window for a few minutes. Turning back around, he reached under his desk. Sam heard the press of a switch. The computer started to hum, the printer beeped.

Preston pounded the keyboard muttering unintelligible remarks. A sinister smile formed on his face. "You deliver on July nineteenth, or July twentieth will be the end of you and your career, just with the press of a button."

Preston straightened his tie, gave his computer one last command, and left.

3

When Sam heard the office door close, she emerged from her hiding place. Checking the computer screen, she noticed that the menu was filled. Preston seemed to have purchased every on-line service available. In the bottom right-hand corner she saw the icon of a lock and key. Her curiosity piqued, she moved the mouse on the icon and clicked.

A question on the screen asked: *PASSWORD*. Sam exited the program and returned to the menu. She pressed the *SCREEN PRINT* key and waited for the page to come off the printer. She folded up the copy and just as she was placing it in her purse, noticed a movement out of the corner of her eye.

"Security," the man said. "Move away from the desk, slowly." He was tall, tuxedo-clad, and aiming a 9mm pistol at her. His eyebrows slowly formed a brown line across his forehead.

"I just wanted to use the phone. There's no need to point..."

"Keep your hands up." The unsmiling eyes and ruddy complexion were almost as threatening as the gun.

Sam rolled her eyes toward the ceiling. This guy was taking his job way too seriously. He probably didn't even know how to use the gun. She imagined him spending his nights as a bouncer in some dance club looking for wiry accountants to bounce off the walls. Anyone who had to spend his Saturday night playing bodyguard to Preston Hilliard led a sorry life. The thought of swiping the Nambe silver ashtray off the desk just to aggravate the hell out of this guy crossed her mind. But he had that stern look in his eyes that said, *not on my watch you don't.*

"Identification." He rippled his fingers back and forth in a *gimme* gesture as he backed up to the door.

Great. She didn't have any on her, not even a driver's license, which was in the glove compartment of her Jeep. The security guard put his hand on the door knob and opened it slowly, as though getting ready to call for assistance. That was when she bolted.

Back inside the closet, Sam slid the back wall open and ran down the stairs. Her right hand retrieved a small flashlight from her purse. Pressing the button, she lit up her path of flight.

But she wasn't alone. She heard footsteps on the stairs behind her and suddenly remembered why she hated wearing heels. Now she was grateful that her skirt, or lack of one, allowed her room for movement.

She ran to the same freight delivery door she had used in the past and in seconds was hit with the dewy smell of fresh air as it opened into the backyard. Seconds after exiting the door she heard her pursuer. She didn't have to see him, she could hear him breathing, hear his footsteps. And he was a lot quicker than she gave him credit for.

The backyard was bathed in soft moonlight. She felt damp grass under her feet. Suddenly, strong arms reached around her and a weight slammed into her as she was tackled from behind.

She cried out as she hit the ground. He was up on his feet in a split second. Rolling over on her back, she propped herself up on one elbow and gazed up at the security guard looming over her. His eyes were glued to her legs. When she looked down, she saw her skirt within two inches of being totally obscene.

Maybe the frail female bit might work about now. She slid her hand down her leg. "I think I sprained my ankle," Sam whined.

One eyebrow on her pursuer shot up. He reached out a hand to her and said, "Get up."

So much for the *Pitiful Pearl* routine. Alternate approach needed. She guessed him to be about two hundred, maybe two hundred and ten pounds. But he had broad shoulders, probably into body building. Would not be easy to handle unless she caught him off guard.

She reached for his outstretched hand. As he started to lift her off the ground, she clamped her left hand on top of his and pulled. Her properly placed heel against his chest aided in flipping him over on his back.

He landed with a thud and a "whoooaaa." She didn't wait around to see if he had broken anything. Grabbing her purse, she ran toward the front of the house by the employee parking lot, away from the main lot and front entrance.

Once inside her Jeep, she scrunched down behind the wheel and watched the front door to the mansion. She closed her eyes briefly and tried to catch her breath. Glancing over at the passenger seat at her purse containing her camera and pictures, she said, "I hope you're worth all this."

"Hey, you okay?" Frank helped Jake to his feet.

Pressing a hand to his stomach, Jake limped along the sidewalk to the front of the house. "Getting away," he breathed hoarsely.

On a bench in front of the entrance sat a parking attendant. Earphones protruded from the sides of his head as his entire body be-bopped to a phantom tune.

"Hey, buddy." Frank tapped the valet on the shoulder. "Did you see anyone run by here in the last couple minutes?"

"Excuse me?" The attendant pulled off the earphones. Frank repeated his question. "Sure, people have been leaving in droves."

"Great," Jake said. "Just fuckin' great."

"What the hell happened?" Frank asked.

Jake leaned over to catch his breath. "I caught someone in Preston's office, trying to access his computer."

Frank followed Jake around the back of the house to the basement. "Where are we going?"

"I'm just curious to see how the intruder found this entrance."

Frank followed his partner up the narrow staircase leading to Preston's closet. "Damn. Someone knew his way around this place." Once in the light of the office, Frank saw Jake's torn sleeve and grass-stained pants. "Hell, that guy really decked you."

"I only wish it was a guy. Him I could have handled." Jake walked over to the bookcase and removed two figurines. He poked a finger through an opening on the bottom right side of the back wall. By pressing a button, a small green light turned to red.

A deep rumble started in the back of Frank's throat. "A frail little lady did this to you?"

Jake flipped down the back of the shelf exposing a video recorder. Attached to the ceiling above the bookcase was a surveillance camera.

"Frail. Shiiiit. She was a goddam she-devil."

Frank pounded the wall and let out a ruckus laugh.

"A woman got the best of Jake Mitchell?"

"That woman," Jake said, as he popped out the

videotape and replaced it with a blank one, "was here for more than just the purpose of using the telephone."

He slipped the videotape into the inside pocket of his tux. His mind flashed back to the woman, the short skirt that had revealed the longest legs he had ever seen, and the most intense blue eyes which seemed to pierce right through him.

They returned to the foyer and followed the hallway toward the kitchen. They located Juanita, Preston's housekeeper.

"Mr. Hilliard?" With her slight accent, it sounded more like *meester heelerd*. Her black dress fit snugly around her petite frame. "He is in the living room. But I don't think he wants you to disturb him."

"We'll take our chances."

Juanita trailed after them. Jake pushed his way in without knocking. He saw the blackjack table and paused.

When Frank saw the attractive, buxom dealer, his eyes glazed over. "Lordy, lordy, am I glad I'm married." He elbowed Jake. "I AM glad I'm married, aren't I?"

A familiar figure turned away from the table. It was Captain Murphy. "Have a problem, detectives?"

Jake didn't reply. He just let his eyes float over the faces of the guests, the councilmen, Judge Becker, some high profile attorneys.

"You have got to be kidding." Jake stared at Murphy. Although Jake himself had engaged in friendly poker games, the fact that Preston had introduced a strong illegal gambling bill last spring was now laughable.

Preston grabbed Jake's elbow and steered him back to the hallway. He turned to Juanita who was attemping a fast getaway and barked, "Stay." Turning to Jake, he said, "I thought you were instructed to keep an eye on the guests." Preston suddenly noticed Frank's presence. "And where did he come from?" He ran his eyes up and down

Frank's body not taking great pains to hide the disdain on his face.

Jake tried to refrain from going for Preston's throat. He could feel Frank pinching his elbow. "You have a very large house, too much for one person to cover. You put me in charge of security. I hired the number of people I thought were needed."

"Well, a great many of the guests are gone now. You can leave." He turned to Juanita and waved his hand as though he were shooing her away. "Go, go. Make sure those illegal aliens you hired for this event aren't stealing me blind." He disappeared behind the oak door, shutting it tightly behind him.

Jake touched the videotape in his pocket and said, "What an arrogant sonafabitch. Remind me to never work for this ass again." As he turned to leave, his cellular phone rang.

4

"Beautiful job. What do you think, Frank?" Jake stepped back from the encroaching dust clouds, brushing his hands against his pants.

"It's about a nine on my scale," Frank replied.

They stepped gingerly through the debris covering two lanes under the 130th Street overpass. Frank flicked the rock dust from his short-cropped Afro. "Yep, this one's a keeper. Department of Transportation is going to love it."

In front of them was a jackknifed semi, its cab wedged against the center support beam, its trailer blocking the northbound lanes of traffic. What had started out as just an accident report had turned into a homicide once the body had been discovered.

High-beam lights had been positioned around the crash site turning darkness into day. Overhead a news helicopter circled, directing its spotlight on the semi. Jake motioned at a beat cop whose thick, curly hair snaked out from under his cap. "Rizzo, move your car around this mess and keep that reporter from getting anywhere near the scene."

Access to the 130th Street exit had been blocked by police barricades. Rush hour traffic had ceased hours ago and only emergency vehicles were on the road.

The two detectives walked over to the driver of the semi. He was holding a Bulls cap in one hand while the other hand scratched his sweat-soaked tee shirt. An entire Lionel train from engine to caboose was tattooed up one arm, disappearing under his shirt.

"Looks like you had a bad day, buddy," Frank said.

The driver nodded. "I had a gole dern Vette, shit ass excuse for a car, cut me off. Had to slam on my brakes." He punctuated his disgust by spitting out a wad of tobacco.

Their gaze followed the landslide of rock and gravel, up the concrete pillar to just below where it connected to the overpass. Enough concrete had broken away to reveal mummified remains, human, perfectly preserved.

"After seven years in homicide, you'd think I had seen everything," Frank said.

"Ain't that a damn sight?" The truck driver ran a forearm across the beads of perspiration on his face and turned to the detectives. "So...do ya think we found Hoffa?"

5

Sam stood on the patio, her hands wrapped around a glass of wine. The humid, evening breeze was doing its best to dry her long, thick hair.

It had taken a hot, fifteen-minute shower to wash what felt like a pound of make-up off and bring some life back to her natural sun-streaked brown hair. Clad in a roomy sweatshirt, her favorite jeans, and a comfy pair of moccasins, she looked up at the stars as if seeking answers to what had gone wrong tonight. At what point did she start to lose control?

Her right hand followed the leather strap around her neck down to a small leather pouch. With a firm clasp she nestled the pouch in her right hand. It was a medicine bundle, a gift from her mother on her twenty-first birthday. It contained sage, pipestone, tobacco, and her umbilical cord and was believed to keep the wearer safe from harm.

Taking a swallow of wine, she thought back to the security guard who found her and wondered where he was from. With any luck he wasn't local.

Lowering herself onto the chaise lounge, Sam picked up her cellular phone and called her client.

"I have them," she told him.

"Thank god," he said softly. "I'll be in town soon."

Sam hung up feeling pleased with herself. Preston can find some other sucker to blackmail now.

Her cellular phone rang. It was Jackie. "Hey, girlfriend. How did things go?" Jackie asked. Sam told her about the fiasco in the study. "Maybe that's what all the commotion was about. Some security guards rushed in to talk to Preston. He escorted them out to the hallway. Did you find what you were looking for?"

"Yes." Sam smiled. "And my client is thrilled."

Jackie Delaney was perhaps the closest friend Sam had, next to her mother. Sam had to pull her share of street duty in her novice days. It was Jackie who showed her how to apply the makeup, how to dress and look the part. Jackie wasn't just a hooker. Back then she was a classy, high-priced call girl. There were oil sheiks who had paid five thousand dollars just to have Jackie on their arm for the night.

"How was the night for you?" Sam asked.

"Oooooweee, baby," Jackie squealed. "I made a little over twelve thousand dollars. Those puppies couldn't even pee straight let alone count their cards. You sure you don't want part of it?"

"No, thanks. You were helping me out tonight. I'm not going to cut in on your action. What about Preston?"

"The old fart wanted me to spend the night. His wife is out of town and he was going to make it worth my while. I just took twelve thousand dollars off of his buddies. How is he going to make it worth my while?"

They said their goodnights promising to meet soon for lunch. Sam was glad Jackie was into a different line of work, even if it was a shade illegal. But Jackie and her connections came in handy. A friend of Jackie's had given them both a crash course on dealing blackjack a couple years ago. Sam was able to infiltrate an illegal gambling ring that had netted over a million a week. The cops got the money and the men. Somehow the blackjack equipment was missing one table and a rack of chips.

Talking to Jackie felt good, better than the wine. But then Sam remembered the security guard and that queasy feeling crept into her stomach again. She poured herself another glass of wine and sank back against the cushions.

6

Mondays were press day for Chief Don Connelley. Reporters had been coming and going most of the day. Connelley was a walking Old Spice commercial from his tanned skin to his full head of well-sculpted gray hair which was slightly whiter at the temples.

Sam sipped her tea as she watched the sideshow through the plate glass partition. The reporters jockeyed for position, trailing behind Connelley and dragging their camera crews and equipment down the carpeted hallways lined with potted ficus trees and pink-leafed caladiums.

Connelley didn't mind. Some people believe he plans it that way. Because on the six and ten o'clock news the citizens of Chasen Heights could see their tax dollars at work in the form of solid oak paneling and chair rails, textured wallpaper, and thick wall-to-wall carpeting. No one would dare tell him that the taxpayers were more interested in additional police and updated weapons to keep up with the gangbangers.

Chasen Heights was mainly a blue-collar town. It hugged the southern border of Lake Michigan just fifteen miles south of Chicago. On a clear night you could see the Chicago skyline from the lake shore. Chasen Heights, whose population was just under fifteen hundred in 1922, had grown close to one hundred thousand. It boasted two golf courses, three high schools, and the second largest shopping center in the state.

Sam's reflection glared back at her through the glass. She had her father to thank for her natural curly hair, which she kept tamed only by pulling it back in a banana clip, and her mother to thank for her high cheekbones.

Connelley's head swiveled toward Sam's office. She attempted to make a quick departure for the day, pulling out her tote bag from the bottom desk drawer. A police scanner, sitting on the oak credenza behind her desk, emitted a weathergirl-type voice belonging to Lydia, the night dispatcher.

Sam tuned out the mundane traffic accident/ suspicious character/false burglar alarm calls. One day seemed to be a repeat of the previous day's calls. But the most interesting call was from Saturday night. Fire Department crews were still chiseling the body out of the concrete pillar. It was a long, painstaking process. Sam had driven by the scene yesterday but the crew wouldn't let anyone near who wasn't wearing protective clothing. And, the crew had to be careful not to destroy any part of the body.

"Sam, glad I caught you." Chief Connelley closed the door behind him. She reluctantly sat down as he settled into a chair across from her.

Sam smiled, her blue eyes flashed, and when she tilted her head her third earring of beads and feathers swayed slightly, brushing against her shoulder.

"Did you hear about the body in the overpass?"

"Not your jurisdiction, Sam. How's your mom?"

"Fine." Her smile slowly faded. This was it. He waited until the end of the day to tell her about Preston. "If it's about my report, it will be on your desk by tomorrow morning."

An uncomfortable silence filled the air. Connelley reached into his pocket and pulled out a picture. "Recognize anyone?"

She studied the picture. It showed two waiters and a waitress carrying platters of drinks and food. The waitress wore a French uniform and what looked like a doily for a hat. Her hair was short and platinum. Sam blushed. It was one of her self-directed undercover jobs from two weeks ago.

"Right," Connelley said. "Seems you didn't think that Mayor Jenkins might have surveillance cameras in his house. You are just lucky he didn't recognize you."

"Would you have?"

Connelley ripped the picture into numerous pieces. "Maybe not at first but I've become accustomed to being suspicious whenever you look bored." There was a slight twinkle behind his clear blue eyes.

"I'll just have to be more careful next time."

Connelley shook his head. "No, you are not, young lady." He held up a finger to stop her from interrupting him. "I wasn't born yesterday. Don't think for one minute I believe this is your first charade."

"Where else do you think I got all the dirt I reported to you?"

Connelley scooped the pieces of paper into the garbage can. "Things have changed. Once your face starts showing up on camera and the mayor asks me to check it out, I know it's time to rein you in. My god, Sam. What if he gave the pictures to the FBI rather than me?"

"My disguises always worked before. I'll just lay low for a while."

"Honey, you're not listening." This time he didn't hide the impatience in his voice. He tugged at the cuffs of his shirt.

Sam stared at those cuffs, admired the fourteen-carat gold cuff links in the shape of bullets. Connelley followed her gaze.

"Your father always did have good taste." He and Samuel Casey had been college roommates, were best man at each other's wedding. Chief Connelley was her godfather and had taken her under his wing since she graduated from the police academy five years ago. Although he claimed he had nothing to do with it, she was promoted to sergeant before her twenty-fifth birthday. "I'm trying to keep you out of harm's way, Sam. I promised your father."

She should have been thankful for his concern. But all she could muster was, "There must be some hidden agenda here, Chief."

"Things have changed now, Sam. Jenkins told me I have a good chance of getting the commissioner's job. Something like this..." His face took on a pained expression as he added, "Hon, face it. You've been bored here. I really think you need to spread your wings. It's for your own good."

"Sounds more like it's for YOUR own good." The words stung but she could see in his face that nothing she said was going to change his mind. Connelley scribbled a name on a piece of paper and shoved it toward her. Her mind wandered, catching the gist of his speech, like how he felt it best she be transferred to Precinct Six effective tomorrow, and she should report to the captain whose name he had written on the piece of paper. It was for the better, he droned on, and he was sure she would understand. Instead, she was thinking of Preston's reception and the security guard. Her gaze drifted to the piece of paper where Connelley had scribbled the name, Captain Dennis Murphy.

7

By the next morning, crews had successfully removed the body from the concrete pillar. Just as Jake and Frank were ready to leave for the medical examiner's office, Murphy appeared.

"In my office," Murphy barked at the two detectives. "Jake only," Murphy clarified as the two started to rise.

"We were just getting ready to go to Benny's office." Jake closed the door and sat down.

"This won't take long. I haven't had the chance to commend you for making an ass out of yourself at Preston's reception Saturday night."

"Sorry. I thought I took an oath to uphold the law."

Murphy slowly lowered himself into his chair. "I've been more than patient with you. You're showing signs of burnout, drinking too much, and you just don't seem to have that enthusiasm anymore. Your chances of being promoted are remote, at best." He smiled as though the very thought delighted him.

"Two beers after work is hardly the makings of an alcoholic," Jake spit out.

Murphy arched one thick brow saying, "You have three in your car before you even leave the parking lot, Detective. Care to try your math again?"

Jake crossed his left ankle over his right knee. Murphy gazed at Jake's gym shoes. Jake was a firm believer in following rules. But he never met a man he

despised more than Murphy, and any way he could find to
irritate the hell out of him, he did. Like refusing to wear
a suit every day. The only reason he wore as much as a
sportscoat was to conceal his belt holster. He preferred
comfortable polo shirts or jersey pullovers, anything that
didn't require a tie. And seeing Murphy cringe every time
he wore his gym shoes brought one of those rare smiles
to his face.

Murphy folded his hands over a manila file folder.
His skin was leathered from the tanning spa, causing deep
crease lines to form around his eyes.

"Your file is impressive. Five years with the FBI,
seven years with CHPD. It seems once you moved from
FBI to police work, your enthusiasm went right down the
toilet."

"All this because I almost halted Preston Hilliard's
illegal blackjack game?" Jake challenged.

Murphy's eyes narrowed. "I could bust you down to
writing tickets if I wanted to. But I need your skills. The
chief is transferring one of his people here, a Sergeant
Sam Casey. I think Casey is a plant. Connelley would like
nothing better than to see me out of here. But I'm going
to stay two steps ahead of him. I want you and Frank to
work with Casey. I'll let Mick know that I want you to
have every opportunity to redeem yourself. I want to
know anything remotely suspicious Casey is working on.
If you can do that, I'll see to it you make sergeant."

Jake's radar went on high alert. Murphy had an
agenda and Jake's suspicions and curiosity were kicking
into overdrive. Jake studied him the way he would a
suspect. "What makes you think I WANT to make
sergeant?"

"EVERYONE wants to make sergeant."

"What if I don't come up with something?"

Murphy leaned over his desk, close enough for Jake

to smell his morning cups of black coffee. "Then you are free to do anything necessary to guarantee that you DO come up with something, if you get my drift."

Jake tightened his jaw, uncrossed his legs and stood up.

Murphy walked him to the door and stuck out his hand. "Good hunting, Detective." Jake looked at the uncallused hand with its manicured nails and walked out.

8

"What do you make of it?" Frank asked Jake as they drove over to the medical examiner's office.

"Goddam prick. He knows how I feel about him. He should make his offer to Brandon Carter. He's the one kissing his ass for that promotion."

"Because Brandon never sees things through. It doesn't take much to sidetrack him."

"I thought I left the bullshit back in D.C."

"Same bullshit, different bull. Besides, Brandon has been pretty vocal about getting into Internal Affairs."

"I don't like owing people, especially Murphy, him with his twelve-hundred-dollar suits and ostrich shoes."

Frank pulled into the crowded lot next to Headquarters. An enclosed walkway over the lot connected Headquarters to the County Medical Building. They parked near the rear of the building and walked around to the front entrance.

"It's no secret he's had it in for Connelley ever since the mayor gave Connelley the chief position over Murphy." Letting out a chuckle, Frank added, "All those connections didn't do Murphy one damn bit of good. You gotta love it."

"And then his damn comments about my drinking..." Jake mumbled.

"Well," Frank started, "you do kinda..."

Holding up a hand like a warning sign, Jake said,

"You don't want to go there, Frank. You take care of Claudia and Justin. I'll take care of me."

An uncomfortable silence hung like a curtain between them. Jake started to despise Sister Lucia from grammar school who had a way of ingraining guilt and shame in her students, sometimes for doing absolutely nothing. The case of the guilts that just grabbed him by the neck and throttled him had Sister Lucia's fingerprints all over it.

Frank took the hint and changed the subject. "Find out anything about the mystery thief in the video?"

"Nothing yet. None of my contacts knows anyone fitting the description. Even Juanita wasn't much help. There were a lot of wives and girlfriends there. I guess they all look alike to her."

Frank laughed that deep laugh that seemed to start at the base of his throat. "That was no wife or girlfriend," Frank said. "That lady was good, a pro. Someone has to know her."

9

King Tut stood propped in the corner of the examining room like an archeological find. Long, fluorescent bulbs lined the tall ceilings giving the starched white tiled floor and walls an even more sterile appearance.

Benny Lau smiled like a proud father. Benny had been the chief medical examiner for the past fifteen years. Small, dark eyes rested under a helmet of jet black hair. His deep olive complexion shielded his skin from the typical aging signs of a man just reaching fifty.

"Unbelievable!" Sam couldn't take her eyes off of the monolith. She detected a pungent odor drifting from the body and waved a hand in front of her face.

"Adipocere," Benny explained. "Due to chemical changes, the body turns to soap, literally. It's the fatty acids from the hydrolysis and hydrogenation of body fats after death that gives it the odor."

Something other than the odor, however, was overpowering her. It was the aura. She had felt it the moment she stepped into the room. That's usually when it is the strongest. Right after the person dies. In this case, King Tut's death aura had been entombed with him.

Sam moved toward King Tut. "May I?" she asked Benny as she started to place her hands on the body.

* * *

Frank signed their names to the log at the reception desk. A young woman with porcelain skin and China-doll features glided gracefully over to the desk. The name on the badge clipped to her white lab coat said *Tamara*. She looked at their names and with a lilting voice said, "Doctor Lau is expecting you."

Jake carried his sportscoat hooked on the tip of his finger. They walked past empty, pristine offices crammed with computers and filing cabinets.

Benny's office was at the far end of the wide corridor. Stacks of reports cluttered a conference table. Two file drawers stood gaping, file folders left slanted like large Post-it™ notes.

Two of the walls were plate glass giving a full view of both the large gymnasium-sized examining room and the smaller room where King Tut stood. The intercom into the smaller examining room was on while Benny's voice and an unidentified female voice filtered through the air.

Jake studied the woman whose back was to them. Her mass of untamed hair was pulled back in a clip. She wore a white lab coat but there was something familiar in the curve of those calves and the tone of her voice.

Sam approached King Tut. Only the front portion of the body was exposed. The back side was still wearing a thin concrete jacket. The right arm hung straight at the side while the left arm rested across the chest. Pieces of skin, brown and leathery, hung like sheets of phyllo pastry.

Fragments of clothing appeared well preserved but fragile. When her fingers touched what looked like a plaid shirt, the weaker sections of cloth crumbled in her hand.

Gingerly she touched the concrete framing the

corpse. Her hand rested on top of the skull, holding it there for several moments like a mother feeling a child's forehead.

"What on earth is she doing?" Frank whispered.

"I don't know." Jake turned the volume up on the intercom.

Sam closed her eyes. Immediately she saw lightning bolt shapes, smelled gun powder, blood. It all overshadowed the odor from King Tut. He spoke to her. Out of his gaping mouth she heard the screams of battle, of war. She sensed fear, terror.

Sam jerked away, stepped back from King Tut.

"Are you okay?" Benny placed a hand on her shoulder.

"Nothing that a little air won't cure." Studying the deceased, she wondered what kind of horrors this man had suffered. "He died about fifteen or twenty years ago, maybe longer." Sam peeled off the latex gloves. "And I believe he knew his killer."

Behind the plate glass window, Jake and Frank exchanged glances. Jake raised an eyebrow in skepticism. Frank's eyes widened; he checked to see how high up the hair on his arms was standing. Benny waved them in.

"Jake, Frank, have you met Sam Casey?" Benny asked.

Sam turned and felt the blood slowly drain from her face. The tousled hair, ruddy complexion, and those interrogative eyes—there was no doubt he was the security guard from Preston's.

Frank stood a couple of inches shorter than his partner, eyes lively and animated. His full lips formed a wide smile.

"Sergeant Sam Casey?" Frank almost seemed to laugh. And then he did, starting with a deep rumble in the back of his throat.

"You three know each other?" Benny asked.

"No," Frank replied. "It's just that we didn't know our new sergeant was a...woman." That low rumble started up again.

He had a contagious laugh and Sam couldn't help but smile. She also couldn't help feeling that a little private joke was going on between Jake and Frank.

Circling King Tut, Jake said, "Damn, ain't he a sight."

Sam exhaled slowly. Maybe Jake's memory bank came up empty.

Jake glanced at King Tut's face, studied the bone structure. "African American?"

"Yes." Benny pointed with a pen to King Tut's eyes. "The eye sockets are farther apart and rectangular-shaped. And there's a little thrust to the lower jaw."

Leaning against a stainless steel sink, Sam folded her arms in front of her and watched them.

Jake walked behind the body again. Sam could feel his eyes on her. She kept her eyes on Benny.

"Any guess yet, Benny, on how he died?" Jake asked.

"We'll run him through the CAT-scan. I prefer not to dissect this gentleman if at all possible." Benny turned to Sam and said, "Of course, Sam might be able to save us a few steps. Sam?"

"This was definitely a hit. No bullets, no knives. They buried him up to his neck just to watch him squirm and then covered him completely. He was buried alive." She spoke matter-of-factly, letting her eyes glance at Jake and Frank only long enough to get their reactions.

In a condescending tone which irritated her, Jake said, "If it's all the same to you, I'd just as soon wait for the CAT-scan."

Sam shot a piercing gaze his way. "I'd say he's been dead about..."

Jake cut her off in midsentence. "The overpass was reconstructed about twenty years ago." He turned back to Benny. "What about fingerprints?"

Straightening up from his close inspection of the body, Frank asked, "You can get prints off a corpse entombed all these years?"

"Sure. The most successful method for mummified remains is the use of disodium ethylenediamine tetracetic acid in a saturated solution of Coleo."

"How long will that take?" Jake asked.

"With luck, twenty-four hours. We'll also get dental and DNA."

"You can still get DNA outta this guy, too?" Frank asked.

"They have successfully extracted DNA from teeth that had been buried for up to eighty years," Benny replied.

A young female intern walked in carrying an object. "Here you go, Doctor Lau."

"Lift any prints off of it?" Benny asked as she laid the pin in the palm of his hand.

"Nothing."

"Our friend here was clutching this in his hand," Benny explained after the intern left the room.

Holding the pin up, Sam could see a similarity to the pin she found in Preston's safe. She wrapped her hand tightly around it. Almost immediately she saw dozens of lightning bolt shapes. The tiny hairs on her body did their own version of the wave as cold swept up her body starting at her ankles. In vivid color, she saw limbs and other parts of bodies lying in a field. *Lightning strike.* The words echoed, the same words, the same smell. Everything was the same as when she touched the pin in Preston's safe.

"Do you know what it is, Sam?" Benny asked.

She shook her head. "I'm not sure...yet." She caught the puzzled look in Jake's eyes, a look she couldn't quite decipher. Taking one last walk around the body, she said, "I would check military records first. I don't believe the deceased had a criminal record."

Jake and Frank shifted their gaze. If she had to place their reactions on a skeptic meter of one through ten, theirs just hit a twenty. But it didn't faze her. It was a typical reaction to which she had become accustomed.

"Do me a favor, Benny," Sam continued. "Don't mention to the press about the pin. I think it might be important."

"Fine with me, Sam."

Frank gazed back at King Tut, searching the body and clothing again as though trying to see where Sam was getting her information.

Reaching behind Benny, Jake picked up a piece of the torn fabric. It was a faded blue plaid. "Any possibility of getting the label off the shirt?"

"I wouldn't count on it," Benny replied. "I'm hesitant to try to chisel any more of the concrete away. I could try. I just don't want to decapitate our friend here. Besides, I think running the prints through military records might be our best bet." He looked around for Sam.

"Where did she go?" Frank asked.

Peering into his office through the plate glass, Benny said, "Probably for some air. She'll be back." He looked at the two detectives and smiled. "You two have never seen Sam in action, have you?"

"In action?" Jake repeated.

Frank's body shuddered. "It gave me the heebie jeebies. How did she know all that stuff?"

Benny leaned closer to them as if he didn't want King Tut to hear. He whispered, "The dead talk to her."

10

"The dead talk to her?" Frank huffed as he carried the video recorder into Jake's apartment.

Jake moved the morning papers to one side and placed the bags of hamburgers and fries on the coffee table. "You've repeated that about twenty times, Frank."

"But she knew how long the body was there."

"She knew how long ago the overpass was built."

Jake slid open his balcony door. Three floors below a young mother was pushing an infant in a stroller. Jake paid six hundred and fifty dollars a month for what seemed like a day care center. Kids outnumbered the adults four to one.

"What about the military? She knew he was in the military."

"It was a lucky guess. Everyone in the military has prints on file. Maybe she recognized the fabric as something one would buy at a commissary. As a process of elimination, it's not a bad place to start. Just don't read more into this."

Frank set the recorder down on the floor in front of the television set. "Okay, how did she know how he died? Buried alive? Benny hasn't even done an autopsy yet."

Taking a seat on the couch, Jake shifted his eyes in Frank's direction and let out a sigh. "Another guess with nothing factual or logical to back it up." Jake opened an envelope and passed several sheets of paper to Frank.

"Sergeant Samantha Casey, twenty-six, happens to be the goddaughter of Chief Don Connelley."

"No shit. This what you stopped off at the office to get?"

Jake flashed him a grin. "Remember that sixty-year-old records clerk who had a crush on me?" Frank nodded. "She's now Connelley's secretary."

Frank studied the personnel records. "You sure you have the right girl?"

"See for yourself." Jake backed up the tape and pressed the PLAY button. "Watch."

"She's bugging the state rep's phone?" Frank asked.

"That's what it looks like."

The screen showed Sam opening the safe, taking out the contents, slipping something into her purse. When she held Preston's pin in her clenched fist, Jake pressed the STOP button.

"My god," Frank gasped. "That's the same way she held the pin in the lab."

"Red wig and plenty of makeup transform any plain Jane into Cinderella. The eyes are definitely the same."

"Not to mention the legs," Frank added with a chuckle.

Jake pressed the PLAY button again. They watched Preston walk in, take a phone call, pound the keys on his computer. Once he left, Sam accessed the computer, printed out a page, and stuffed it in her purse.

"I would be curious to know what she printed off of Preston's computer," Jake said.

"I couldn't help but laugh when I saw who Murphy is paranoid about...a woman. But now I think Murphy might have something to be paranoid about." Frank hooked up his recorder, inserted a blank tape, rewound the tape in Jake's machine, then proceeded to copy the tape.

Jake pulled out newspaper clippings of murder cases.

"Check these out. Press makes her sound like some psychic who just sits behind her desk with a crystal ball."

Frank unwrapped a burger and sat down next to Jake. "You saw what she did with King Tut. I'm telling you, Jake, there's something strange going on."

Jake pulled the articles from Frank and tossed them back into the envelope. "You WOULD be a believer. Your relatives come from a long line of New Orleans voodoo priests." He studied his notes and added, "I did find out something interesting. Seems Connelley received a disturbing photo from the mayor. My source tells me Casey has disguised herself on numerous occasions and shown up at secret political meetings, sometimes as a waitress, bartender. Connelley has looked the other way in the past, even welcomed some of the information she would pass on to him."

Frank's smile broadened. "I think I'm going to like this lady."

"Well, Connelley is up for a big promotion. If his little snitch were to be exposed, Connelley would probably end up writing parking tickets somewhere." After taking a swig of soda, Jake added, "This lady is flying by the seat of her pants. According to Mary, Chief Connelley had a fix on Sam's test scores, threw her into a desk job after only six months. I would bet she couldn't shoot a target if she were standing in front of it."

"I guess patronage still reigns. That shouldn't surprise you." He glanced at the videotape. "So, what's your next step? Are you going to take the video to Connelley?"

Jake ejected both tapes, studied them, then shook his head slowly. "No, I have other plans for this tape."

11

Sam looked down the three rows of back-to-back desks filling the center of the fourth floor at Precinct Six. There weren't any attractive modular units, potted plants in brass urns, or employees dressed in the latest power suits. Just men in sweat-soaked shirts with the sleeves rolled up, and clerical staff casually dressed in skirts or slacks.

Offices lined the outer walls and a file room occupied the farthest corner. No pictures on the walls. No piped-in music. She scrutinized the tiled floor, which was yellowed from age and losing its design pattern to harsh cleansers. She looked at her white, ankle-wrap espadrilles and wondered if they would still be white by the end of the week.

A stale, moldy odor permeated the air combined with a hint of burnt coffee and the lingering body odors from witnesses and suspects who had been shuttled through the doors over the years.

Ed Scofield, the resident desk sergeant, eyed Sam suspiciously over his bifocals as he handed her a new I.D. badge. Reluctantly, she accepted it and clamped it on her collar.

This was not Precinct One, which she was used to. The First was a state-of-the-art building that boasted a full-time cleaning crew who walked around picking up abandoned coffee cups and periodically cleaning the coffee machine.

Dust was not allowed to settle at the First, which was visited constantly by press, public officials, and dignitaries. Even security was tight. You had to be buzzed in by the desk sergeant to gain access. But here at the Sixth, the desk sergeant wasn't always at the front desk. Any drunk could wander in and use the bathroom if someone didn't stop him in time. The thought crossed her mind that maybe the tile wasn't yellowed from age or cleansers. She shivered and pushed that thought out of her head.

The Sixth's jurisdiction included the most diverse neighborhoods, from two-million-dollar homes on its northern boundaries to low income housing apartments to the south. In between comprised a vast melting pot.

As Sam made her way down the center aisle, at least a half dozen sets of eyes were focused on her. Maybe it was the medicine bundle or her third earring of beads and feathers that hung from within one inch of her left shoulder. Or maybe it was just their way of scrutinizing the *new kid on the block*.

She found Murphy's office at the far end of the room. No one was there. It was a little too tidy, suggesting a man who either delegated well or had next to nothing to do. Walls were covered with pictures and plaques. Several manila folders sat near the edge of the desk. A vase of fresh-cut roses sat on the back credenza next to a family picture of a woman with a Buster Brown haircut and two teenage girls who had inherited their mother's plain, just-scrubbed look.

Strolling past the front of the desk, Sam's finger flipped open a file folder. It was hers.

"Sergeant Casey?" Murphy closed the door behind him and looked at the folder.

"Just making sure my name was spelled right." Sam's first impression of Murphy when she had seen him at

Preston's hadn't changed. He looked like a used-car salesman from his all-tooth, fake smile to his picture-perfect hair.

Murphy extended his hand to her. "Welcome aboard, Sergeant. Although I expected you sooner." He glanced at her choice in jewelry.

Sam's smile was just as fake as she grasped his hand firmly. "I was preempted by a homicide." She released her grip quickly. So far, there were no quizzical stares, no *have we met before* questions. "Chief Connelley did tell you I work alone."

Murphy's eyes narrowed. "You're on my turf now, Sergeant. You work with whomever I say." Murphy raised his hand toward a figure in the outer office.

Lieutenant Anderson was in charge of the homicide unit at Six. He was a human Cabbage Patch doll with batteries. His pudgy cheeks were a permanent flush pink and his stomach looked a few weeks shy of eight months pregnant. Papers flew off of desks as he rushed to Murphy's office. Mick didn't have a low gear. Murphy made the introductions.

"Ready for your tour, Sergeant?" Mick asked.

After a half-hour of shaking hands and constantly checking over her shoulder for Jake and Frank, Sam was led to her twelve- by-eighteen-foot office. At least it had windows.

She surveyed her office walls with their numerous nail holes and immediately missed her wallpapered office and hanging plants. Her finger made a trail through the dust on the surface of the wooden desk. After making a mental note to bring in some plants from home, she cranked open one of the windows. Two mourning doves looked up at her curiously. She made another mental note to bring sunflower seeds for her two friends.

Murphy breezed past Sam's door. He didn't look Sam's way, didn't pause with a sudden hint of recollection. Sam breathed a sigh of relief. Maybe she had nothing to worry about.

12

Preston took a long swallow of his Bloody Mary. He leaned back in the throne-high chair in the living room, the evening paper spread out in front of him. He read the latest article on the body found in the overpass. The update wasn't detailed enough for him. He dialed Murphy's home phone.

"Any news yet?...Is your medical examiner done with the autopsy yet?...Keep me updated."

Preston hung up the phone. He scanned the pictures and plaques on the walls. Having served as state representative for twenty years, he was retiring and entertaining the idea of something more powerful, more prestigious. His name had been touted around as a possible running mate for Governor Avery Meacham, seeing as how Lieutenant Governor Arthur Ashburn was returning to private law practice, a decision prompted by his wife's ill health.

Juanita knocked on the door. "You have a guest."

Trailing behind her was a bulk of a man who looked put together by spare parts. His features seemed to have been rearranged on more than one occasion. His head and neck were the same width...a tree trunk with ears. And he walked with a rolling gait, as if his legs hadn't come off the same assembly line.

Cain Valenzio, a former boxer, had street smarts and connections—two attributes in his favor. More than twenty years before, an unknown informant had passed him an envelope containing ten thousand dollars. All he had to do was follow Loren Stuble around for a week and take pictures. Loren Stuble had been Preston's opponent in the race for state representative. Stuble was the incumbent, very popular with the voters and far ahead in the polls. The pictures were of Stuble with a prostitute in a motel in Lansing, Illinois.

Somehow the newspapers received copies of the pictures. It cost Stuble the election. Preston had been more than satisfied with Cain's work over the years.

"Thank you for flying in so quickly." Preston ushered Cain to the sofa and offered him a drink.

"I read the newspaper in the airport." Cain's voice was thick and cottony.

"An unfortunate incident, but things do happen."

"Will you be all right?"

Preston handed Cain a scotch on the rocks. "I'm fine." Preston returned to his throne seat. "I have people on top of it who will let me know the developments. That's why I want you close by." Preston studied Cain's calm demeanor. "You are probably the only person I truly trust."

Cain's fingers started to twitch, just like before a big boxing match. He smiled slightly, revealing too many teeth even for his size mouth. And they were going in different directions.

"I'm here for as long as you need me."

13

The dishwasher hummed silently. Sam sat at the kitchen table deep in thought. The kitchen was large and airy with terra cotta tiled floors and light oak cabinets.

Sam's mother, Abby Two Eagles, stood at the island counter in a long skirt and colorful blouse, her dark hair hanging in a long braid down her back. Abby poured hot water into two cups, placed a cup of tea in front of Sam, then gently stroked her daughter's hair.

"Something is bothering you."

Sam blew at the steam wafting up from the cup. "It's nothing. I'm just stinging from my transfer to the hell hole on the lake."

"Hmmm. Nothing more?"

Abby kissed the top of Sam's head and with her *Indian Country Today* newspaper from South Dakota tucked under one arm, went upstairs to bed.

Sam placed the pictures on the table in front of her. Tim Miesner, the town geek, had dropped them off earlier. With an I.Q. of one-eighty-five, Tim's interests were mainly in computers and the latest technology rather than in sports and girls. Developing Sam's film and inventing listening devices immune to scramblers were more exciting than a homecoming dance.

The letters Preston had in his safe were interesting but vague—some from other state reps offering support for various bills in exchange for his endorsement of road projects, social reform—all cleverly worded so as not to sound suspicious.

She had given Tim the printout of Preston's menu screen but ordered him to study for his finals first. What intrigued her most, what she regretted not taking a picture of, was the pin Preston had in his safe, the one that was a possible match to the one found on a body that had spent its last twenty-one years holding up an overpass on the Bishop Ford Freeway.

The pictures were all starting to blend together. She pressed her fingertips to her head and massaged her temples. Maybe in the morning things might make sense.

She shoved the photos to one side, grabbed her cup of tea, and walked out onto the patio. The landscaping lights flooded the darkened yard with a warm white glow.

She pulled on a sweatshirt over her thin shirt to ward off the damp chill brought earlier by a moving storm front. Uneasiness crept into the back of her throat. Jake had not asked questions, nothing to indicate he knew beyond a doubt that she was at Preston's Saturday night. Maybe he didn't recognize her or maybe he just wasn't sure.

But a nagging voice told her he was a panther, lurking in the bushes, waiting for the right time. She again cursed herself for not being more patient. It was too late now. There wasn't anything she could do to change what had happened.

She finished her tea and turned toward the patio door. That's when the chill washed over her body. Someone was standing at the bottom of the stairs by the house.

"Not a bad bungalow on a cop's salary," the voice said. The figure climbed the two stairs, out of the dark. It was Jake.

Her eyes followed him, watched him as he studied the two-story house, the balcony that ran the length of the house, the expansive flagstone patio. He had a menacing look about him, the same look he had at Preston's...no smile, thick eyebrows, a ruddy complexion that looked as if he were on the wrong side of the bars.

And there was something else. He seemed somewhat regimental, almost too disciplined in the way his eyes deciphered the size of the house, the grounds, even Sam's every move.

When he was done surveying what little he could see in the landscaping lights, Sam asked, "Take a wrong turn, Detective?"

Jake gave a half-hearted smile. "Thought I did. For a moment I thought I was back at Preston's mansion. The damn driveway is just as long as his."

"I wouldn't know."

Jake's smile faded. "I think you do, Sergeant. And I need answers to some questions."

"Is this an interrogation?"

Jake walked closer, saying, "We can do it here, or we can do it downtown."

Sam gave a slight laugh. "You have got to be kidding. What are the charges?"

"I don't know. Breaking and entering for starters." He tossed something clad in a cardboard jacket on the table while his eyes followed her casual movement toward him.

Sam gave the object a passing glance and wondered who he could be working for. Preston?

"What's that supposed to be?" she asked finally.

"Bet you didn't know Preston had a video camera."

She shrugged and said, "State Representative Hilliard? I told you. I've never had the honor of being in his house so I have no idea what you're talking about."

Jake straightened up, shoved his hands in his blue jean jacket. "You don't have to play it now. It's your copy. I have more where that came from, and I'm sure Chief

Connelley would love to know your whereabouts Saturday night."

The hair at the nape of her neck tugged at her nerve endings. "If you must know, I was on official assignment for Chief Connelley."

Jake flipped open his cellular phone. "Why don't I just call Chief Connelley and confirm that." He started to punch in the number.

Sam bristled. "You're on the wrong side of town, Detective."

"And you're on the wrong side of the law, Sergeant."

As though a light flickered inside her head, her eyes seemed to take on a glow, seemed to bore right through him. "You wouldn't be blackmailing me now would you, Mitchell?"

Jake grinned, the kind that tugged at only one corner of the mouth. "Let's just say I'm leaving my options open."

"I'm the last person you want to mess with."

"On the contrary, Sergeant. I'm the last person YOU want to mess with."

Grabbing the videotape from the table, she stormed past him and into the house, slamming the patio screen door behind her.

Jake savored the moment, although he didn't get any answers to his questions. Grinning like a Cheshire cat, he quietly pulled out the chaise lounge and sat down. He was in the middle of a full stretch when a wet spray hit him square in the face. He jumped to a sitting position and was greeted by a woman holding an opened beer can in her outstretched hand. Jake jerked himself to a standing position and smiled at her. He gladly took the beer in one hand and reached out his other hand to her.

"Jake Mitchell."

Her handshake was firm, as was his. "Hello, Jake Mitchell. I am Abby Two Eagles." She grasped his hand with both of hers and held it for several seconds.

"I didn't think anyone would mind. I was just taking a walk around the patio." He finally sat down once she took a seat next to him.

"You work with Sam."

"Yes, and I have to add...it's quite an experience." Jake peered over his beer can at her—eyes dark and mysterious surrounded by lines of wisdom, skin clear and bronzed, cheekbones so pronounced she seemed to be smiling even when her mouth wasn't. Her long, gleaming hair was streaked with sparkling silver. She was average in height and weight although her skirt made her look a little thick around the middle.

"The house looks massive. Does anyone else live here?"

"Just the two of us. Alex lives in the carriage house out back."

"Alex?"

"He does our gardening and handiwork."

"A house out back, too. This place must be something to look at in the daylight." Jake pulled out a cigarette and looked at her for approval. She nodded and handed him an empty can for an ashtray.

"Maybe you would like to stop in sometime and see the house."

"Thanks. I might do that." As he took a long sip from his beer, he noticed a small buckskin pouch hanging from Abby's neck.

She followed his gaze and lifted the pouch. "It is a medicine bundle." She leaned over so he could get a closer look. "It is sacred, a protector. Each is different because each contains something of importance to the individual. Mine has blackgold dust, sage, tobacco, and my umbilical cord."

"You're kidding." He felt the weight of the pouch. "Tell me something, Miss Two Eagles."

"Abby, please," she insisted.

"Abby...Does Sergeant Casey seem a little strange to you?"

"I'm not sure I know what you mean by strange."

He took a long drag from his cigarette, flicked an ash in the empty can. "She looked at a body, touched it, claimed to know how and when he was killed. That is logically impossible."

Abby smiled and said, "Sometimes things cannot be looked at logically."

Abby peered through the blinds by the front door and watched as Jake's car pulled away. She had heard bits and pieces of his conversation with Sam, had studied him as she held his hand on the patio.

At first glance he appeared cold and harsh. But when she spoke to him, his smile gave a devilish twinkle to his eyes. It had been a warm, genuine smile. She had felt the sincerity and gentleness in his touch.

He gave off mixed signals, but she had seen him before. At least six months ago in a vision. It had been on more than one occasion. She was sure of it. The chiseled features, the boyish grin that changed his threatening glare to a mischievous though kind face, and his strong shoulders.

"Finally," Abby said in the darkened foyer as the blinds snapped shut. "I knew you would come."

14

Sam poured water on the miniature rose bush, azalea, and other assorted potted plants on the windowsill in her office. She touched one of the buds on the azalea bush as if coaxing it to bloom. She lacked Abby's and Alex's green thumbs. All of her office plants were usually taken home just before last rites, resuscitated by Abby or Alex, and then returned to her office only to have the whole process repeated again in four to six months.

"Good morning, Sergeant," Jake said. "How did you sleep?"

Sam poured the last of the water on the wilted African violet and glared back at Jake and Frank.

"What's your game plan, Mitchell? I'm not a patient person."

"I am." Jake pulled up a chair and sat down near Frank.

Mick walked in requesting an update on King Tut. He leaned against the door frame while Sam retrieved a file folder.

"We've confirmed that the overpass was rebuilt twenty-one years ago," Sam explained. "The CAT-scan didn't reveal any gunshot or stab wounds. Right now Benny's calling it asphyxiation. He thinks the skin pads should be ready to go to the Crime Lab sometime today."

"I want him to do an autopsy, even if it's a partial," Mick said. He turned to Frank. "Any I.D. on that pin?"

"Not yet. I showed the picture to several jewelry stores but it isn't anything the jewelers recognize. I also checked out Decker Construction who did the work on the overpass. Business has been shut down for quite some time." A wicked smile turned up the corners of his mouth. "Little problem with using substandard materials. Haven't located the owner yet."

Jake clasped his hands behind his head and rocked back on his chair. "Maybe we should check for more bodies in the overpass." This brought a hardy laugh from Frank.

A commotion in the outer office interrupted the meeting. Sergeant Scofield could be heard calling out after a dowdy brunette.

"Aw, jeezus, not again," Mick said.

"What's going on?" Sam asked as they filed out of her office.

"Camille Carter, Brandon's wife. She's made a couple trips here in the past to confront her husband," Mick replied.

"You know the rules, Camille," Sergeant Scofield yelled. "You need a pass."

But the brunette kept walking. Gelatinous thighs stretched the fabric of her yellow jogging suit. Her straight pony tail swayed across her back. When she reached down into the handbag hanging from her right shoulder, every cop in the place reacted to the familiar move and headed for cover.

"Holy, shit." Mick motioned for the clerical staff to get down. The brunette approached to within twenty feet of Brandon Carter, who was bending over a cute blond seated in front of a computer. The blond took off for the safety of the filing cabinets. Brandon looked up, slightly annoyed.

"I warned you, Brandon," she cried out. Camille,

Brandon's wife of ten years and mother of his four children, pointed a .357 Magnum at him.

"Camille, you don't want to do this," Scofield called out.

"Get away," she screamed, "all of you."

"I'm not moving, just stay cool." Scofield stopped in his tracks sending his bifocals bouncing to the tip of his nose.

"You lousy son of a bitch," Camille yelled, a rush of tears streaking down her face.

Sam didn't know Brandon but she knew his type. He had Hollywood good looks and a swagger to his walk. She had seen him earlier in the break room hanging over one of the part-time clerical workers, a petite redhead with green eyes and dimples.

He was a beat cop with aspirations for Internal Affairs. Unfortunately, no one had told him *affairs* didn't mean his own. Seeing Brandon sweat gave Sam a perverse pleasure. She cautiously approached Camille eager to get a front row seat.

Brandon, his face red from embarrassment and anger, slowly raised his hands in front of him. Gone was the arrogant, self-assured smile, the cocky tilt to his head. Even his hair, which was never out of place, lay matted to his forehead by beads of perspiration.

"Just take it easy, Camille. You know you haven't been feeling well lately. Just a little PMS." He tried a nervous laugh to ease the tension. But the room was silent, except for the droning of the ceiling fans.

Camille raised her left hand to help steady the gun. "How the hell should I feel after your high school girlfriend called to tell me the results of her pregnancy test?"

Gasps could be heard from some of the women crouched behind their desks. Scofield maneuvered himself to where he could be seen to Camille's right while Sam approached on Camille's left.

"I've been true to you, Camille." Camille's voice mimicked him. "I've been faithful, Camille." Several sobs escaped her throat. "You lying sack of shit." She squeezed the trigger, sending a bullet directly over Brandon's shoulder and into a picture hanging on the wall. Shards of glass sprayed in all directions.

"Are you nuts?" Brandon yelled, moving away from the desk with sudden boldness.

Sam smiled and casually walked up to Camille, first looking at the gun and then Brandon's nervous face. She placed her left hand on Camille's wrist and lowered the gun until it pointed well below Brandon's waist. "That was a little too high, Camille. I bet if you spend some time at the range, you could improve your aim dramatically."

Some of the observers couldn't contain their laughter. She could hear Frank's deep, resonant chuckle somewhere behind her. Camille's hands began shaking as she started sobbing uncontrollably. Sam took the gun away from her.

Brandon walked over, smoothing his hair down. "Baby, she's lying. You know how these teenagers are," he whispered.

Sam handed the gun to Scofield and turned to Brandon. "All she asks for is a little honesty. You've slept with half the women in this building. Why don't you just admit it?"

Camille let out another sob and sank into the nearest chair.

"Sarge, what are you doing?" Jake asked.

"Stay out of this," Brandon yelled at both Sam and Jake.

"Why don't you just divorce the jerk?" Sam asked.

Camille shook her head, dabbing her eyes with a tissue. "I still love him."

Sam threw up her hands in disgust as Murphy approached, his overpowering scent of aftershave trailing behind.

He shook his head at Sam saying, "You're not even here a week, Sergeant, and already you're causing us grief."

15

Jake and Frank stood on the front steps of Sam's house looking back at the three-hundred-foot-long brick drive.

The home, nestled in a partially wooded area near Lake Michigan was surrounded by a black wrought iron fence with a remote control gate, which Abby rarely closed.

A variety of colors welcomed them in the shape of peonies, potentillas, roses, and spireas. Flowering magnolias and red buds hugged the fence along the brick drive.

Frank let out a long whistle and said, "Shit, I never knew the sarge lived in a mansion."

The house had been constructed with flagstone and a concrete mixture that gave it a stucco appearance. A large overhang by the front door protected them from the noon sun.

"It certainly didn't look this huge last night."

Frank gave him a puzzled look. "You were here last night?"

Suddenly, the door pulled open and Jake found himself staring into the mysterious eyes he had met on the patio.

"Jacob." Abby greeted him warmly.

"Frank Travis, Abby. My partner."

Abby reached out and shook Frank's hand.

"Nice to meet you," Frank said.

She turned and led them into the house. Her patterned

skirt hung to within inches of her moccasins and her printed blouse was accented by some of the most eye-catching turquoise jewelry they had ever seen.

"I'm sorry, Abby. I probably should have called first," Jake said.

"No problem," she replied. "I was expecting you."

Frank gave Jake another puzzled look. He then inhaled deeply. "Damn, somethin' smells good."

"I've been baking."

"This REALLY isn't a good time," Jake apologized.

Abby patted his arm. "I just finished. And besides, I prepared lunch for you."

Jake could feel Frank's quizzical eyes on him. And Jake had no way to explain how Abby knew they would be by for lunch.

The two detectives gave a quick glance up a slightly curved staircase which led from the quarry tile foyer to the second floor.

"I'll just make it a quick nickel tour." Abby led them through four-thousand square feet of pottery, sand paintings, area rugs, Navajo-style upholstered furniture, and windows with remote control blinds. She moved gracefully, as reserved as a First Lady giving a tour of the White House, yet had a casual air about her that made them feel comfortable.

The house had been built thirty years earlier when solid oak flooring and trim were standard. All four fireplaces had been recently converted from wood-burning to gas.

The men marveled at the intricate hand-carved designs on the fifteen-foot-long dining room table, the huge bay windows in the dining room, the restful ambiance of the Florida room.

A fragrant breeze swept through the kitchen from the opened patio door. Jake slid open the screen and walked out onto the massive flagstone patio surrounded by a three-foot high brick wall.

"So this is where I was last night."

"How much land do you have here?" Frank gasped.

"I'm not sure. Maybe seventy-five, one hundred acres. Alex knows the exact figure. There's a pond out back which Alex has surrounded with a variety of wild flowers and natural settings. It's also nice that we are bordered on two sides by forest preserves and one side by the lake, so we have maximum privacy."

Jake turned and faced the house, wondering just why they needed so much privacy. He gazed up at the long balcony which shaded part of the patio.

Frank whistled. "It certainly isn't a house you could buy on a sergeant's salary."

Abby led them back into the kitchen as she explained, "Mrs. Casey's father built this house as a wedding gift. When Samuel and Melinda died, Sam inherited the house. The only expenses are insurance, upkeep and taxes."

It took a great deal of effort on Abby's part to pull Frank from the full-sized gym with whirlpool and Jake from the study with its bar, entertainment center, and Sam's computer terminal which was hooked up to Headquarters.

The tour ended upstairs in the master bedroom. In all, five bedrooms, three bathrooms, and two fireplaces comprised the second floor.

Jake noticed the tape recorder on the coffee table. The red message light was blinking.

Abby checked her watch. "I really should put lunch out or you two will never get back to the office."

"You two go ahead," Jake said. "I'm just going to use the washroom here." He waited until they had left, then walked back to the recorder and pushed the PLAY button.

* * *

Abby stopped at the top of the stairs to catch her breath. She had a better look at Jake in the daylight. He was definitely the one she had seen in her vision. His eyes were the color of doeskin, the softest brown she had ever seen. He was handsome, in a rugged sort of way. She felt as giddy as a schoolgirl. Smiling, she started down the stairs, her skirt brushing softly against the carpeting.

Catching up with Frank she said, "Maybe some night I can have you and Jake and your wives over for dinner."

"My wife would just love to see this place," Frank replied. "We're planning on building a house and I'm sure this place could give her lots of ideas." His hand glided over the solid oak railing as he added, "Jake isn't married."

Abby stopped and looked at Frank. She tried to sound sincere as she said, "Well, he can certainly bring his girlfriend."

"Nope. Jake's kinda a loner these days."

She let Frank pass her on the stairs as she smiled broadly. Without realizing it, she started to whistle.

Jake listened to Preston's voice on the recorder. Preston had received a call from his wife informing him she wouldn't be home for another month.

The second call was from a Bill Simpson, who was looking for votes for a labor bill being introduced. Nothing out of the ordinary.

"My, my, we certainly are talented." Just as his finger touched the eject button he heard the cocking of a gun just above his right ear.

"Don't even think of taking that."

Slowly Jake straightened up, leaving the tape sitting

up in the chute of the recorder.

"Never crossed my mind." He turned and stared down the barrel of Sam's 9mm stainless steel Taurus. He clenched his jaw in anger. "Don't EVER point a gun unless you plan on using it."

She grabbed the gun with both hands. "What makes you think I won't?"

Abby entered smiling. "There you are. I thought I heard you come in. Lunch is ready," Abby announced, appearing unconcerned about Sam's armed threat. As Abby turned to leave she looked back at Jake and said, "Don't look so nervous, Jacob. She never keeps it loaded when she's in the house."

Sam dropped her arms and shot Abby an accusing look. Jake breathed a sigh of relief. With a soft laugh, Abby turned and left.

16

By the time Sam finished her phone call to the Crime Lab and glanced over the daily log, Jake and Frank were already halfway through with their lunch. On the table in front of them were the pictures from Preston's safe.

"Just make yourselves at home," Sam spit out. "Go through the mail in my mail box while you're at it."

"The gym will be fine for starters, thanks," Frank said.

"There's not much here. Exactly what were you hoping to find?" Jake asked.

She gave a shrug of her shoulder in response and took a sip of iced tea.

"Who hired you? Do you have any idea what would happen to your career if you were caught?" Jake tossed the pictures toward the end of the kitchen table.

"I work alone." She threw her napkin on the table and stood up saying, "You ruined a perfectly good dress."

"Dress? What about my tux?" Jake argued. "And we can also talk about my bruised ribs."

"Sounds more like a bruised ego," Frank mumbled.

"And what about Preston's computer?" Jake continued. "What did you print off of it?"

Sam explained the menu and how Preston seemed to be unusually interested in something he had typed after receiving a call.

"Do you know who called him?" Jake asked.

"No," Sam lied. Setting her plate in the sink, she added, "If you were half as good of detectives as you two claim to be you would have noticed something interesting on the videotape. You keep focusing on my being where I shouldn't have been rather than focusing on Preston having something he shouldn't have."

"If you mean the pin, we already noticed it," Frank replied. "They may be close, but we don't know for sure if it connects Preston with the deceased."

"I held it in my hand. The same visions were there as when I touched King Tut in the lab." She looked into their skeptical faces. "I know this sounds crazy to you. But all I can tell you is what I sensed."

Jake walked over to the counter. "What exactly did you...*sense*...when you touched King Tut?"

Sam explained the vision of lightning bolt shapes, the smell of gun powder, screams of battle. The men were silent for a while.

"Why don't we stick with what we know right now. The pin that a presumed murder victim held is the same as a pin owned by our state representative," Jake said.

"Weelll, let's not exclude everything," Frank said slowly.

"Finally, someone with flexibility," Sam whispered, loud enough for them to hear.

"I prefer logic," Jake clarified.

Sam jabbed her fists onto her hips. "Let's try this for logic—Preston had something to do with King Tut's murder. And once we get an I.D. on the victim, I'll shove the logic right down your throat."

17

Sam circled Skip Foley's desk impatiently. He looked up from his phone conversation and signaled that he would be another minute. Skip had been the print technician at Headquarters for the past fifteen years. During his first month on the force, he had tried to break up a fight in a local bar, only to take a bullet in the leg. It shattered his knee cap and left one leg two inches shy of the other. He refused to go on disability. Instead, he trained with the FBI and became one of the best print technicians in the state.

Skip hung up the phone and swiveled his chair around to the computer. Jake and Frank leaned over his shoulder. Sam continued to pace.

"It's a positive match?" Sam asked.

"Absolutely." Skip punched the keys on the computer and pointed to the screen. "Who's the primary?"

Frank jerked a thumb toward Jake. "He always gets the good ones."

"No. I always get the unsolvable ones."

"No case is unsolvable," Sam said simply.

"Military records?" Frank asked eyeing the report coming off of the printer.

Sam ripped off the printout. "Harvey Wilson, born July 10, 1930, in Huntsville, Alabama. African American. Father, James, a postal worker. Mother, Ruby, a homemaker. Let's see," she ran her eyes down the form, "joined the Army out of high school, stationed in Hawaii."

"Not a bad assignment," Skip commented.

"He was part of the Twenty-fifth Infantry Division dispatched to Korea in June of 1951," Sam continued. "Last assignment was to delay the advance of North Korean troops in Mushima Valley." Sam read the rest in silence, then looked up. "He was reported AWOL August 13, 1951."

18

"AWOL?" Frank repeated, as if his mind had been in a fog during the ride back to Precinct Six.

Sam cranked the windows open in her office. Tossing a handful of sunflower seeds on the sill, she clicked her tongue, then called out in a language the two men didn't understand. Immediately, two mourning doves flew over, looked up at her and started pecking at the seeds.

"You're going to have a windowsill full of bird shit," Jake pointed out as he sat down and draped his long legs over Sam's desk, crossed just above the tennis shoes. He pulled out a notepad and started writing.

"Where are you going to start?" Sam asked.

"Try to locate a relative," Jake replied. "The father died twenty-five years ago. The mother died ten years ago. There's a sister, Matilda, who lives in D.C. Frank, I need you to make out a list of the men in his division, his commanding officer. Hopefully, someone is still alive. See if anyone remembers him."

"That's a long time to hide out," Sam said, eyeing Jake's tennis shoes as she sat down. "Do you mind?" He slid them off the desk.

"If I were a guy with the threat of prosecution if the military caught up with me," Frank started, "I would avoid stepping foot back home. I'd probably..."

"Stay in Korea," Jake said.

"Right." Sam picked up her pen and started doodling,

drawing lightning-bolt shapes as she thought back to the pin in Preston's safe. "The pin has stayed out of the papers, right?"

Frank glanced over his shoulder and saw Murphy walking down the aisle. It didn't matter that the door was closed. Murphy walked in without knocking.

"So." Murphy rubbed his hands together. "I hear we I.D.'d the fossil." He said it as if he personally had something to do with it.

Sam eyed him suspiciously, then turned her notepad over. "Yes," she replied.

"I read Benny's preliminary report. Asphyxiation. Horrible way to go." This time he let his eyes rest on Sam, "What's with the pin that was omitted from Benny's report?"

"We're still looking into it," Sam replied. "It could be a key piece to identifying who he might have been in contact with."

"Looks like you have your hands full with this one. Trying to retrace this guy's steps after all this time should keep you busy for a while."

Sam forced a smile. "Which is why I need as much uninterrupted time as possible." Murphy took the hint and left. Sam flipped her notepad over again and stared at the drawings. "I'm personally going to handle finding out how Preston is connected to Harvey Wilson."

"So, you're really going to go through with this," Alex said. He and Abby sat in the shadows on the patio enjoying a glass of iced tea.

Alex's dark eyes were framed in sharp, angular features. His strong body had been toned by judo, a sport he had learned years ago during his two years in the Army. Enlisting had saved him a trip to reform school for siphoning gasoline.

"It is tradition. As Sam's mother it is only right that I choose her husband."

Alex shook his head in disbelief. "She should marry Lakota. Besides, I have watched them, listened to them when I've worked around the yard. They hate each other. You can see it in their eyes," he argued.

"I know I saw him in my vision. Besides, when they are together, all I see are sparks. They are attracted to each other."

"Sparks," Alex muttered. "They are sparks generated by a lot of friction."

Abby raised her hand to silence him. "We will let the spirits decide. You must prepare the sweat lodge. We need large rocks, they hold more heat. And sage. It is important we have a lot of sage."

"I have plenty of sage."

They heard the slamming of car doors from the side drive by the garage followed by loud voices. They watched as Jake trailed Sam up the steps and across the patio.

"Act with your head this time, dammit," Jake yelled. "I don't know how you ever made sergeant. It sure couldn't have been from common sense."

Sam slid the screen open and rushed inside with Jake close behind. "All I want to do is take another look at the pin. Is that so wrong?"

"He has a surveillance camera," Jake added as he slammed the screen shut behind him.

"I can get around it."

Once inside, the arguing continued, although the voices seemed more muffled. Alex shifted his gaze from the house to Abby and said in a dry, humorless voice, "I think we need more sage."

19

By the next morning, the identification of the body in concrete had made the front page of every major newspaper, and the one living relative had been notified.

"Are you sure I can't get you any coffee?" Carl Underer asked.

The elderly woman lifted her eyeglasses to wipe her eyes. She looked well preserved for her seventy years.

She smiled through her tears. "He was such a bright boy, Harvey was. And always smiling." Her face lit up as she spoke of her brother. "That's why we nicknamed him Happy, *Hap* for short." Her bottom lip trembled, the tears fell freely.

Carl walked around his desk and wrapped a consoling arm around Matilda Banks' shoulder. She patted his hand as though he were the one who needed consoling. Mattie had worked for the FBI for thirty years in their Housekeeping Department. She had outlived her husband. Her one and only child, a daughter, had died of leukemia at the age of two. Other than memories, all she had left of Hap was in the shoe box sitting in her lap.

Carl propped himself against the edge of his desk next to Mattie. The morning sun sliced through the blinds, spraying lines of striped sunlight across Mattie's face.

"Do you need help with the funeral arrangements? I'm not sure when they will release the body."

She shook her head no. "I would never ask you for

anything, Mr. Underer. I know you are a busy man. But..." She started to cry again. The shoe box fell off her lap spilling its contents on the dark blue carpeting.

Carl picked up the letters, all with the same handwriting, all with an APO return address. Mattie motioned with her hand for him to keep them.

"I want you to read them," Mattie said. "I never believed the Army when they said he deserted. The Army was his life." Her eyes pleaded, her hand gripped his wrist. Holding back sobs, she cried, "Would you help me? Find out what happened to my brother."

The files from storage sat on the FBI security director's desk. Carl pulled off his horn-rimmed glasses, ran his hand through his thinning gray hair, and rubbed his eyes.

Chasen Heights was a long way from D.C. But if his memory served him correctly—he found the file he was looking for and picked up the phone. When his assistant answered, Carl said, "Book me on a late afternoon flight to Chicago. Reserve a car at the airport and a hotel suite in Chasen Heights."

Carl hung up the phone and opened the file folder. The name on the folder read *Jake Mitchell.*

20

"You read all these letters?" Jake asked Carl as he fanned through the envelopes on the conference table.

"On the flight over." Carl poured two cups of coffee and handed one to Jake.

The suite on the top floor of the Suisse Hotel had a wall of glass overlooking Lake Michigan. Decorated in contemporary European with fine lines and tiny flowers in the furniture, drapes, and wallpaper, the suite screamed *expensive* from every fiber.

"Hope I didn't pull you from that nice warm bed of yours." Carl grabbed reports from his briefcase and slid them across the table.

"Midnight?" Jake laughed. "I can't remember the last time I got to bed by midnight." He leaned back and studied his former boss. Professional and detail-oriented were two words that had described Carl when Jake first met him twelve years ago and the words still fit. Every category of backup material had its own folder labeled in bold lettering. Jake noticed the folders were even alphabetized in Carl's briefcase.

"Do you have any connections in the Pentagon to get us Hap's military records?" Jake asked.

Carl smiled. "Did better than that. I have all the original depositions from the guys in the Twenty-fifth Infantry Division including the commanding officers."

"You've saved me a lot of footwork. Thanks." Jake

studied the list of names. "Was this your war?"

"Please," Carl laughed, "I'm not that old. But I've read a lot about it and I had an uncle who was right on the front line."

Jake took a sip of coffee and winced. "It's a little too late for coffee. Do you have anything that foams?" He walked over to the bar and retrieved a beer. "What did your uncle say?" Jake returned to the conference table.

"Well, it wasn't a pretty sight," Carl replied. "According to what I remember Uncle Paul saying, approximately eight or nine thousand POWs or MIAs are still unaccounted for. Over thirty-four thousand men were reported missing the first week of the war, and that was from the Republic of Korea Army. Our troops were poorly trained and physically unfit. They threw these troops in so quick they didn't even have time to unclog their machine guns or set their sights."

"Sounds more like a suicide mission," Jake said. He gestured toward the stack of letters. "What was the gist of Hap Wilson's letters?"

Setting his horn-rimmed glasses on the table, Carl said, "When he talks about the Army it's like listening to a kid talk about football. He mentions nicknames of some of the guys in his unit. Basically, he was proud, patriotic, for god and country, that sort of thing." He studied the coffee ring in his cup and told Jake about the bond between Mattie and her brother.

"That lady," Carl continued, "would dust my pictures and framed awards. She thought cleaning the office of the FBI security director was the most important job in the world. She would have coffee ready, leave home baked goodies on a paper plate. Everyone loved her."

"Confirmed bachelors bring out maternal instincts in many women." Jake thought about Abby and smiled.

"Tell me about Sergeant Casey," Carl said.

Jake took another long swallow of beer. "She has a great Indian lady for a housekeeper and cook. And Sam's hell-bent on proving that State Representative Preston Hilliard had something to do with Hap Wilson's death."

Carl straighten up at the mention of Preston's name. "What on earth would make her tie Representative Hilliard to Hap Wilson?"

Jake handed Carl a picture saying, "This is what Hap Wilson was holding."

Carl stared at the picture, put his glasses back on and studied it closer. He was silent for a while, then asked, "Any prints?"

"No, we couldn't lift any."

Carl put the picture down. "What does this have to do with Preston?"

"Sergeant Casey found an identical pin in Preston's safe."

21

A dull rhythm jarred Sam awake. Staring at the ceiling, she willed her body to move which was always a chore before nine in the morning. In her sleep, it seemed as if the dull sounds were the exercise equipment calling for her to make one of her too infrequent visits to the pain room. Her feet slowly hit the floor. She struggled into her sweat shorts and top and trudged downstairs.

"Aw, jeezus." Sam pounded the door jamb at the entrance to her gym where Frank and Jake in sweat-soaked gym clothes were working out. "Six in the morning and I get to put up with you two."

Jake climbed off the rowing machine sporting a five o'clock stubble and a look of pain on his face. "God, do you always look this bad in the morning?" Frank gave a half-hearted wave from the stair-stepper.

She stared them down with contempt. Sheet marks lined her face. Her hair was making a desperate attempt to unleash itself from the fabric tie. Jake met her in the doorway, gave a nod toward the room and said, "A lot of dust on those machines." He brushed by her and headed out to the backyard for a jog.

The sun was peeking over the trees. The dew on the wet grass stained Jake's tennis shoes as he made his way to an asphalt path past the gazebo.

He followed along a six-foot-high wrought-iron fence in which ivy had been allowed to crawl through and over. Sculptured multi-tiered gardens had been designed using perennials in increasing heights. A maze of trees blocked his view of the house.

His mind kept replaying his meeting with Carl. He wondered why Carl wouldn't just have his Chicago office handle the investigation. He may have a soft spot for Mattie, but surely, Carl must have better things to do back in D.C.

As Jake turned the corner he noticed a small, ranch-style home which he assumed was the gate house. He didn't stop. Not too far from the house was a timber-framed structure covered with heavy blankets.

One hundred feet beyond the structure he came to an abrupt stop. Standing before him was a thirty-foot-tall tipi. Jake touched the hide skin that had been tanned to a silky finish, then ducked his head and entered. Tall lodgepole pines supported the cone-shaped structure. There were enough tall trees around that only a pilot would be able to detect the tipi.

Hides covered all seven-hundred square feet of ground except for the center where charred remains of wood lay. Bowls and what looked like cooking pots and utensils hung by ropes nailed to the large timbers that stretched up toward the peak.

Jake slowly backed out and continued his run. His mind returned to Carl. Jake had gotten the distinct impression that Carl had seen the lightning bolt pin before. Jake saw a glimmer of recognition in Carl's eyes. All Carl said when Jake had pressed him was, "I'll look into it." Then Carl asked him to keep an eye on Sam and to report back if anything new develops.

The well-manicured lawn was beginning to blend into taller rye grass. Off to the right was a vegetable garden. Past a field of what looked like hay the lawn narrowed to just a few yards wide.

Jake slowed to a walk and then stopped to take a few deep breaths. The air was filled with the sounds of nature. What lay ahead looked like it had been left to grow thick and natural. Creeping phlox meandered through the rye grass and over the rocks surrounding a sizable pond.

It was there, sitting on the rocks by the side of the pond that Jake saw him. The mahogany-skinned face was stoic and weathered. A red and white bandanna was wrapped around his forehead and tied just above his gray ponytail. The body under the blue denim shirt seemed firm and muscular. His neck and wrists were adorned with coral and turquoise jewelry.

Jake watched the Indian gently apply a salve and then wrap the foot of a squirrel while talking softly to it in a language Jake didn't understand. In the back acres of Sam's property Jake felt he had been thrown into another world.

The squirrel saw Jake first. It fled for the safety of the tree by the vine-covered fence. The Indian and Jake locked eyes. Neither said anything. The Indian's eyes contained a lifetime of distrust. He gazed briefly at the coral-handled knife that lay next to him.

Jake saw the knife, too, and wondered with amusement how many other men were lured to the back acres and never made it out, their scalps left hanging out to dry in the tipi.

"Nice morning, isn't it, Alex?" Jake remembered Abby mentioning his name the first day he met her.

Alex eyed him suspiciously but after a few seconds acknowledged his greeting with a nod. Jake quickly broke into a jog and then a run and never looked over his shoulder until he reached the patio.

22

Sam watched as the printer spit out pages of background information on Preston Hilliard. She had skimmed through the sections about his pompous father and socialite mother, the boarding schools. Libraries went a little too in-depth about the family life.

"Aren't you going to the office today?" Abby asked.

"I just needed to run some reports first." She looked at the wool blankets Abby was carrying. "Are you going to the sweat lodge?"

"Yes. We will be there tonight. I made some chicken and potato salad for your dinner."

"Thanks, Mom."

Abby paused at the doorway and added, "I made more than enough in case you want to invite anyone to dinner."

Sam looked up from the printer but Abby had left. She shrugged off the comment and returned her attention to her computer. She scrolled through newspaper articles going back to Preston's original campaign for state representative. She printed every article she saw about him, even the pictures of him kissing babies and attending church socials although he admitted that he had no particular religious affiliation.

His campaign promises had been all rhetoric—housing for the homeless, jobs in the form of bringing large corporations to Illinois, revenue in the form of casinos.

One paragraph caught her attention. It was Preston's military record citing his various awards—Purple Heart, a Distinguished Service Cross, and a Congressional Medal of Honor. He had been a member of the U.S. 8th Infantry Division and had served two years in the Korean War.

She scrolled to the beginning of the article. It had appeared in the April 26, 1977, issue of the *Chasen Heights Post Tribune*. The reporter's name was Samuel Casey.

Sam walked into her office to find Jake nestled comfortably in her chair, legs propped up on her desk, telephone to his ear. He was doing a superb job of trying her patience.

"What would you suggest? You must have some Internet pen pals in South Korea." Jake waved a hand at an attractive brunette seated at a desk just outside Mick's office. Janet, the department secretary, appeared seconds later with a cup of coffee.

Sam watched Janet's rolling gait as the stiletto heels carried her diminutive frame back out to her desk. Sam leaned on her desk and glared at Jake, whose eyes were glued to Janet's legs.

"I'll have a couple photos of Hap Wilson shipped overnight to you," Jake spoke into the phone. "His sister has some pictures of him in his uniform." Jake looked up at Sam and raised his coffee cup as if offering her some.

Her eyes glazed over his peach-colored knit shirt that hugged his chest. She looked away quickly, opened her tote bag and pulled out a thermos and a foil-wrapped package.

"Good, Elvis. Anything you can do, the Sixth would be entirely in your debt. Thanks." Jake hung up, pulled his legs off the desk, and ripped off a piece of Sam's fry bread.

"By all means, help yourself."

"You're late." Jake motioned through the window to Frank, then moved to one of the chairs in front of the desk.

"I didn't know you were the keeper of the time clock." She looked at the phone and as an afterthought asked, "Elvis?"

"Hangor Pannabuth," Jake replied. "He's a homicide detective at the Second Precinct, which is in the heart of Little Korea. He has relatives in the police department in Seoul and in Korean communities across the U.S. He's a big fan of Elvis." He handed Sam several photos. "He's going to put Hap Wilson's picture in the *Korean Today* newspaper."

"Where did you get these?" The pictures showed a handsome black youth, a wide smile that displayed even white teeth.

"Mattie, Hap's sister. The D.C. police sent the pictures by courier." Jake shoved the photos into a brown envelope.

Frank appeared in the doorway. "Ummmm, I can smell that fry bread all the way out there." He ripped off a piece and shoved it in his mouth. Inspecting Jake's hair he said, "Nice haircut."

Jake patted the back of his head. "Abby does a nice job."

Sam jerked her gaze to Jake's hair, opened her mouth to say something, but was interrupted by Frank who handed her a list.

"Here's a copy of the depositions from the men who were in Hap's division. These were taken over forty years ago when they were questioned after Hap went AWOL," Frank explained.

"More than half of them are marked as deceased," Sam pointed out.

"Twelve are considered MIAs or POWs. Not all of them died in the war, Sam," Frank clarified. "After all, most of the men would be close to seventy by now." He pointed to a section of the depositions. "There was one deposition they weren't able to obtain—a house boy by the name of Ling Toy. The base commander was pretty fond of him. He went out with Hap's unit but never returned."

"Do we have a picture of him you can give to Elvis?" Sam asked.

Frank shook his head no. "Maybe Elvis can put some feelers out."

Jake scribbled a note to Elvis and placed it in the envelope with Hap's pictures.

Sam fanned the sheets of paper. "How did you get this information so quickly?"

"Some of us start at the crack of dawn," Jake remarked.

"I was working at home, if you don't mind," Sam snapped back.

"On what?"

Sam handed them copies of newspaper articles on Preston Hilliard. "The top article is the one I found most interesting. It seems Preston served in Korea. Even earned himself some medals," Sam said.

"Mushima Valley?" Jake looked up from the page. "Isn't that where..."

"Yes. That's where Hap Wilson was last seen. Preston and some of his men supposedly risked life and limb to carry injured soldiers out of the valley. The injured were members of Task Force Kelly from the Fifth Regimental Combat Team."

Sam let them read the articles while she read the

report Frank had given her.

"Eight men were rescued, four died on the ride back to base," Frank read from the first article. "I guess I have four more veterans to contact."

"Wait a minute." Jake pointed at the byline. "Samuel Casey?"

"My father was an investigative reporter. He followed Preston's campaign," Sam replied.

"From the sound of the articles, he wasn't too fond of our esteemed state rep," Frank pointed out.

Glancing over the top of his copies, Jake said, "It seems his daughter inherited his distaste for politicians."

Frank thumbed through the copies of the articles. "What happened? There aren't any more articles by your father?"

"He died," Sam replied simply. "Car accident."

There was a brief silence until the phone rang. It was Tim Miesner, the teen computer geek. He might have a way to make the device she had requested. She was smiling when she hung up.

"Good joke?" Jake asked.

"Just admiring talent." As she spoke she drew shapes of lightning bolts on her pad of paper. She had to see Preston's pin again. Posing as a reporter, she had called Juanita earlier and learned that Preston would be gone most of the night on Friday. So Sam knew Friday would have to be the night.

23

The rocks had been on the fire for most of the day. Alex carefully carried them inside the square structure and set them in a pile on the ground. The sweat lodge was situated between Alex's house and the tipi. The ground was bare except for the blankets they sat on.

"We are ready," Alex announced.

Once he pulled the tarp down the entire lodge was sealed off. Alex proceeded to pour water onto the hot stones. Steam filled the air.

Abby sat on her blanket across the hot stones from Alex. Her long hair was pulled around to the front, gathered in two thick ponytails adorned with beads and feathers. They hung strategically over her naked torso, concealing her firm breasts. Her thin skirt was hiked up to her thighs exposing muscular legs.

Alex wore a traditional breechcloth, his bare chest exhibiting a sprinkling of gray hair. The glow from the rocks provided the only light.

"Do you have the *cannunpa wakan*?" Abby asked, referring to the sacred pipe.

"*Hau,*" Alex responded. "Where is the medicine bundle?"

Abby touched the unwrapped bundle next to her. She lifted up a small glass jar and passed it to Alex. He stared at the contents and grumbled.

"I know you are not enthused about this," Abby said.

"The purpose of a sweat lodge is to pray for the sick, to communicate with the spirits in helping someone in need. Not for this. You are trying to control fate."

"Fate has already been determined. I'm just trying to hurry it along. This is necessary for Samantha's mental and emotional health. We are to pray for our loved ones and that is what I am doing. I call this laying the foundation for Sam's future."

Alex moved around uncomfortably. "I call this sweating my ass off."

"Shhh," Abby whispered. "You will anger the spirits."

"YOU will anger the spirits, foolish woman. Using the spirits to play Cupid."

"Go, then. I will pray on my own. I do not need a nonbeliever in my midst."

Abby took her rattles and bags of tobacco from the bundle.

"You would probably mess things up; it's been too long." Alex tossed more water onto the rocks. Sweat trickled down his chest as he unscrewed the bottle cap. Abby handed him a lock of Sam's hair. He carefully dropped it into the bottle where it lay haphazardly among the hair clippings Abby had saved when she cut Jake's hair.

They worked silently. Alex tied the bundles of tobacco to the sticks that surrounded the fire. Abby drew a circle in the dirt and placed the glass jar and a handful of medicine beads in the center. Alex picked up the horned rattle and shook it as he sang, *"Ah Hey Yah."* Abby lit the pipe, and after pointing it to the four directions beginning with the east, she took a puff and passed it to Alex.

* * *

Sam checked the clock on the stove. Seven-thirty at night.
The house was uncomfortably quiet. It shouldn't have
bothered her, but for some reason the silence was
deafening. She opened the refrigerator and studied the
contents.

Her uneasiness had a lot to do with Benny's call. He
had apologized for not calling her earlier but had wanted
to wait until his visitor left—a forensics expert with the
Bureau. She assumed a soldier missing since the Korean
War was probably going to attract the Pentagon. But the
Bureau?

The cold from the refrigerator was chilling her legs,
but she wasn't even looking at the chicken or potato salad.
Instead, her mind was wandering, thinking back to Hap, a
line drawn from him to...where? To Preston for one. And
to many others whose faces were blank right now. Her
father's byline kept creeping into the picture. And the
lightning bolt shapes. *Lightning strike.* The words again
echoed in her head.

The doorbell interrupted her thinking. She was
surprised to see Frank and Jake. Frank carried a briefcase,
Jake an accordion file folder.

"I'll just set it all down here." Frank laid his briefcase
on the dining room table and snapped it open.

Sam removed the grapevine tree trunk arrangement
from the center of the table. She heard the refrigerator
being opened and walked into the kitchen to find Jake
setting out plates and silverware. He knew exactly where
everything was which made her wonder just how many
visits he had made here to see Abby.

"Let's see, chicken, potato salad, kidney bean salad."
He looked up at her. "Anything else you'd like to eat?"

She surveyed the buffet he had spread on the island
counter. "Fruit salad."

Jake opened the refrigerator again and located the

fruit salad. Sam brought out a pitcher of iced tea.

"Benny called," Sam announced. "Seems the FBI has sent a forensics expert from their Chicago office to examine Hap's body."

"That's not unusual," Jake said.

Frank loaded his plate and followed his colleagues into the dining room. "The guy was AWOL. I guess someone in Washington would be interested." He found an empty spot between the papers strewn around the table.

"So, why not the military instead of the Bureau?" Sam cranked open the bay windows to welcome the mild breeze. The sun was disappearing behind the trees, casting the last of its warmth on the west side of the house.

The two men didn't respond. They ate as though they hadn't had a decent meal in months. Abby had a way of making even leftovers taste like a two-hundred-dollar meal in an upscale restaurant.

"One thing that Benny discovered was that Hap had a bullet wound." Sam read from a fax. "A bullet perforated the left clavicle, first rib, resulting in a depressed fracture." She slid the printout across the table to Jake and Frank. "It's Benny's conclusion, and the FBI examiner was in agreement, that at one time in his life Hap had been shot in the back."

"Any idea how long ago?" Jake asked.

"The FBI called D.C. and talked to Hap's sister. She said he wasn't in any gangs in his youth and never had any type of bullet wound before he went to Korea," Sam said.

"How about a cause of death?" Jake asked.

Sam looked up from her notes. "Inconclusive. Benny said it's difficult to determine if he died before being put into the concrete. There were ligature marks on the neck but not defined enough to point to strangulation. Neck wasn't broken but there was a slight skull fracture. It's possible he was hit first with a blunt instrument."

Jake smiled smugly and said, "So much for asphyxiation."

24

"Why was that left out of the report?" Preston sat behind the mahogany desk in his study, the picture on the wall was pulled away, the safe opened. Preston held the gold lightning bolt pin in his fingers. He had just placed a call to Captain Murphy.

Murphy's voice blared from the speaker phone. "It was the call of the primary on the case."

"And who's that?" Preston snapped his fingers and pointed toward the bar. Like a lap dog, Cain obediently rose from his seat and lumbered over to the bar.

"Jake Mitchell."

Cain returned with two glasses of Jack Daniels, handed one to Preston, and then sat down across from him.

"He handled security for me last Saturday night, right?"

"Yes," Murphy replied. After a few seconds, he added, "I understand from the medical examiner's office that the FBI sent a forensics expert to examine the body."

Preston closed his eyes and pressed his fingers to his temple. He opened his eyes again, swallowed the contents of the glass, and waved it in front of Cain to signal he wanted a refill.

"What's the Bureau looking for?" Preston asked.

"The deceased is an alleged deserter, not to mention an African American. We'll be lucky we don't have the

NAACP, Jesse Jackson, and god knows who else looking into this case."

"Great, just fucking great," said Preston. "I have to have another dead nigger screwing up my..."

"What was that?"

"Nothing. I just don't need this grief right now. I'm leaving it up to you to play this down. He's been identified. He was drunk, a victim of strange circumstances. Make sure the autopsy report shows a high level of alcohol, or..." he snapped his fingers, "drugs, a high level of drugs. Then just let the story die. The headlines will be filled with something else in no time and people will forget."

"It may not be that easy." Murphy's voice sounded strained.

Cain eyed the contents of his glass while keeping one eye on Preston. Cain always seemed to know how to respond based on Preston's reactions. And right now, he didn't like the sound of Preston's voice.

Preston's voice softened, a sinister smile spread across his face. "Did I tell you we are creating a police commissioner post? This qualified person will be over the Board of Police and Fire Commissioners, even the Chief of Police." Preston's smile broadened. He had hit a hot button. "You know our city is just growing too fast and one police chief isn't enough, yet it doesn't make sense to have two."

"I...yes, I agree." Murphy was practically salivating over the phone.

"It will take someone who is tactical, efficient, who really gets the job done. And, of course, being my home town, I will have a great deal of input."

The speaker phone was silent, except for Murphy's breathing which bordered on panting. Cain smiled at Preston's skillful art of manipulation.

"The only problem I foresee is the sergeant on the case. Casey may not let it die."

Preston straightened up, stared at the phone as he repeated, "Casey?"

"Yes, Sam Casey."

"Sam? Wasn't he a reporter?"

"That was her father. But it may as well be her old man. She's just as tenacious."

Now it was Preston's turn to be silent and breathe heavily. He regained his composure quickly, saying, "A good organizer, an excellent candidate for police commissioner, would find a way to control his people."

Preston ended his call, leaned back in his high-backed chair, and studied the brown contents in his glass. His left hand squeezed tightly. The names Samuel Casey and Harvey Wilson pounded in his head. His temples throbbed, his jaw tightened.

The glass burst in his hand, scattering shards and spraying whiskey on his desk and the front of his blue silk shirt. He looked at the blood running down his hand.

Cain seemed unaffected, as if the scene were a frequent occurrence. Preston casually started to pull the glass shards from his hand as he told Cain, "I think it's time to put together a plan."

25

"Beer?" Frank handed a can to Jake without even waiting for a reply. They sat around the table on the patio. Moths flitted through the still air. The sky was the darkest blue, one shade before total darkness. Candles glowed on tall bamboo rods standing guard at the corners of the patio.

"We didn't really expect the major general to be alive anyway. He would have been what? Seventy-six?" Jake took a long drag from his cigarette and exhaled. "There must be a subordinate who's still breathing."

"I've left half a dozen messages. I'll have to see how many return calls I get tomorrow." Frank raised his head, listening for something, then shrugged. "Why don't we just question Preston?"

"I don't want to tip my hand. I'd rather get more information first," Jake replied.

"I agree," Sam said. She picked up her cellular phone and dialed. She smiled when she heard the familiar voice. "Hi, Tim. I need a favor. Have a pencil handy?" She waited a few seconds, then continued. "The dates are 1950 to 1953. Yes, the Korean War. I need information on a place called Mushima Valley. I'm interested specifically in a Private Harvey Wilson and anyone who might have been close to him. Yes, just send the information through to my printer. Thanks, Hon."

Sam hung up smiling.

"What pipeline do you have?" Jake asked

suspiciously.

"A high school computer genius. He's been quite helpful to me in the past."

"And exactly where does he plan on getting all this information?" Jake dropped the butt of his cigarette into his empty beer can.

"He's going to tap into the Pentagon files."

Frank turned and spit a mouthful of beer onto Abby's pot of pink geraniums. He coughed and sputtered in between his howls of laughter.

Jake glared. "You are encouraging this kid to break the law?"

"And I suppose you've never done whatever it takes to solve a case?"

"Shhhh," Frank held his hand up and cocked an ear toward the darkened yard. "Do you hear that?"

Only if one listened closely could the chants and rattles be heard from the deck. The rhythmic singing blended into the sounds of the night.

The drum beats stopped and seemed to signal the animal kingdom to be silent. The sounds began to diminish—the owls, frogs in the pond, insects, until the silence became uncomfortably eerie.

"Do you hear that?" Frank whispered.

Jake strained to hear. "I don't hear anything."

"Right. Everything stopped." As quietly as the drum had stopped, it started up again. "There they go again." Frank walked out to the edge of the patio. "Now do you hear it?"

It was vague at first but then intensified. The longer Jake listened the stronger it became.

"You're right. It sounds like a drum beat." Jake joined Frank at the edge of the patio.

Sam remained calm, sipping her wine.

"What are they doing out there, Sam?" Jake asked.

"It's a sweat lodge," Sam explained.

"A what?" Frank asked.

"*Inipi*, a purification ritual. Someone back home must be sick so they are cleansing their bodies and praying for a speedy recovery."

"They wouldn't be smoking anything illegal out there, would they? Like peyote?" Jake asked.

"It's going to go on all night, get used to it. We have more important things to think about."

The drum beat was replaced with a defined series of rattles.

"What's that?" Frank's eyes widened. What may have started out as only two rattles was magnified to an entire orchestra.

"They are calling upon the spirits to intercede," Sam explained. "The spirits are responding by adding their rattles to the ritual."

"Jake, do you believe this shit?" Frank whispered. Jake didn't respond, just stared out at the darkened yard.

As if a storm front had whipped around the corner, the umbrella on the patio table shook back and forth wildly. The pattern of the wind could be traced from across the patio through the lilac bushes toward the sweat lodge. In the distance, the flag of the sovereign nations could be seen flying high on a lighted pole near Alex's house. It whipped around furiously under the illumination of the moon, even though the umbrella had stopped vibrating and the lilac bushes became still.

They listened as tree branches whipped with as much fury as the flag. Wind moved through the acreage like nature holding a hand blower over the landscape, shifting it from side to side.

As the drum joined the sound of the rattles, the flag fell limp, the wind whipped back across the patio. Frank watched as the wind tossed Sam's hair around and then

Jake's. Frank, only five feet away, was untouched.

"Sammmm?" Frank's voice rose to a falsetto as he backstepped his way to the table.

Sam whispered, "You can feel their presence." Her eyes seemed spellbound, in awe at the unexplained power around them.

Jake looked around for a logical explanation for the wind tunnel. "We're probably blocked by the house back here."

"Uh," Frank gulped the last of his beer. "I think I'm going to go home. See you tomorrow."

Sam watched in amusement as Frank stumbled out of the yard. "He doesn't feel very comfortable about the thought of spirits and rituals."

"Do you blame him?"

As though purposely timed, the rattles and drum stopped and the animal kingdom came alive again.

"It isn't easy for people to understand. Sometimes it's best not to." She picked up her wine and walked inside the house. Jake looked out toward the darkness. A strong curiosity pulled at him to take a walk out there, just to watch, or maybe wait.

"Don't even think about it," Sam said from behind the screen door.

Jake looked over his shoulder at her and then back toward the direction of the sweat lodge. He reluctantly followed her into the house.

He insisted on cleaning up the kitchen and loading the dish washer all the while trying to talk Sam out of involving Tim in anything illegal. She ignored him.

She emptied the coffee grounds from the coffee maker, wiped the dining room table and counter. They worked silently, in unison, almost with surprising ease.

"Is it my imagination," Jake asked as he scraped food into the garbage disposal, "or do you people purposely leave food on your plates?"

"They are offerings to the spirits. It's customary, a part of our heritage."

He leaned against the counter and in all seriousness asked, "Don't they take cold, hard cash?"

She had to look hard to find the twinkle in his eyes. He wasn't smiling. There was no way for her to tell if he were joking. If he were, he had the driest sense of humor she had ever known, except for Alex's.

She slid onto a stool at the island counter. "Does the phrase *lightning strike* mean anything to you?"

Jake shook his head. "Where did you hear it?"

She explained how she had heard it when she touched Hap and the two pins. "Preston is a primary player here. He was in Mushima Valley. So was Hap. He has the same pin Hap was holding. There is a connection."

"If it IS the same pin," Jake added.

"I guess there's only one way to find out."

26

"So, you have a renegade cop," Carl commented. He struggled with his tie as he stood in front of the mirror in his suite.

Jake watched Carl mentally gauge the knot of the tie as if making sure it was symmetrical. "Let's just say we have a cop with an overactive curiosity and a bizarre—to use our medical examiner's term—mystic power." Jake explained the visions Sam had described seeing when she touched the remains of Hap Wilson, his pin, and Preston's pin.

Swiping a brush through his hair, Carl stared at Jake's reflection in the mirror. "You ARE kidding, I hope."

Jake shrugged. "Benny's sold on her. According to newspaper reports, she has solved some pretty tough cases. And you know how the media likes to blow things out of proportion."

Turning from the mirror, Carl said, "And what's your take on Sergeant Casey?"

Jake followed Carl to the living room. "She's stubborn, has a hard-on about politicians, isn't too thrilled about Captain Murphy, or me for that matter, has a housekeeper who talks to spirits, a gardener who talks to animals, and she herself hears voices that tell her who the bad guys are. Enough said?"

Carl smiled. "And you wanted to leave the Bureau to find more exciting work." He picked up the autopsy report on Hap Wilson and sat on the couch across from Jake.

Jake handed him a packet. "You'll find this interesting. We obtained information on Task Force Kelly. Lieutenant Colonel Joe Kelly, the creator of the Task Force, had dispatched his men to Mushima Valley on August 9, 1951. Frank is going to speak with him this morning. He's about eighty years old. Lives with his daughter in Phoenix."

Carl thumbed through the pages. "Jake, these are Pentagon files."

"Let's just say Sergeant Casey has extraordinary resources and I think our creative artist is going to make another trip to Preston's."

"For what purpose?" Carl asked.

"Probably take a picture of the pin. I think we all would like to have the comparison confirmed." Jake pulled the carafe of coffee toward him and filled his cup.

"Want me to order you some breakfast?"

"No, thanks. Coffee is fine." Jake drank half and refilled his cup. "Why don't you make a house call to Preston's?"

"Oh, no. I don't even want Preston to know I'm in town. I have our St. Louis, Milwaukee, Chicago, and Springfield bureaus to visit. That will keep me busy while you do what you do best."

Jake peered at Carl over the rim of his cup. "Ever hear of the term, *lightning strike*?"

Carl put his cup down a little too quickly, spilling remnants into the saucer. "Where did you hear that?"

Jake explained what Sam had heard when she touched Hap's body and the pin. "I know it sounds like something from *X-Files*. And if I could find an explanation for what she sees and hears, I would be the first to tell you." He studied Carl's pensive look. "Carl, do you know what *lightning strike* means?"

"I'm not sure yet, but I'll check it out."

Jake no sooner left then Carl pulled out a phone from his briefcase and dialed. When his call was answered, he said, "This is Director Underer. I need to speak with the President."

27

"I really don't feel comfortable having my father discuss the subject, Officer Travis."

Frank listened as Joy Engle, Joe Kelly's daughter, explained by phone her father's fragile condition. Frank could hear kids talking in the background and Joy telling them to go outside by the pool.

"But you did explain to your father why I was calling? The case we're working on?"

"Yes, and I know he agreed to talk to you. It's just that his health is not..."

"Joy, give me the phone, Dear."

Frank could hear another voice, then muffled voices as the mouthpiece of the phone was covered. Seconds later, a man's voice came on the line.

"Officer Travis?"

"Please, call me Frank, Lieutenant Colonel Kelly."

"Only if you call me Joe."

"All right, Joe." Frank explained the case and how they were trying to piece together Hap's whereabouts since Mushima Valley. "What can you tell me about Mushima Valley?"

Joe sucked in a deep breath. "A night doesn't go by that I don't think of those boys."

Contrary to his daughter's concerns, Joe sounded sturdy, youthful, as if he still did fifty push-ups every morning. His voice was deep, confident, with just a slight hint of the emphysema that racked his lungs.

"I dispatched my men to Hill Fifty-Six at sixteen-hundred-hours. We knew the North Koreans had a massive front organizing north of Hill Fifty-Six but we weren't sure of their strength. Our orders were to wait for the Marines and the air power. And, if necessary, delay the advance of the North Koreans."

"How many men comprised your task force?"

"Forty-five of the best men in the Army. They were like the Navy Seals and Green Berets combined. But the columns of civilians our planes saw hours before were a smoke screen. We lost communication sometime during the night. Didn't know what to think except the worst. Ended up a battalion of North Koreans and Chinese was waiting in the brush at the top of Hill Fifty-Six. They mowed down my men like they were sitting ducks." Joe's breathing sounded labored. "Damn, what a waste of good lives." His voice broke. Frank could hear Joy in the background saying, "Daddy, you don't have to do this."

"How did Hap Wilson's unit, the Twenty-fifth Infantry Division, get involved?"

"Montgomery, that's Major General Stanton Montgomery, offered to send a detail out to check on my men."

"Do you know their names?"

"No, just some of Montgomery's black boys." Joe coughed, wheezed. "Damn," he muttered under his breath.

"Black?" Frank's voice and diction usually did not give away his African American heritage. And right now, Frank wasn't about ready to tell him.

"Yes. The Twenty-fifth was a black unit."

"I thought the infantry was integrated. If I remember my history class, it was banned in 1947 or `48."

Frank swiveled in his chair to survey some of his fellow workers. Andy Branard and Maury Jackson, the newest recruits, one Caucasian, one African-American, were high-fiving each other, laughing. There was mutual respect in their eyes. Sergeant Ron Dorsey, due for retirement in a couple months, sat two desks away, complete disdain written all over his face as he watched the young detectives. They came from two different generations. Sometimes you hope things have changed.

"In principle only. There was too much in-fighting. Many commanding officers would rather separate the troops and have peace than try to follow the executive order and have fights and disorder among the ranks. Besides," Joe went through a ten-second coughing spasm before continuing, "what D.C. ordered and what actually happened thousands of miles away, hell, it was two different worlds. I had a couple of blacks in my task force. Never had a problem with my men. We had bigger fish to tackle." Joe heaved a sigh. "My men. Damn."

"Have you ever talked to the men who made it out?"

"I met with each of them at the hospital. All four had been unconscious when they were pulled out of there.

"So they don't remember anything about the rescue."

"Just what they were told...that four men from the Eighth pulled them out and drove them back to base. Those boys were decorated heroes." Joe coughed and wheezed again. Frank could hear Joy mumbling something.

"Just one last question, Joe. What does the term *lightning strike* mean?"

"That's when the North Koreans conducted a full assault, threw the whole damn shit load at us. It was quick and deadly. I guess you could say that's what my boys got."

28

"I received my medical examiner's preliminary toxicology report," Murphy whispered into his phone. "It's negative. Did you hear me, Preston? Negative on the drug or alcohol theory."

"I have confidence in you, Dennis. Get your people in line. I have a major announcement that I can't talk about right now. I don't need a full-blown story about the death of some black deserter to overshadow my campaign. I've had a flawless record when it comes to introducing laws to keep down the crime in Chasen Heights. This would diminish everything I have worked for. It would certainly look bad for you and anyone in law enforcement. How could I even entertain the thought of your promotion in the necessary circles if this unfortunate occurrence tarnishes our efforts?"

Murphy shook his head. Preston was good. No wonder he was in a high-ranking elected office and Murphy was just a patsy, doing Preston's bidding.

"I can't ask my medical examiner to falsify his report."

"You don't. You order him."

Murphy listened to the dial tone, then dropped the phone in its cradle, as if it were as repellent as Preston. He walked over to the glass partition and scanned the outer office. He watched Frank and Jake walk into Casey's office.

He pursed his lips, walked back to his desk and buzzed Janet.

"I need you to take a letter, Janet."

29

"That doesn't make any sense." Sam closed the door behind them. "If," she continued, "*lightning strike* is a North Korean term, why the lightning bolt pins?"

"Maybe they really don't have anything to do with it." Frank laid his notepad down, tossed his pen on the desk next to it. "I just wish Joe Kelly knew a little more about Hap's unit. I wish Hap's commanding officer were still alive."

Maury knocked on the door before entering. His tailored white pin-striped suit and pink shirt, a sharp contrast to his dark skin, looked right out of a *Miami Vice* television program. His aftershave was subtle yet pleasant.

"I've tracked down a couple of the guys in the Eighth." He handed Frank a sheet of paper with the names from Preston's unit, then left, closing the door behind him.

"Leonard Ames...wonderful..." Frank read, "died in a car accident in 1976. George Abbott is in a VA hospital in Dallas. I'll get Janet to look up the phone number, see if I can talk to Abbott." He punched the intercom on the phone.

Sam looked over at Jake. He was too quiet, ever since Frank explained the term *lightning strike*.

"Anything you care to share with us?" She studied his face, looking for any telltale sign of life behind those private eyes. There was an undercurrent in the air, electrical. She found herself admiring his chiseled features and rugged good looks.

"Not yet," was all he replied.

She had to force herself to pull her eyes off him to check her watch. Tim was supposed to call her after he delivered his package to her house. Without his device, she would not be able to make her trip to Preston's tonight.

30

Lincoln Thomas shuffled to the kitchen in his modest three-bedroom brick house in San Francisco. From his kitchen window he could see the Golden Gate Bridge lighting up the night sky.

Again he had been unable to sleep. He told himself it was because of business. He should have hired an accountant rather than try to do his quarterly taxes on his own.

His daughter, Nina, had been by earlier to bring him dinner. She knew he never stopped to eat when he had to figure out his taxes. She had a key to his house and stops by to clean and do his laundry. He had resisted her offer for him to move in with her, her husband, Raymond, and their son, Raymond, Jr.

Lincoln had always been independent, didn't want to be a burden on his family. He considered himself successful, accomplished what he wanted in life. Nina had been his greatest pride. She looked just like her mother, Sia. Dark hair, dark eyes. He had buried Sia ten years after Nina was born. Pancreatic cancer, the doctors had said.

Lincoln owned a successful employment agency with a staff of eight. Raymond was the vice-president. Thomas Associates was responsible for placing over three thousand Koreans in varying jobs, from offices to hotels, cleaning services, bakeries, retail stores, hospitals. Every type of market. And he made sure they all took night classes to learn English and skills that would make them more marketable. The people saw him as their savior. And it gave him an overwhelming sense of pride and satisfaction.

He walked through the tidy living room, past the awards hanging on the wall from the Chamber of Commerce, the mayor, the California Businessmen's Association. Next to a picture of Sia and Nina was his certificate of U.S. citizenship, framed in oak, matted in light peach to match the peach floral couch. He ran his fingers down the frame. That had been his lifelong dream since he was five years old. He would sit and listen for hours to his uncle's stories of life in America. He knew that was where he was going to live once he was old enough to travel alone.

He carried his cup of tea to the enclosed breezeway where he sat in the dark. On the coffee table in front of him was a copy of yesterday's *Korea Today* newspaper. He could still hear Nina's voice saying, "Didn't you tell me once that you were in the war, Papa?"

Even in the darkened breezeway he could see the outline of the man on the front page of the paper. *Do You Know This Man?* the headline asked. It gave the man's name as Harvey Wilson. A black man, young. Back then, they had all been young, too young. Lincoln himself had been fourteen. He had closed his eyes to that war, but obviously not his mind. Because in his sleep, he started to re-live it. Started to remember. Back then, Lincoln Thomas had been known as Ling Toy.

31

"You didn't have to come," Sam whispered. The closet was dark. She could feel Jake's body pressed against hers.

"Baby-sitting is not exactly my way of spending an evening either," Jake whispered back. He wrapped his hand around the knob and slowly opened the door.

An earlier phone call to Juanita, Preston's housekeeper, confirmed that Preston would be attending the Chamber dinner tonight.

"Wait." Sam took a small remote control from her pocket, peered out at the bookcase to her right, and aimed the remote at the shelf which housed the video recorder. A tiny red beam located the one-inch hole which exposed the recorder's control panel. With the press of a button, the remote sent the recorder into pause mode.

"Clever. Where did you get that?" Jake asked, stepping from the closet.

Sam smiled coyly. "A friend."

"How much time does it give us?"

"About two minutes." Sam opened the safe and pulled out several items. "There it is."

Jake pulled Hap's pin from his pocket to compare the two. Once Jake snapped pictures of the pins side by side, Sam placed Preston's pin and the remaining items back into the safe.

"What are you doing?" Sam watched as Jake unscrewed the mouthpiece on the phone.

"Getting rid of evidence."

"But I need..."

"We don't have time to argue. Let's go."

Sam pressed the remote again to turn the recorder back on. They exited down the staircase in the closet, through the basement and out into the darkened yard.

They heard Jasper's voice and the Dobermans in the distance, which prompted them to hightail it to the back fence. Sam remembered from her previous visits that it was a straight shot to the back of the property as long as they stayed close to the fence. No ponds or maze of gardens to run through.

Their feet hit pavement as they located a narrow access road used by the lawn service.

"How much farther?" Jake huffed.

"Not much." Her arms pumped but she matched him stride for stride. "There are large boulders...we can use them to...get over the fence."

The barking intensified, as if the dogs were right on their heels. Jasper had obviously unleashed them.

"Shit!"

"It's just up ahead," Sam said as the dark shadows of the boulders came into view.

They leaped onto the stair step boulders. As their feet hit the top of the wooden fence, Jake wrapped an arm around Sam and pulled her toward him, cushioning her fall onto the damp grassy hill.

They rolled together down the hill to Frank's waiting car.

Sam slid open the patio door to find Abby emptying the dishwasher. Frank followed close behind, an arm wrapped around Jake's waist.

"He's hurt, Abby," Frank said. Streaks of crimson ran

down Jake's face.

Abby, dressed comfortably in a nightgown and lightweight robe, quickly pulled her hair back and wrapped an elastic tie around it, preparing for whatever the emergency might be.

"It's just a scratch." Jake lowered himself onto a chair at the kitchen table. The hill they had rolled down had not been a smooth grassy knoll, but a hill speckled with rocks and debris.

"Let me see." Abby pulled the bloody handkerchief from Jake's forehead. "You might need stitches." She placed his hand back on the handkerchief. "Hold it there." Turning to Frank, she said, "There's a first-aid kit in the gym." She told Sam, "Get me a pail of hot water, a washcloth, and soap." Next, she called Alex. Within minutes, Alex arrived with medicinal pastes.

"How did you manage to do this?" Abby pressed the hot wash cloth to Jake's head. Her face was masked in concern and apprehension, but never panic.

"Two hundred and ten pounds hitting an immovable object," Jake replied. His face was smudged with dirt, his jogging suit torn.

Sam grimaced at the sight of the deep cut. "Are you sure you didn't break anything?" Sam asked.

"Maybe he should have X-rays," Frank suggested.

Alex elbowed his way between the spectators. "I need room."

Sam went to the counter to put on a pot of coffee. Frank joined her.

"Did you bring the berry root paste?" Abby asked Alex.

"Yes."

"The berry what?" Jake asked from under the washcloth.

Gently washing the rest of Jake's face, Abby

explained, "The paste has a numbing agent which should ease the pain somewhat."

"Did you at least see the pin?" Frank asked.

Jake pulled the Polaroid pictures from his pocket. "Identical. In size, shape, type of clasp. They are the same pins."

"Damn. What a pity we can't do a thing about it. No cause to present a search warrant. And we certainly can't say how we got the pictures." Frank sat down on a stool to study the pictures closer.

"Why can't we just knock on Preston's door and show him Hap's pin?" Sam suggested. "Ask if he ever saw it before. After all, he was in Mushima Valley. He might have known Hap. It's part of our investigation."

"Not yet," Jake said to Sam from behind Alex. "We still don't know how Preston ties in. And if there's even a hint we're suspicious, he's going to either start covering his tracks or get rid of the people who are suspicious."

Alex taped a gauze pad to Jake's head. "I put on a butterfly bandage so I don't think you need stitches. Too bad," Alex mumbled, "you'll live."

"By the way." Sam spun on her heels, away from the cabinet where she had been pulling out cups and saucers. "What gave you the right to take the bug out of Preston's phone?"

Abby looked up from the pail of water. "You bugged the state representative's phone?"

Alex let out a hearty laugh.

"It IS inadmissible," Frank pointed out.

"I wasn't going to use it for evidence. Just information, for my own use."

Jake lightly touched the gauze bandage, his eyes hooded in pain. "When and if Preston is arrested, how do you think it will look in court when that bug is found?"

Once the makeshift emergency room was cleaned up,

Alex left and Abby disappeared down the hall.

Frank rolled up his shirt sleeves as he informed Sam and Jake of his call to George Abbott's hospital room in Dallas. Abbott had been with Preston in Mushima Valley.

"His doctor said I can call him in the morning. He just had surgery earlier today. They removed his right leg ... diabetes. Other than that, he's of sound mind and body. Should be coherent enough to answer some questions."

Returning to the kitchen, Abby announced, "You will stay here, Jacob. I want to keep an eye on you should you develop a fever during the night. I have made up the hide-a-bed in the study."

Sam shot Abby a look that did not go unnoticed. They exchanged words in their native language and it was evident that Abby had the last word.

"That's nice of you Abby, but..." Jake started.

"I don't take refusals very well, Jacob." Abby swept out of the kitchen before Jake could respond.

Sam caught up with Abby at the bottom of the staircase. "You're carrying hospitality a little too far. He could have gone home with Frank."

"He would have been over here in the morning for breakfast anyway, Dear." She kissed Sam lightly and walked up the stairs.

Clenching her teeth, Sam debated on whether to say anything more. Subconsciously lifting the collar of her jumpsuit, she inhaled the scent of Jake's aftershave which was clinging to her clothes. She could still feel his arms locked around her when their bodies had rolled down the hill. Sam shook the thoughts from her head.

32

The rubber-soled shoes were silent against the sterile white floors of the Dallas VA Hospital. The young, dark-haired nurse didn't even give the orderly a passing glance as he walked by carrying a tray.

The door to Room 321 was slightly ajar, the television set tuned to CNN. Thin white window drapes were shut. The light from the television set cast an eerie light in the room. A slim figure in the bed was asleep, defenseless. Three blankets were pulled up to his chin. A glass of ice chips was on the nightstand.

The orderly took a syringe off his tray and injected the contents into the IV tube running into George Abbott's left hand. He watched for several seconds, then carried the tray down the hall to the laundry chute.

Once outside in the darkened parking lot, Cain changed his clothes. He would find a dumpster on his drive back to the airport, where he would discard his orderly uniform. By the time his flight was airborne, George Abbott would be dead.

33

Sam answered the phone on the first ring.

"I'm sorry to be calling in the middle of the night," the voice said.

It was her client. "It's okay. Are you still coming to Chasen Heights?" The voice was in a whisper. Sam had to strain to hear him.

"I'm in town now. I wanted to let you know I would swing by at seven-thirty this morning. Is that too early?"

Sam pulled the covers back and slipped a cotton robe over her pajama short set. "No, no problem. I'll be up."

Sam checked the clock on the nightstand. It was just after three o'clock in the morning. She crept downstairs, cursing herself for not removing the pictures from the hiding place she had stuffed them in after her caper at Preston's. Of all nights Abby had to invite Jake for a slumber party.

Because the door at the foot of the stairs would make too much noise when she slid it open, she walked around to the kitchen and entered the study door across from the gym.

She found the light switch for the track lighting above the bar and gently pushed it up, casting the room in the faintest of light. She quietly pulled out the books where she had placed her client's pictures. They weren't there. Maybe she had the wrong shelf. Maybe the wrong books. She pulled them aside, searching between the encyclopedias and forensic research books.

A voice in the shadows asked, "This what you're looking for?"

Sam screamed, dropping two books to the floor. Jake snapped on the lamp on the end table, the pictures clutched in his hand.

"Just great." She shoved the books back into their slot on the bookshelves and stormed into the kitchen. Jake pulled a CHPD tee shirt on over his gym shorts and hobbled after her, holding his hand to his head.

"You are a piece of art," Sam continued. "Abby nurses you, offers you a place to recuperate, and you thank us by snooping?" She slid onto the stool by the counter and buried her face in her hands, kneading the sleep from her eyes. "I promised my client the utmost in secrecy." She slowly poured out two aspirin on the counter. Jake filled two glasses with water, setting one in front of her, then took a seat on the stool next to her.

"Don't tell me you're blackmailing the governor." Jake winced as he moved his head a little too quickly.

"No." It came out as a painful whisper. "Preston is. Governor Meacham hired me to get the pictures back."

"Hey." Jake wrapped a hand around her right arm and pulled it away from her face. "I'm not the enemy here. Trust me."

"Trust you?" she forced a laugh. "Last time I looked, you had copies of a videotape of me."

"I haven't used them, have I?"

His skin felt warm, almost hot. Maybe he had a fever, maybe she did. She looked into his eyes. There must be something trusting about him if Abby liked him. His hand slid down her arm and clasped her hand, gave it a squeeze. He must have felt the same heat because he let go of her hand and wrapped it around his glass of water.

"You certainly don't give me much of a choice now."

Sam downed two aspirins with several gulps of water, then searched through the pictures in the envelope.

"They are all there." Jake popped two aspirins into his mouth and swallowed them dry. "I don't have to know all the sordid details. I'm just curious what Preston wants from Governor Meacham."

Sam glanced at the pictures of two men in compromising poses. It was easy to conclude the two men were in a motel room from the sign by the phone listing extension numbers.

"Preston wants to be governor. He wants Meacham to not seek another term and throw all of his support to Preston. Preston is power hungry."

"Who's the other man in the picture?"

Sam gazed down at the faces in the picture. "I'm surprised you don't recognize Archbishop Simon Carmichael."

Jake shrugged. "I don't really follow the papal circuit." He drank half a glass of water in one long gulp. "What will Preston find when he checks his safe?"

Sam smiled. "Baseball trading cards."

Jake flashed a weary smile. "Good ones?"

"Mickey Mantle, Hank Aaron, among others."

"Those are too good for Preston." Picking up the pictures of Meacham he asked, "Did you notice these were Polaroid pictures?"

"Yes."

"My guess is they are the only copies."

Sam's eyes brightened. "You think so? That's what I had hoped but Preston doesn't seem to be the type not to cover his bases."

"True. But I don't see him walking into a Walgreens and asking to have copies made. He couldn't chance someone seeing these pictures and trying to do his or her own blackmail scam."

"He could have had someone on his payroll make copies."

"One more person who knows is one too many. He would be left with too many people to pay off."

"Or knock off." She swept a hand across the top of her head, lifting a mass of springy hair that she thought must look frightful. "Are you going to tell Frank?"

"Not if I don't have to."

Sam closed her eyes in relief and whispered, "Thanks."

34

Since Jake's head wasn't up to exercising, he took a quick shower instead and slipped into a pair of jeans. The early morning rays were already heating up the patio. The chaise lounge was cushioned, comfortable. Jake stretched out and smelled the new morning dew.

He thought back to last night. He and Sam had talked for an hour. After Sam had gone to bed, Jake spent some time thumbing through the photo albums in the study. The smiling child with the sun-bleached hair had tugged at his heart. There were pictures of Sam with her adoring father, a handsome man with curly blond hair. The woman in the photo he assumed was Melinda Casey. She was barely five feet tall with milk glass skin and brown hair. Many of the pictures from Europe and Asia were only of Samuel and Melinda Casey.

He guessed Abby to be about nineteen or twenty in most of Sam's infant pictures. Sam's olive complexion seemed a sharp contrast to Melinda's milk glass skin. Sam's cheekbones were well defined even at such a tender age. There was a secrecy that seemed to pass between Sam and Abby that only the camera caught. If he were a betting man, he'd say that Melinda Casey was NOT Sam's mother.

What Jake found strange was that there were no pictures of Sam after 1977. That, Jake remembered, was when Samuel and Melinda Casey had died in the car accident.

"I thought I smelled coffee." Abby poured herself a cup. She checked his bandage. "How is it feeling this morning?"

"Better, much better, thanks." Just like in the pictures Jake found himself drawn to Abby's features. She hadn't changed much from the pictures in the album other than adding a few pounds and smile creases around her eyes. Time had not been unkind to Abby. Jake smiled at her.

"What?" Abby gathered her skirt around her legs before taking a seat.

"Why didn't you tell me you were Sam's mother?"

"I guess I assumed Sam had told you."

Jake shook his head then told her how he looked through some photo albums last night. "But, Melinda was his wife, right?"

"Yes. It really isn't too complicated. Samuel and Melinda picked me up just outside Chamberlain, South Dakota. I was hitchhiking. Going...anywhere." She took a sip of her coffee. "They helped me through some rough times. They brought me back here to live. I insisted on working for my keep. I cooked, did laundry, helped Melinda mail out invitations to a variety of social events."

The picture Jake was formulating in his mind of Abby and Sam's father having a torrid love affair just didn't fit the woman sitting in front of him whose integrity seemed above reproach. Luckily, he didn't have to ask the question.

"When Melinda discovered she couldn't have children," Abby continued, "I agreed to be a surrogate mother. It was the least I could do to thank them."

"It must have been difficult for you, having Sam call another woman Mommy."

"There was a bond between Sam and me that no one could come between. When she was old enough to understand, I didn't have to tell her. She just knew."

Jake thought back to Hap's body, how Sam had touched it, touched the pin. How the words *lightning strike* seemed to have popped into her head. Jake always dealt in logic. And what Sam supposedly did was not logical to him. She seemed to know things that defied logic.

The sprinklers bordering the patio turned on, spraying a fine mist over the geraniums, irises, and lilies. Abby gazed lovingly at nature's pastel colors, as if seeing them for the first time.

"Tell me something, Abby." He told her about Hap Wilson and some of the revelations Sam had come up with. "How does she do this little mind-reading act of hers?"

"Sam has a unique gift. Ever since she was small she seemed to be able to sense things about certain people or places. It was confusing for her to interpret at first. We spent several years on the reservation after Mr. and Mrs. Casey passed away. My grandmother was a powerful medicine woman and taught Sam how to interpret these feelings."

"What kind of feelings?"

"She can sense the aura left in a room or surrounding a body that can tell her things about a killer or the victim." Abby flashed a smile filled with pride and affection. "My grandmother used to say that the victim either had to be cold to the touch or cold-hearted in order for Sam's powers to work."

Jake eyed her strangely. "And you believe this?"

Abby's dark eyes danced. There was a secret world behind those eyes of hers, a secret world that only Sam and Alex seemed to have a key to.

"There are many unexplained things in life, Jacob. We can't see electrical currents, but we know they work.

We can't see radio waves or even gravity, but we have no doubt they are there."

"That's true," Jake agreed, "but, unfortunately, our judicial system requires solid evidence and logical conclusions. And these little visions Sam has just don't fall anywhere in line with those requirements."

A comfortable silence surrounded them. A large bee droned over to a cluster of day lilies near the patio. A gathering of finches splashed in the birdbath near the Florida room. Jake could feel Abby's eyes on him, studying him, probing. Probing what?

"One thing you have to understand about Sam, she hasn't had it easy. I don't want to make excuses for her."

Jake shifted his gaze to Abby, her smiling eyes, the genuine love in her voice whenever she mentioned Sam's name.

"She withdrew after Mr. and Mrs. Casey died. She didn't talk much and children can be cruel. Then when the visions started, kids thought she was a freak. Adults understood she had a powerful gift. Until..."

Jake arched one eyebrow.

"There was a murder on the reservation," Abby explained. "A young boy. The authorities thought he had played with matches and accidentally set himself on fire. But Sam walked through the rubble of the boy's house. She saw what had happened to him, somehow knew who did it."

"I would think everyone would be thankful that the truth came out."

"Yes, but tell that to the young men who were afraid to even talk to Sam for fear she could read their every thought. Tell that to the adults who suddenly realized she might be able to discover secrets about them."

Jake pondered Abby's comments as he studied the remnants of coffee in the bottom of his cup. His face must have displayed his unswayed skepticism because Abby asked, "You still doubt Sam's ability?"

"Well, you have to admit," Jake added, "it isn't something I run into every day. And I can almost see people taking two steps back whenever she walks into a room."

"Grandmother told Sam that people are more receptive to healing powers. But other powers should not be advertised. Unfortunately, Sam chose a line of work where she can use her powers. I guess I should be glad she is callused enough to survive the opposition she encounters." After a few moments she added, "Sam also tends to take lightly the danger she puts herself in. Promise me you'll keep an eye on her."

For the first time since he met her, Abby's eyes showed genuine fear. He touched her hand and said, "Of course." Jake leaned over to place his cup on the patio table. His shirtless torso was tan and muscular. He felt Abby's hand on his back, a back he rarely exposed. When he heard her gasp, he stood up, felt his face flush. He thought he saw tears edge their way to the corners of her eyes. He departed abruptly explaining, "I should get dressed."

Abby watched Jake leave. She leaned back against the table shaking her head in shock. Raised welts, old scars, had criss-crossed Jake's back starting at the shoulder blades and disappearing below the belt line.

When she placed her hand on one of his scars she saw a vision of a boy, no more than six, shielding a woman, his mother perhaps, who was cowering in a corner. A leather strap cut across the boy's back, literally ripping his shirt off.

The visions had come quick, split frames like

watching a slide projector. The one that came into clear focus was the boy tied to a bed on his stomach, naked, his back and rear cut and bleeding profusely and then the strap slapping across the back once more, sending blood spraying onto the walls and sheet.

She knew more than ever that she made the right decision to use the sweat lodge. Jake had built an emotional wall around himself and now Abby knew that only the spirits would be able to penetrate that wall. Only they would be able to help him open his heart.

35

Jake watched Frank through the glass partition in Sam's office. Frank was on the phone with the Dallas VA Hospital.

"I thought Abby had told you she was my mother," Sam said.

"She thought you had told me. All this time I thought she was your housekeeper." Jake watched Frank hang up the phone and lean back in his chair shaking his head. "This doesn't look good," Jake observed.

Frank walked in and closed the door. "George Abbott, one of Preston's fellow Army buddies, conveniently passed away last night."

"Complications from surgery?" Sam asked.

"The doctor thinks there was a problem with his insulin. The nurse on duty said he received his proper dosage at six o'clock. But he seemed to have a suspicious amount in his system. I talked to the Dallas P.D. Told them Abbott was an integral part of our investigation and we would like them to treat it as a homicide."

"That's just great. Someone is picking off our witnesses one by one. First Leonard Ames dies in a car accident in 1976. Who's next?" Sam asked. Janet buzzed Sam on the intercom. Benny was on the phone. She pressed the speaker button. "I hope it's good news, Benny." Benny informed them that Captain Murphy would be issuing a press release to the *Chasen Heights*

Post Tribune informing them the Hap Wilson case was closed. Murphy's memo to Benny requested that Benny report the preliminary tests were inconclusive on the cause of death but that drugs had not been ruled out.

"Hc can't do that." Sam looked up at Jake. "Can he do that?"

"He's doing it," Frank chimed in.

"I've already received the toxicology report, Sam." Benny's voice blared through the speaker phone. "It's all negative. Basically, what Murphy says is correct. Cause of death is inconclusive."

"But you and I both know Hap was murdered. How could he possibly want you to infer in your report that drugs might have played a part?" Sam argued.

"He's closing the case is what he's doing, and my hand is being held to the fire to sign off on it."

"Can't you stall him?" Frank asked.

Jake leaned on the desk, close to the phone. "How much longer can you hold the body?"

"As long as necessary."

Sam ended her call with Benny and started pacing. The more she paced, the angrier she became. "It had to be Preston. He's pressuring Murphy to close the case. Murphy is such a sonafabitch. He should be fired." She picked up the phone and dialed Chief Connelley. "Do you know where he went, Mary?" Sam sat down at her keyboard and pounded out a note to Connelley on the computer. "That's okay. I'm sending him a message. Do me a favor and read it to him when he calls in and have him call me ASAP."

"What do you want your memo to accomplish other than pissing off Murphy because you went over his head?" Jake asked.

"That's good for starters." She pressed the ENTER key. "I don't care what he says, I'm not giving up on this case. You two can do what you want." She watched as the two men exchanged eye contact. Years of working together made Jake and Frank think like one. Sam never had the experience of knowing or even appreciating how that felt. "You think I'm crazy?"

"Other than ancient depositions, Sam, we've got nothing to work on," Frank confessed. "The depositions revealed nothing other than that Hap was a respected, honest soldier. No proof that he might have deserted. But no proof that he hadn't."

"Elvis hasn't come up with any responses to the ads he placed in the Korean newspapers," Jake added. "Our backs are against the wall here and we're coming up empty-handed. That, added to the lack of a relevant cause of death..." Jake let his comment trail off.

Sam held her hands up in surrender. "All right. Okay. Enough already." She peered through the window toward Murphy's office. He wasn't in. She studied the two detectives. There was something in their eyes. Chief Connelley had told her she had it. And maybe that was what she was seeing. When she looked at their eyes she saw the hunger, the desire to get at the truth. Unrelentless.

She smiled slowly and said, "I don't believe you. I don't believe either one of you can walk away from Hap without knowing the truth."

36

A normal day for Lincoln Thomas was twelve hours. From seven in the morning until seven at night. He always brought his lunch and ate at his desk.

Some evenings were filled with meetings with local organizations and new business owners who were building hotels or convention centers and might need the assistance of Thomas Associates.

Lincoln had picked his American name from two presidents—Abraham Lincoln and Thomas Jefferson. It wasn't that he lacked pride in his given name. After the war, he had stowed away on a ship to Seattle. He had been afraid he would be hunted down.

He could still hear them yelling, "You can't hide. We'll find you. And when we do, we'll cut your tongue out." He had run as fast and as far as he could that day. Never returned to the Base Commander.

The thought of them having a nationwide hunt for Ling Toy was his worst fear. So he had changed his name, found someone in the Korean underground to give him fake I.D.s, and hid himself deep in the Seattle Korean community.

He slept in a storage room above a bakery at night, helped with the baking between three and seven in the morning, then went to school. Melee, the bakery owner, was the biggest Korean woman he had ever seen. The Korean War had made her a widow. No children but enough friends and connections to help her open her own business in the States.

She never asked Lincoln about his nightmares, but would stay by him until he went back to sleep. She had a great business sense and within three years opened a small restaurant next door to her bakery.

Lincoln had been with her for seven years. He had no idea she had no living relatives. So it took him by complete surprise that she had willed him her businesses.

After a few years, Lincoln sold the businesses and headed south to California, to San Francisco. He had admired pictures of the bay and the Golden Gate Bridge when he had seen the colorful postcards at the command post. Now he would see them for himself.

Lincoln knew he had been blessed finding Melee. She had always told him that if each person returned a favor given to him, the whole world would be a lot happier.

"Mr. Thomas, this is the last of them." Sherita, a young black high school student who worked after school at Thomas Associates, placed a stack of newspapers on his desk.

"Thank you, Sherita."

Raymond, his son-in-law, passed Sherita in the doorway. Raymond was tall by Korean standards, at least six feet.

"Do you need help, Lincoln? Are you looking for something in particular?" Raymond flipped through some of the papers. "*Chicago Tribune, Sun-Times*. How was Sherita able to find all these back issues?" Raymond's slicked-back hair revealed a distinct widows peak.

"The hotel across the street usually keeps their leftovers. Saves them for the school paper drives." Lincoln carried the papers to an oblong conference table. "I believe there is a conference in Chicago I wanted to go to. I thought the paper might have an ad."

"I'll help you."

Lincoln placed his hand on the stack of papers, saying a little too quickly, "That's okay. Really. I need a diversion right now." He checked his watch. "Why don't you meet with Mr. Hensen? And maybe you and Nina can plan on attending the museum reception tonight." Raymond gave a puzzled look as he retreated. There was rarely a benefit or meeting that Lincoln missed.

Lincoln remembered the article in his Korean paper stating Hap Wilson's body had been found in Chasen Heights, a suburb south of Chicago. Since none of the hotels or stores sold newspapers from Chasen Heights, he decided there had to be something in the papers in the largest city closest to the suburb.

With a pair of scissors he cut out all the articles pertaining to the body found in concrete. He read about the investigation and circled the names of the detectives.

Then he went through each of the papers a second time to make sure he didn't miss anything. He was surprised to read that the police were closing the case since there was no evidence of foul play. He was also surprised that the article intimated that Hap was possibly a deserter. Lincoln sat back and rubbed his eyes. Where had Hap been all those years since the war? He thought for sure he had been killed with all the rest. Briefly, Lincoln closed his eyes and thought back to that hot August day in 1951.

> *"Do you think they'll make it, Sergeant?" Hap Wilson asked Booker, a muscular black man with a shaved head and eyes that naturally bulged.*
>
> *Ling Toy looked up at the two men as his hands bandaged the shattered*

remains of a soldier's leg. Ling Toy understood English better than he spoke it. The injured numbered eight and they were all unconscious.

Ling Toy shook his head in despair. "Need doctor." He looked past Hap and Booker, beyond Bubba's bulky frame hovering over the combat radio and Shadow who was studying the picture of his wife and baby, down the tree-lined dirt road which led to the killing field where they had found the ambush victims.

"Yeah, we're going to get them a doctor," Booker said clapping a hand on Ling Toy's back. "Just try to keep them alive until we can get them back to Base."

Hap crumpled an empty cigarette package and patted his pockets. His hand touched damp fabric. They were all covered with dirt, sweat, and the blood of war. Booker shook out two cigarettes from his pack and held them out to Hap.

"Thanks, Sarge." Hap broke out in a broad smile. His trembling hands had trouble striking a match so Booker lit one for him.

Ling Toy marveled at the camaraderie of the black men and the loyalty of the Americans to their cause. But he still couldn't understand why there were separate units for blacks and whites.

Hap took a long drag off his cigarette and winced.

"Still got those cramps?" Booker lowered his muscular frame onto a flat rock next to Hap.

Hap nodded. "Feels like someone's puttin' my intestines through a wringer."

"Bad river." Ling Toy stood up, his clothes hanging loosely over his frail body.

Booker sucked long and deep off his cigarette, savoring one of the few luxuries of combat. "That's what you guys get for bathin' in that river two days ago. I told you there's enough stuff floating in these rivers to make you sick for a month. Even a guy your size, Hap."

Hap nodded toward Bubba and Shadow. "Did Base confirm that the injured are the guys who were missing?"

"Yes. We're looking at what's left of Task Force Kelly. They were dispatched to Mushima Valley yesterday. Supposed to climb Hill Fifty-six and report back. It doesn't seem they ever made it up that hill. The last communications Base received yesterday was that the civilians they had found were decoys."

Along the horizon, a number of smoke trails spelled the demise of more villages. Beyond kelly green rice fields, Ling Toy could see the sun, a huge yellow ball setting quickly. He listened, deciphering the words Hap and Booker spoke, how they wondered how the

North Koreans could be so brutal in their killing by the looks of those who didn't make it out of the valley.

"Not Korean," Ling Toy offered. He waved a hand toward the injured. "Chinese. They do this."

"Bull shit. There ain't no damn Chinese here." A figure stepped out of the shadows and flicked a cigarette butt at Hap's feet. He wore his khaki shirt tied at his waist in such a way that his Sergeant's stripe and several odd-shaped pins were exposed. He glared at Hap with eyes that were sinister, mysterious, and dangerous, as his shoe slowly ground the lit butt into the dirt.

Ling Toy didn't like the white sergeant who was called P.K. There were four white soldiers who had shown up right after the survivors had been pulled from the valley, claimed they had been separated from their unit. All four of them treated the black soldiers cruelly. But the white sergeant, he was the worst. He eyed Booker's unit and even Ling Toy, as if they were the lowest form of life.

Lincoln awoke with a start, the memories too vivid, too painful. He shivered, wiped the sweat from his forehead and pushed the papers away. One of the *Chicago Tribune* papers opened part way. He froze when he saw the picture. He'd remember those cold eyes anywhere. The leering smile was a mask of lies and deception. After all these years, Lincoln would never forget that face.

He read the description under the picture about the Illinois state representative who had recently held a reception at his home in Chasen Heights. The picture was of Preston Kellogg Hilliard. Lincoln knew him as P.K.

37

"You've been staring at the screen all day. You didn't finish the dessert that lady brought you," Janet said. She looked over at the platter of cookies and brownies and took one of each.

"Ummmm," Jake mumbled.

"Who was that woman?" Janet asked.

"Abby? That's Sam's mom. Great lady."

"She just kinda snuck up out of nowhere. Scared the hell out of me."

"She has a way of sneaking up on people. It's in her genes."

He leaned back and watched the computer screen freeze as it processed his command. The second shift was drifting into the room. He looked at his watch. Sometime within the last hour Sam had left for home.

"Captain Murphy never came back?"

"No. Sam asked me six times. Guess she didn't like that memo Dennis wrote."

Jake looked up at her. She was leaning on the corner of his desk. Her white skirt hit her mid-thigh. The hot pink blouse didn't have enough buttons to conceal her cleavage. A gold necklace around her neck held a small gold typewriter that had the pleasure of resting comfortably in the valley of that cleavage.

"If you don't have plans for dinner, Jake, I have spaghetti sauce simmering in a crock pot at home."

Jake smiled. Janet was a catch for any lucky guy. He had taken her to dinner once years ago. He had no intention of it being any more than a friendly dinner. But she took him home to meet her two young kids. She had been newly divorced at that time and scared to death of being a single parent. She was looking for a father for her kids, but Jake wanted no part of it.

"Thanks, Janet, but I'll have to take a rain check." He handed her the container of cookies and brownies. "Here, take these home to the kids."

He watched her walk away and felt guilty that he couldn't even bring himself to have a friendly dinner for fear he might give her the wrong impression. She was too nice to be used. That's basically what he did—used women. And they used him. They each knew ahead of time that the relationship would be purely physical, maybe dinner every now and then. But never any family-type dates like a trip to the zoo or shopping, where the woman would gush over furniture and place settings and make subtle remarks like, "When WE get a place of our own," or "Wouldn't it be nice to have...?"

He rubbed his eyes with his palms and stared back at the computer. The printer beeped. He pressed the paper feed button and stood to rip the pages off.

Brandon swaggered in from the break room. "How's the Dragon Lady? That broad had a hell of a lot of nerve planting ideas into Camille's head." He worked a toothpick around between his teeth.

"You should be concentrating more on getting your home life back in order and less about Sergeant Casey." Jake gathered the pages into a file folder and headed for the elevator.

"My home life is fine, but do let me know if you need any help with your project. It would be my distinct pleasure," Brandon called out.

Jake stepped onto the elevator and stared back at Brandon. The prick Murphy had filled Brandon in on their conversation.

"Not in this lifetime, ass," Jake whispered as the elevator doors closed.

Sam closed the glass doors of the fireplace in the study. The flames engulfed the photos, the edges curling up, the paper disintegrating into ashes.

Governor Avery Meacham leaned back against the sofa and heaved a sigh of relief. Due to unexpected meetings, he had been unable to make it to Sam's until late in the afternoon.

Not an overbearing figure, Governor Meacham looked more like someone's math teacher. An accountant by trade, he had managed to balance the state's books with money to spare in the three years he had been in office. He had abolished the school boards his first year, insisted on more parental involvement, and more accountability by the teachers.

Creases had deepened around his eyes as if the whole ordeal had aged him ten years. "I thought I could handle it myself. I thought, naively, that the threats were just that...threats."

Sam took a seat on the sofa next to Governor Meacham. "What is the significance of July nineteenth?"

"My wife and I are flying to England on the eighteenth to spend time with our son. He's stationed there, in the Air Force." Governor Meacham clasped his hands together prayer style. "I wanted my family out of the country if Preston decided to go public with the photos."

Seeing that the photos had been reduced to ashes, Sam turned off the fireplace just as someone knocked on the study door.

"Are you ready, Dear?" A petite blond wearing a tailored navy suit and a quick smile, peered into the study. Nancy Meacham cradled a box in her hand. Abby followed her in.

"Abby was nice enough to take me out to Alex's house. He finished repairing my bracelet."

Avery smiled wearily and stood up. "We really should get going. Our plane is waiting."

"Thank you for hosting the tea, Dear," Nancy said to Abby.

"My pleasure." Abby turned and clasped Avery's hand.

Sam winced at the sight of Avery's hand in Abby's. Sam's powers were strongest with the dead, but Abby's were with the living. Sometimes a touch could tell Abby a lot, sometimes nothing. Sam didn't see any reaction on Abby's face.

38

By eight o'clock in the evening, Jake and Frank had completed the investigation of a homicide at Stateline Liquors. Beat cops had found the nineteen-year-old stock boy four blocks away still carrying the Glock 9mm. A homicide once a month on State Street wasn't unusual for Chasen Heights.

"You didn't have to give ALL the cookies to Janet. You could at least have saved me one," Frank moaned.

"I'm sure Abby has more at home. Quit whining."

"This kid better do some fast confessing. I don't plan on spending all night dancin' around with him."

Jake's cellular phone rang. It was Elvis calling to update him on the blurb he had placed in the *Korean Today* newspaper.

"Anything new?" Jake pulled out a notepad from his shirt pocket. "What time?" He scribbled five-thirty and underlined it. "Call me at the following number." Jake gave him the phone number for the Suisse Hotel. He wanted the conference call to take place in Carl's room.

"Elvis has something?" Frank asked after Jake hung up.

"He set up a conference call at five-thirty in the morning. There's a woman in a town called Yongchou, South Korea, who recognized Hap's picture."

39

Sam walked up behind Tim Miesner, who was hunched over Sam's keyboard. A fluff of youthful, sand-colored hair stood straight up on the top of his head. He stared intently at the screen through rimmed glasses.

"I'm sorry finals tied me up."

"How did you do?"

Tim flashed a smile. "Straight A's." Sam patted him on the back. Tim pointed to the screen on her computer. "This lock and key icon on the menu is a tricky one."

"Just take your time. I only need it yesterday." Tim looked sharply at her. Sam smiled. She wrote CAIN on a sheet of paper. "Also, see if you can find anyone by this name with a rap sheet."

"You mean like CIA or Interpol?" His eyes grew wide with anticipation.

She laughed and ran her hand through his hair. "Police, FBI, CIA, whatever your heart desires." She stood at the door, "Don't let anyone in but me."

Jake and Frank walked in through the back door carrying their sportscoats. Frank's tie was loosened. The front of Jake's cream-colored knit shirt was damp.

"The motor pool better have the air conditioning in that car fixed by tomorrow or I'm just going to drive my own," Frank said.

"How did you get in here?" Sam demanded.

Jake dangled his keys in front of Sam, then snapped

them away before she had a chance to give them a closer look.

"You made a key to MY house?"

"Abby gave me a spare." Jake tossed his sportscoat over the back of a kitchen chair.

Sam raised her hands in an *I give up* gesture. "I want you to listen to something." She pressed the button on the tape player sitting on the counter.

The two men listened to Preston's threatening call to Murphy, demanding that he close the case on Hap Wilson. But the most interesting call was to someone named Cain. All Preston had said was, "I have a job for you."

"This was the morning before Abbott died. The morning before YOU," Sam pointed an accusing finger at Jake, "removed the bug."

"That's reaching, Sam." Jake pressed the STOP button. "*I have a job for you* does NOT mean he hired a hit. The guy could be an auto mechanic."

Frank checked his beeper, then carried Sam's cordless phone to the dining room to call the office.

"Sam..." Tim stopped when he saw she had company.

Jake reached out a hand to him. "You must be the boy genius."

"I guess so." Tim turned back to Sam. "I'm going to need more time on that lock and key icon menu. And I better use my modem at home to access the CIA and Interpol files."

Jake asked, "Am I going to want to know what you want with CIA files?"

"No," Sam replied, steering Tim toward the back door. "He's just going to run Cain's name through the files." Turning to Tim she asked, "How soon can I have something in my hands?"

"I have to write a program in order to cross-check the

name. That may have to run all night. I'll write the program right after dinner. As far as the menu, I'll keep working on it. There may be a password within a password, and those can be tricky."

"They can trace it, you know," Jake said after Tim left. "And if the paper trail leads to Tim, you're putting him in a compromising position."

"Tim's good. He never leaves tracks."

"There's always a first time."

"If I remember correctly, you were the one breaking and entering with me the other night at Preston's."

"Self-preservation. You get busted, it reflects on the entire department."

"Sam," Frank called out. "What's your fax number here?" Sam wrote the number down and gave it to Frank. Minutes later, Frank ended his call and joined them in the kitchen. "Jim Ludders, who's investigating Abbott's death in Dallas, said they would leave the case open for a couple of days in case we come up with anything on our end but, as far as their department is concerned, George Abbott died of natural causes."

The fax machine started humming. They walked into the study and stood vigil over the paper-spitting machine.

"The family lawyer accessed Mr. Abbott's safety deposit box," Frank explained. "It contained only one item. Ludders wasn't sure if it had any significance. But when a man bothers to rent a safety deposit box for over forty years..."

"Forty years?" Sam interrupted.

"Yes. And all he kept in it was one piece of jewelry." Frank pulled the sheet out of the fax tray.

"Sonafabitch," Jake whispered.

The picture was of a pin in the shape of a lightning bolt.

40

Carl opened the door to his hotel suite wearing a robe, his face covered in shaving cream. "I see you are still an early riser," he told Jake.

"Old habits are hard to break."

"Help yourself to coffee." Carl returned to the bathroom. "Any luck on the survivors in Mushima Valley?" Carl called out.

"According to Lieutenant Colonel Joe Kelly, none of the survivors of his Task Force was conscious at the time so they wouldn't be able to tell us anything anyway."

Jake carried his cup of coffee to the large picture window. The sun was making a stunning appearance on the horizon, dwarfing the fishing boats and a large tanker off in the distance. He walked over to the dressing area where Carl was rinsing off the shaving cream.

"Murphy closed the Wilson case. He received the order from Preston."

"I thought you removed that bug from Preston's phone." Carl hung his robe up in the closet and slipped into a light blue short-sleeved shirt.

"These were calls made before I removed the bug. Preston is bribing Murphy with the police commissioner post. Claims he can't have any negative publicity in HIS town before his announcement."

"What announcement?"

They moved to the couch in the living room. Jake told

Carl that Preston was blackmailing Governor Avery
Meacham. "I'm not at liberty to explain the extent of the
blackmail. It has been neutralized, for now."

Carl shook his head in disbelief. "That man has no
conscience. State rep wasn't good enough. Now he wants
to be governor?"

Jake told Carl about the phone call from Murphy to a
man named Cain.

Carl slid several pictures across the table. "My
surveillance team took shots of this guy coming and going
from Preston's house numerous times. Recognize him?"

Jake studied the picture. The man looked like a retiree
from the pro-wrestling tour. "Hate to meet him in a dark
alley."

"His name's Cain Valenzio. Former boxer from New
York. We think he was a runner for the Gambino family at
one time. We could never get anything to stick. For his size,
it's surprising he's able to slip in and out of the darkest
recesses of a city without being seen. If he's used aliases,
we haven't pegged any on him yet. But give us time."

"He didn't happen to hop a plane to Dallas recently,
did he?"

"I'm embarrassed to say he gave my men the slip that
night. His name wasn't on the flight log but he could have
used an alias. Our Dallas office showed Cain's picture
around the VA hospital. No one recognized him."

Jake showed him a copy of a fax. "The family attorney
found this lone item in Abbott's safety deposit box.
According to the bank, the box hadn't been accessed since
1957."

Carl studied the picture. "Damn. That's the same pin."

At exactly five-thirty, the phone rang. Jake pressed
the speaker button on the phone. They exchanged
introductions and pleasantries. The woman's name was
Phong Lee. Elvis translated for Phong Lee who said she

hoped she could help.

"Phong Lee tells me she was twelve years old when Hap washed ashore in their village of Yongchou," Elvis explained in his slight accent.

"Does she remember a date?"

Elvis relayed the question to Phong Lee.

"No. She says she only remembers it was hot, so it had to be August or September. And since she had turned twelve the month before, it had to be 1951."

Jake read off a list of questions slowly so Elvis could write them down. Elvis relayed the questions one by one to Phong Lee.

"She says the black man was delirious. He had a bullet in his back and he also had malaria or something. He told her his name was Duke."

"Does she have any idea where he went after he left Yongchou?" Carl asked.

"She says men stopped by the village for food and he left with them. The men had painted faces and spotted clothing. They frightened her. They were American. Duke was frightened of them at first but then after talking with them he shook their hands. Duke told her father that he lost his papers to get home and the men would help him get some made up. He mentioned something about Honolulu."

"Mercenaries," Jake said under his breath. "One last question, Elvis. How does Phong Lee know this Duke was the same man pictured in the paper?"

After a while Elvis replied, "She says it was his smile. She had never seen anyone smile the way he did."

Jake ended the call and looked over at Carl. "He had a whole new set of I.D.s made up."

"Which might prove the desertion theory. Why else would he need to change his identity?"

Jake got up to leave, then turned back to Carl, rested his gaze on him, his brows furrowed. "Are you sure there isn't some information you want to share with me?"

Carl shoved his hands deep in his pants pocket, studied the patterned carpeting. For a moment, Jake thought Carl might finally tell him what was bothering him. Instead, Carl patted him on the back as he walked Jake to the door.

"Have patience."

41

Preston walked up behind Cain. "What are you looking at?"

Cain's thick fingers were parting the white sheers hanging from the window in the ballroom. "There was a dark car following me from the hotel this morning."

"Could have been a coincidence."

Cain shook his head. "Maybe, maybe not. I made a detour through the shopping center and eventually lost him."

"Did you get a look at the driver?"

"Dark windows. Could be cops."

"You are jumpy." Preston walked over to the silver tray on the bar and poured himself a glass of orange juice. His heels clicked against the polished marble floor. "You did an excellent job in Dallas. They have made it official. My dear friend, George Abbott, died of natural causes. No witnesses. Another clean job."

"What about Parker Smith?"

Preston reached into the inside pocket of his linen jacket and pulled out an envelope. "Parker is a vegetable. He's no threat. Ames is already dead. That takes care of everyone." He handed Cain the envelope. "There's a little bonus in there, too. The helicopter should be coming soon. I'll be leaving shortly for a meeting in Springfield."

"When will you be back?"

"Late this evening or early morning, depending on

the weather."

Cain watched a blue Jeep ramble up the drive. "Are you expecting company?"

Preston looked over Cain's shoulder. "Come." Preston led Cain down the hallway to the living room. He motioned for him to wait around the corner in the dining room. A few minutes later, Juanita knocked on the door and announced his visitor.

"Hope this isn't a bad time, Mr. Hilliard," Sam said with a somewhat monotone voice that said, *I don't really give a damn if it is.* Preston extended his hand which she clasped firmly.

"I'm leaving in a few moments. What can I do for you, Sergeant Casey?"

Sam took a seat on the Queen Anne sofa. Preston chose a regal high-backed chair. "I'm sure you've read about the body discovered in the overpass."

"Yes. A syndicate hit, wasn't it?" Preston smiled slightly, then added, "or was it a drug buy gone bad?" Hearing a helicopter droning nearby, he checked his watch.

Sam watched him closely, her eyes dissecting his every move, her mind digesting and storing the information for future use. She pulled out a picture of Hap Wilson from her purse and said, "I understand that you served in the Korean War. Mushima Valley seemed to be where you made a name for yourself."

Preston picked up the picture of Hap and studied it. "He wasn't one of the wounded I carried out."

"No?" Sam asked with an innocent, wide-eyed expression.

"There weren't any blacks on that killing field. I would have remembered that."

"You don't recall during your tour of duty in Korea of ever seeing this man?"

Preston gave a half-hearted laugh and tossed the picture on the coffee table in front of her. "My dear girl, that war ended over forty years ago. Where has this man been all that time? He has been reported missing from duty while the rest of us risked life and limb. And you expect anyone to have any interest whatsoever in where he has hidden himself all these years?"

Preston pulled a piece of lint from his pants and held it up as if scrutinizing this foreign object that dared to soil his clothing. Standing up, he straightened his floral silk tie and buttoned his suit coat over his trim torso. "I saw a lot of men die in that war, Sergeant. I myself was wounded. I won't spend one more second discussing a cowardly deserter."

He was ending the meeting. Sam watched him walk to the door. She picked up the picture and followed him.

"Did you know George Abbott?"

Preston turned, his hand on the front door knob.

"Abbott?" He furrowed his brow in thought. "Yes, he was with me in Korea, for a brief time. I'm ashamed to say I didn't keep in touch with anyone after Korea." He held the front door open.

"The Dallas police are looking into Abbott's death as a possible homicide."

"Oh, really? The papers say the police closed that case."

"That's what the police want the press to print." She handed him a picture of Cain. "What about this man? His name is Cain Valenzio and it's possible he might be tied to Abbott's death. Maybe he has some vendetta against Korean War vets."

Preston grew silent. Overhead, the helicopter was sweeping around for its landing in the backyard. The updraft sent tree branches swaying.

Sam could tell by the way his temples pulsed that she had hit a nerve. "Well, I see your ride is here." She motioned for him to keep the picture of Cain. "Have a safe trip, Mr. Hilliard."

Sam smiled as she walked to her Jeep. She had ruffled his feathers, and ruffling a few feathers was always her favorite way to start out a morning.

As the pilot carried Preston's suit bag and briefcase onto the helicopter, Preston made a quick call.

"You need to rein in Sergeant Casey or we are going to have problems."

42

Murphy stopped by Sam's doorway. He didn't wait for her to look up. He just bellowed, "Casey, I want you in my office, NOW."

Sam didn't think it would take long for Preston to call Murphy. He probably called him from the helicopter. She saw the look on Jake's face as she headed down the aisle. It was a look of, *What have you done, this time?*

Murphy didn't bother to close his door. He liked an audience when he was chewing out one of his subordinates. He planted his knuckles on his desk. "What the hell were you doing at our esteemed state representative's house this morning?"

"Just tying up loose ends."

"Loose ends on a case that's closed?"

"It's routine."

"Routine?" His voice raised a few decibels. "I'll say what's routine and what isn't. You usurped my authority when I specifically..."

"You closed the case too soon," Sam countered. "I didn't know you were the kind of cop to bury a case under a ton of red tape."

"You have a problem, Sergeant?"

"My problem is with you. How dare you interfere with an ongoing investigation? Chief Connelley would never go behind his detectives' backs. He obviously is a man of character and principle." Sam kept in control but made no effort to keep her voice down. If Murphy wanted an audience, she would give them something to hear.

Murphy's face reddened. "Who the hell do you think you are talking to, young lady?"

"At this moment, I'm not really sure." Her feathered earring whipped across her face. At one point it got caught in her hair. She was aware of the spectators in the outer office. Some lived and breathed for confrontations like this and Camille Carter's visits. It fueled the break room gossip mongers. From the corner of her eye, she saw Jake heading her way, but Frank stopped him.

Perspiration started to form on Murphy's forehead. The meeting would be short-lived because Sam knew the last thing Murphy wanted was to sweat in his one-hundred-and-twenty-five-dollar silk shirt.

"Sergeant, I think you need some time off to think about this. You are suspended. Take three days to rethink exactly what kind of future you want in this department. No, make it a week." He raised his arm in a theatrical gesture. "Now get the hell outta here."

Sam glared at him. Her hand instinctively found her medicine bundle. Oblivious to the stares and whispers, she returned to her office. All she did was chant in her native Lakota while she clasped her medicine bundle firmly in her right hand.

"Sam, you have to think first before you open your mouth," Jake said.

She ignored him, walked over to the window in her office and cranked it open, all the while chanting. She packed up her tote bag with her notes. Janet poked her head in to tell her Chief Connelley wanted her to call him. It was important.

"Sam," Jake called out after her as she headed for the elevator. He stopped at Janet's desk and stood next to Frank. As Sam waited by the elevator, the two mourning doves streaked through her doorway and into the office. Maury and Andy made a dive for the floor. One officer pulled out his gun and aimed it at the moving targets.

"Hey, shoo them birds out of here," Sergeant Scofield yelled, rushing out from behind his desk. "And put that gun away."

The two mourning doves flew into Murphy's office where they each made a deposit on Murphy's desk right in the middle of the report he was writing to put into Sam's file.

Murphy jerked back screaming, "Sonafabitch!"

One dove snatched a yellow rose from the vase of flowers on Murphy's credenza. It flew over to the elevator where it deposited the rose in Sam's outstretched hand, and then flew back to its mate on the windowsill.

The laughter that erupted when the birds visited Murphy's office ended abruptly when the rose was dropped into Sam's palm. She scanned the silent office slowly, her turquoise eyes seeming to take on a glow. Inhaling the sweet fragrance of the rose, Sam smiled and stepped into the waiting elevator.

"Mitchell!" Murphy stood at his doorway with his hands on his hips.

"What happened to my day-to-day reports on Casey?" Murphy closed the door eyeing the bandage on Jake's head but not curious enough to ask him what had happened.

"You said to report anything suspicious. I haven't seen anything suspicious. Just routine police work." Jake looked at the residue the mourning doves had left on Murphy's desk and smiled.

"Routine? You call anything Casey does routine?" He used a notepad to scoop the littered papers into the garbage can. "JANET!" Murphy yelled into the intercom.

"Circumventing a homicide investigation isn't exactly routine either."

Jabbing an index finger toward him, Murphy warned, "You watch it or you'll be suspended along with Casey."

Janet appeared in the doorway. He pointed toward some of the bird droppings that had missed the papers and stained his desk. "Get something to clean this up."

A few seconds later, Janet appeared with a can of disinfectant and a wad of paper towels. She set them on his desk and announced, "I'm going to lunch."

"Wait." Murphy watched Janet scurry out. "Shit, you expect me to clean this?" He stared at the mess and winced. Gingerly, he ripped off one of the paper towels and took a half-hearted swipe at the droppings.

Jake moved toward the door. "What's the saying? Ye sow what ye reap?"

"You just remember our agreement and keep up your end of the bargain."

"Now that Sam's suspended, she can't very well get into any more trouble."

Murphy straightened up from his sanitizing chore. "Trust me. The worst thing in the world is to give Sergeant Casey time on her hands."

43

Jake dried off and pulled on a pair of clean blue jeans, thanks to Abby. Little by little, more of his clothes were ending up in the locker in the gym. He heard soft flute music floating through the intercom system on the wall. A lit, scented candle on the counter emitted a faint, pleasant aroma.

His hair still damp from the shower, Jake opened the refrigerator and felt for the coldest beer can he could find. He didn't open it, just held the can to his head.

Abby materialized in the doorway. "You left work early." She poured two glasses of iced tea and handed Jake one. Taking the can of beer from him and placing it back in the refrigerator, she said, "Have a seat and I'll change the bandage."

Subtle, yet effective. Jake had to smile at how smoothly Abby did that. She had a certain air of respectability that made it difficult to defy, deny, or criticize her. She was Mother Theresa in a headdress.

"Is Sam around?" Jake flinched as Abby pulled off the bloody gauze pad.

"Upstairs, I believe." She applied more of the salve and a fresh bandage to his forehead. "Alex and I are going to try a new Mexican restaurant in town. Sam doesn't care to join us."

"She's probably still pissed about her suspension."

"Sam was suspended?"

"She has a habit of sticking her foot in her mouth. Now she has a whole week off."

Abby had him hold the bandage in place while she cut strips of tape. "Maybe I should stay home." She finished the bandaging and pressed the back of her hand to his face.

"Don't worry. Sam planned it that way," Jake said. Abby's look of confusion prompted him to explain. "This way she has more time to work on a case that Captain Murphy closed."

Abby shook two aspirins out of a bottle and handed them to Jake. "You have a slight fever. Other than that, the wound is healing."

"How can I thank you and Alex?"

Patting his hand, Abby said, "You don't have to thank me."

"There has to be something I can do for Alex. It was his medicine. Although I'm sure he doesn't want anything from me."

Fabric rustled as Abby sat down. She gazed out at the backyard where Alex was riding up the asphalt path in the golf cart.

"Actually, there is one thing Alex would like." She told Jake about an Irish Setter at the pet shop next to a spice emporium. Alex would go next door to play with the dog while Abby shopped. Alex had a similar dog on the reservation but it had been run over by a truck. "He denies that he has a soft spot for that dog and, knowing Alex, I'm sure he feels he would be imposing on Sam."

"But it wouldn't be here in this house. It would stay with Alex."

"I know, but Alex..."

Alex walked in looking dapper in blue jeans, a navy blue sportscoat, navy blue shirt, and a silver conch as a tie. His long gray hair was pulled back in his usual pony tail. His navy hat had a matching conch.

He gave a nod toward Jake, looked at his head. "How is it doing?"

"It lets me know it's still there when I try to do too much, but I'll live."

"Are you sure you don't want to come?" Abby asked.

"No, thanks."

"There are leftovers in the frig and cake in the cake saver."

Once they left, Jake walked into the study. There was a plexiboard on the wall. With magic markers Sam had written the word HAP on the left side of the board. A line extended to the right where she wrote the year Hap allegedly died. Another line continued to the date Hap's body was found.

Jake picked up a red magic marker. By Hap's name on the left he printed, YONGCHOU. A little to the right of that he wrote HAWAII.

44

Sam took a breather, settling back on the lumpy couch in the master bedroom. She had spent the afternoon cleaning out the walk-in closet. Boxes were marked with colored tape based on whether they were for the church rummage sale or storage until the remodeling was complete.

The master bedroom had fond memories for her of how she used to climb into bed and get lost in the mounds of pillows. She would curl up on her father's side just to smell his aftershave, feel as though he were always there even though he was half way around the world on a news story.

The room looked out of place now. Not just because the decor didn't match the rest of the house, but because it seemed so empty, so...she couldn't bring herself to say the word dead. She pulled a mahogany jewelry box onto her lap and opened it. Inside were cuff links, tie tacks, and a variety of sterling silver bracelets and necklaces with inlaid turquoise and coral.

Her fingers picked through the tarnished silver and leather wristbands until a familiar-looking pin caught her eye. She slammed the lid shut and hurried down the staircase.

"Abby?" Sam clutched the jewelry box as she ran through the dining room into the kitchen.

Jake strode in from the study with his typical gait, long strides, similar to her father's. Maybe it was their height. Even at the precinct, she noticed Jake had a purpose to his walk. It wasn't an arrogant strut. Jake's head would be bent slightly forward, always kept straight, but his eyes would sweep the room from left to right under those thick brows.

"Abby and Alex just left," Jake said. He opened the refrigerator and checked the contents.

Sam cocked her head slightly, looked up at Jake's wet hair and his clean knit shirt that smelled of Abby's fabric softener. "This isn't a goddam hotel, Mitchell. You're getting your clothes washed, your bandages changed ..."

Jake slammed the refrigerator door shut, knocking some of the magnets off the front panel. "I'm outta here."

He slid the screen door open just as Sam said, "Wait." She opened the jewelry box and mumbled, "I need your help."

Jake jerked his head around. "Excuse me?"

Sam took a deep breath despising the fact that she had to repeat herself knowing full well he had heard her the first time. "I said I need your help." She looked at him and tried to stop the tears that were welling up. She whispered, "Please." Jake closed the screen door and walked over to Sam. "I found this in my father's jewelry box." She held up a gold pin in the shape of a lightning bolt.

45

"And you never looked in your father's jewelry box before?" Jake asked.

"I had no reason to. Everything has been packed away since his death."

"Damn." He held the pin between his fingers. "It's definitely the same. But he was too young to have been in the Korean War."

"Hap had one, Preston, Abbott, and now my father. It doesn't make any sense."

"We can't think on an empty stomach." Jake set the bowls of leftovers on the counter and they loaded their plates.

Sam picked at her food as Jake fingered the heavy silver bracelets and leather bands. He found a matching men's necklace. Her gaze swept over his muscular arms and the magnificent way he filled his blue Henley knit shirt. The room was filled with the subtle scent of his woodsy aftershave. She felt a warmth spreading rapidly through her body.

He held up a silver arrowhead on a leather cord. "Beautiful jewelry."

"Abby used to bring back jewelry from the reservation. That's how she met Alex. These are some of his earlier pieces."

"Tell me more about Alex."

"Alex Red Cloud. He's a fantastic jewelry maker,

herbologist, animal doctor, does great rain dances..."

Jake arched one eyebrow. "Rain dances?"

"He came here about ten years ago. Said that in a vision the spirits told him he had been chosen to protect *wicasa wakan*."

"What's that?" Jake retrieved two liqueur glasses from the cabinet.

"It's a holy man or medicine man, someone who speaks with the *Wakinyan Oyate* and *heyoka*, the Thunder-Beings and spirits. Abby is a *wicasa wakan*."

"Medicine woman?" Jake almost dropped the glasses on the counter. "Abby is a medicine woman?"

Amused by his reaction, Sam added, "Any powers I have that you try to dismiss logically were inherited not just from my grandmother, but also from my mother. Watch your thoughts around her, Jake." She smiled coyly. "She can see into your soul."

Jake seemed to be deep in thought, worry lines creasing his forehead. He snapped out of it, poured two glasses of Tia Maria liqueur and said, "Come on. I want to show you something."

She followed him into the study. They stood in front of the plexiboard.

"Who added this?"

"Guess I forgot to tell you." Jake told her about his conference call with Elvis and Phong Lee.

"And you didn't include me?"

"It happened too quickly. Then you were shooting off your mouth at Murphy. I left several messages that you conveniently ignored."

Sam walked up to the plexiboard, drew another line down from Hap's name, and wrote Preston's and Abbott's names. She drew a small lightning bolt by the three names.

Jake took the marker from her and wrote Samuel

Casey's name near the date that Hap had died. He drew a lightning bolt by Samuel's name.

Sam pointed at the empty space between 1951 and 1977. "We still have to fill a pretty large gap."

"DMV hasn't been of any help," Jake said. "Records weren't computerized back in 1951. We're kind of at a standstill."

He sat down on the couch and propped his feet up on the coffee table. "Tim find out anything about Preston's computer?"

"Preston's using some kind of fail-safe code. Tim found the first password—BYRON. But the program is set up so if you don't get the second password on the first try, something is executed. Tim's not sure what it is that is activated but he doesn't want to take any chances." Sam sat down next to Jake, resting her feet on the table by his.

"What about the CIA files?" Jake's arm found its way across the back of the couch behind her.

"He struck out there, too. So he focused on flight logs but he didn't find anyone by the name of Cain. Cain probably used an alias." She could feel the heat radiating from Jake's arm and tried to focus on the plexiboard in front of her. "Tim will find a way to circumvent that password."

Sam pulled her father's pin from her pocket and studied it. "It's funny. When I first touched Hap's and Preston's pins, I got the distinct feeling that I had seen them before. Then, when I touched my father's, I saw the shapes again—drawn, sketched, traced, childlike drawings." She looked over at Jake, his chiseled features, his strong jaw line. She caught him staring at her legs and wondered if her cutoffs were too short.

She took a sip of the flavorful liqueur, then another. She felt warmth in the back of her throat. But what felt even better was Jake's protective arm. It felt good, too good. The phone rang. The portable unit was sitting on the end table. She had to reach over Jake to pick it up. His breath felt warm on her neck. The track lighting seemed to dim. The smell of burning logs permeated the air yet the fireplace wasn't on. Soft music played in the background, but the music had been turned off after dinner. It was becoming unusually warm in the room.

Jake picked up the phone and handed it to her.

"Hello?" Sam could hear someone breathing on the other end. "Hello, Casey residence." Then there was a dial tone. Sam looked at the phone and shrugged, setting it down on the coffee table.

Jake took the pin from her. "Maybe Frank's suggestion might pay off, to talk to the grandfather of one of Claudia's pupils. He served in Korea." Frank's wife, Claudia, was a part-time teacher. Frank had offered to pay the grandfather a visit. "Did you talk to Chief Connelley?" Jake asked.

"Yes. He thinks I should take a much-needed vacation. He keeps harping on how everything I do reflects on him and he'd like Abby to tuck me away on the reservation til things blow over."

"Not a bad idea," Jake said under his breath as he set the pin on the coffee table. He moved his arm away from Sam and straightened up.

Sam checked her watch. "Where could Abby be? It's almost midnight."

"Maybe they went to a show. I'll wait for her if you want to go on up to bed."

"Maybe I will." She gave the board one last inspection.

"I think you are avoiding one crucial point."

She swung her gaze back to him. "What's that?"

"Don't you find it a little curious that Hap Wilson's death and your father's accident happened around the same time?"

46

After Sam went up to bed and Jake called Carl to tell him of their latest finding, Jake filled the whirlpool, stripped out of his clothes, and climbed in. Only the verdigris patina sconces on the wall were turned on, giving the gym a tranquil mood.

The whirlpool was in the far corner, bordered on two sides by five feet of tiled wall. Above the tiles, jalousie windows were cranked open for ventilation.

The low hum of the jets propelled tiny fingers of pressure over his tired body. He leaned back against one of the jets and let the force work its magic on his lower back.

The more he tried to clear his head, the more the plexiboard puzzle cluttered it. But then he found his thoughts drifting to Sam. He could picture every flawless detail of her face, her eyes that were the color of an azure sea, the mass of curly hair he wanted to plunge his hands into.

He spent his life drifting from one woman to the next. It was safer that way, emotionally. Valerie had been the last. Jake met her two years ago when he responded to a call for a drive-by shooting in an upscale complex. In interviewing the neighbors, he knocked on the door of Valerie Tweed, a high school English teacher, twenty-six years old, short blond hair. She came compact, five-foot-three inches, with an hourglass figure. Except for the times that she corrected Jake's grammar (occupational hazard, she had explained), Jake felt they had a good relationship.

Valerie had a pouty mouth, kind of a young Joey Heatherton. Unfortunately, when she opened it she sounded more like a truck driver. Jake thought it was cute in the beginning. But it wore thin real quick.

He rarely called before going over (occupational hazard, he had explained). Once a month for servicing, completely understood by Valerie, or so he thought.

But last month he had knocked on Valerie's door and interrupted a bridal shower...Valerie's. He had the pleasure of meeting Valerie's fiancee. Jake was livid. Not over having been dumped but that she had been sleeping with someone else while he was dating her. Risky sex these days was frightening enough to drive a person to have his entire body hermetically sealed.

Valerie set him straight in front of Jim, the geek science teacher fiancee; the white-haired grandmother who wore a blue pill box hat and sipped champagne through a straw; and all the bridesmaids and other guests.

Suddenly the pouty mouth didn't look that cute, her compact size was too petite, her hair too short and the color too fake. She had always been far too demanding and flaunted her master's degree every chance she had.

It took a lot to get Jake to lose his composure. But he exploded that day. "You slept with another man while you were sleeping with me?" he demanded.

"Wrong, asshole," Valerie replied. "I was a convenient place for you to drop by any time you felt like it. You never called. We never went out except maybe to dinner once in a while. You usually drank until you passed out, then you got up from your little nap and went home. I saw you once every other month, Jake. We haven't had sex in almost a year."

Almost a year. The words had reverberated in his head. He slinked out of Valerie's apartment red-faced. When he confessed the ordeal to Frank, Frank laughed and commented that it was a wonder his dick hadn't atrophied and fallen off.

Jake had done major backpedaling in his day when it came to women. But for some reason the pedals weren't working now. Something was sneaking up on him and he seemed powerless to stop it.

He inhaled deeply in an attempt to push Sam, Valerie, and Hap Wilson out of his head. Suddenly, his senses detected Sam's perfume, that faint clean scent, like the morning dew. Not that sickening floral worn by some women. This was more like walking through a forest after a heavy rain. He heard the flute music in the background becoming louder and wondered if there was a control somewhere else in the house. He could swear he had turned off the CD player.

Slowly he opened his eyes. Through the mist snaking up from the whirlpool he saw Sam. She was walking through the doorway, nude. A leather cord necklace dangling feathers and beads lay against her chest. Another ring of feathers rested around her hip hanging just low enough to cover strategic areas. Her hair hung loose, the natural curl framing her face. Lips were parted slightly, inviting, and her eyes had a sultry gaze which was riveted on him.

Soon the music faded, replaced instead by the pulsating beat of a drum, a drum similar to what he had heard in Sam's backyard.

There was something too dreamlike about this. But his eyes were open. He knew he didn't have THAT much to drink.

As Sam moved her body to the drum beat, Jake felt her eyes burning a hole, drawing him into her. He wanted to move his arm, just a finger, something to prove to himself he was awake. But his arms refused to budge. He tried to speak but his mouth failed him, too. The brown tips of the white feathers touched softly against her breasts. For a strange moment, Jake felt as though they were his fingertips that touched her.

Then she started to drift, not walk, but float toward him, into the whirlpool. Or was it through the whirlpool? She stood close enough for him to reach up and touch those dangling feathers.

He forced himself to move, forced his hands to push himself off the concrete seat. He slid under the water and came up gasping, the bandage on his forehead soaked.

He winced as he swiped his hands across his forehead and face to clear the water from his eyes. Looking around the gym, he saw that he was alone. The door was closed. All the traces of the hallucination were gone—the drum beat, feathers and semi-nude body—but the lust was overpowering. He stumbled to the shower and let the ice cold water pour over his body. It took ten minutes for him to regain his sanity.

He pulled on his jeans and went out onto the patio. His hands shook as he lit a cigarette. The night air felt clammy. Thunder rumbled in the distance. Flashes of lightning brightened the skies. He didn't try to rationalize what had just happened.

He flicked the cigarette butt into the azalea bushes on the opposite side of the brick patio wall and went back inside. As he made his way to the study, something caught his eye. It was lying outside the door to the gym. Stooping down, he picked up the object. It was a white feather with a dark brown tip.

47

Jake rubbed his eyes, downed two aspirins, and waited for Janet to close the door to Sam's office. Sleep had been anything but restful. The scene from the whirlpool had played havoc with his sleep. To avoid Sam, he had met Frank for breakfast.

Janet put through the call from Sheila Ames, the daughter of Leonard Ames who had served with Preston in Korea, and died in an accident in 1976. Once Jake introduced himself, he explained the Hap Wilson case and how her father might have met him in Korea.

"I'm sorry I haven't gotten back to you. I've been out of town. But, Korea. Detective, that was so long ago and Daddy died more than twenty years ago." Her voice had a slight southern accent and was unusually high-pitched, as if she were a fragile, petite woman.

"Did you have a chance to look at the photo I faxed you this morning?" It was a picture of Hap Wilson.

"Yes, I did. Unfortunately, his picture means nothing to me. I did go through the box of Daddy's things in the attic as your fax had suggested."

Jake could hear thumping in the phone as though she were tossing things back into the box.

"There are a lot of letters," Sheila explained. "It would take me a long time to read through them again."

"I'm more interested in the pin." Along with Hap's photo, Jake had faxed a picture of the lightning bolt pin.

Jake looked up. Through the glass window he saw Frank wave. Frank was on his way to South Holland to speak with Amos Washington, the Korean War veteran who was the grandfather of one of Claudia Travis's students.

"Sorry to disappoint you, Detective. To my knowledge, Daddy never owned such a pin. It's not in the box with his medals. He never wore jewelry so he didn't have a jewelry box."

Jake could hear papers rustling. "What about your mother? Would she possibly know?"

"She died five years ago. I remember her telling me that Daddy had a lot of bad dreams after the war. She couldn't do much for him. He was despondent most of the time. She remembered him being so fun-loving before the war. She told me he was always cracking jokes. That's what she loved about him...his sense of humor. But when he came back from the war, he didn't bring his humor back with him. She said it got progressively worse. Especially a couple of days before he drove his car over the ravine."

Jake hesitated, not sure he heard her correctly. "Are you saying your father committed suicide?"

"Here it is." The rustling of papers could be heard again. "Yes," she replied. "Didn't you know? There weren't any skid marks. It was a dry, December day, no ice. No sign of brake problems. His car just drove right off the cliff."

"I'm sorry to bring up such painful..."

"It's okay. Like I said, Detective Mitchell, it's been a long time. Now, I found Daddy's desk calendar. I was only in high school at the time he died," Sheila explained. "He kept his appointments in here."

"Did he ever see a doctor for his sleep disorder?"

"Like a shrink? No. Daddy never went to a doctor."

"Did he have any close friends he might have confided in?"

"As I recall, my mother said he became sullen, absorbed himself in his work." She spent several seconds locating the date in the calendar book. "Okay, Daddy died on December 23, right before Christmas. On December 22, he has the time of five-thirty in the evening circled and Columbus Park written on it."

"Columbus Park?"

"It's just a local park by the court house. I'm not sure of the significance of the time."

"What about the previous days?"

"I'm checking." After a few seconds, Sheila gasped, "Oh, my."

"What?"

"He drew it right on the section marked December 21. It's that shape, the shape of the pin."

48

Frank found it hard to believe the spry man leading him out to the enclosed breezeway was seventy-five-years old. Amos Washington walked tall, proud. The only hints of his age were the leathery skin and bent joints in his fingers from arthritis.

Amos lived in a brick bi-level on a tree-lined street in South Holland. The four-bedroom home had to have cost at least one hundred and sixty thousand dollars, Frank guessed. Four people lived here. Zeke and Alicia Washington were at their jobs at the post office. Latoya, Amos' fifteen-year-old granddaughter, was spending her summer vacation doing odd jobs around the house and catering to her grandfather. She was a pretty girl, with a devilish twinkle in her eye and a Janet Jackson smile.

"Anyone ever tell you that you look like Denzel Washington?" she asked Frank as she set down the tray of soft drinks and cookies. Her staring was making Frank uncomfortable.

"No, not recently," Frank stammered. "I hear more Eddie Murphy and Wesley Snipes. Although I wouldn't mind having any of their paychecks."

"Well, you can bust me any day."

"Latoya," Amos cautioned. "Didn't your mother have a little talk with you about this very subject?"

Latoya straightened up, suddenly appearing as innocent as a Sunday school choir girl. "Sorry, Sir. Guess

I'll get back to cleaning my room."

Once she left Amos said, "Hope you don't have any girls."

"No, just one boy."

"Good. These girls are a handful after the age of twelve."

The breezeway overlooked a tidy backyard, two-car detached garage, and a vegetable garden. The lush, green lawn was edged and manicured to perfection.

Frank looked at the tattoo on Amos' forearm. It was faint under the dark skin but he could make out the shape of a hula dancer.

"Yep, I've seen a lot in my day, officer." Amos ran a hand over his thinning gray Afro. His dark eyes resembled oil drops in a bowl of milk.

"Frank, please," Frank requested.

"Yep, Frank. If it's war you want to talk about, it's war you're gonna get."

"Korea is what I'm interested in." Frank took a sip of his soda as he watched a light rain dot the sidewalk leading to the back fence. He pulled out a notepad from his jacket pocket.

"Terrible war. We had no damn business being there any more than Viet Nam. Those damn gooks fought a mean fight on the ground. We were not prepared. Hell, our troops were physically unfit." Amos offered Frank a cigarette. Frank declined.

"I thought our military always had state-of-the-art equipment and training."

Amos laughed. "Are you kidding? You ain't never been in the military, I take it."

"Sure. I served four years in the Army."

"Ever see action?" Amos glared. "Unless you been in the trenches, you don't know shit." After a few seconds of silence, Amos added, "Even that Desert Storm fiasco was a laugh. They sent our boys with gas masks that were fifty damn years old." Amos scoffed. "All this military spending going on and we spend it on billion dollar planes to make our defense look good. Meanwhile, our boys still carry the same M-16 rifles that were used in Nam."

"How many years were you in the service?"

"Thirty years. I got out at fifty. Went to work for the post office. Got my boy, Zeke, a job there."

"What did you make it to? Colonel?"

Amos laughed again. "Lieutenant. Ain't no *nigra offisahs* in the military. That's what our commander always said."

"But we've come a long way. Look at Colin Powell."

Amos smashed his cigarette in the ashtray and reached for a chocolate chip cookie. "Look at the swastikas still being painted on the doors at the barracks. It's been in the news." Amos passed the plate of cookies to Frank who took a couple. "They can write all the laws they want, Frank. But what happens out there in the trenches, the White House either refuses to see or covers up."

The rain started coming down heavier, pounding the roof of the breezeway. The skies were dark but there wasn't any lightning or thunder. It was just a hard pounding summer rain, enough to knock the aphids off the rosebushes and drench the thirsty vegetable gardens and lawns. Amos walked over to close the windows where the rain was being carried in by a gentle breeze. He returned to the cushioned rattan love seat.

"What about that 1948 executive order?" Frank asked.

"Wheweeey. Yessir, boss." Amos gave a mock salute. "Congress said that segregation was banned. So, poof." Amos motioned with his hands like a magician.

"Segregation be gone."

"Nothing changed?"

"Hmmmrf," Amos snorted. "We had all black engineering units in WWII and Korea. We were construction battalions. We went ahead to build the bridges, sweep the mine fields. We weren't allowed to fight in WWII. We did the menial tasks. They didn't even train us for combat. Our own damn Army loaned us to the French. And the bigoted press did their bit to fuel the prejudice. We *niggers* were subservient, they said. Always drunk, disorderly, disrespectful. We always went AWOL. And why bother promoting us. We always conducted ourselves unbecoming an officer. Bullshit. All goddam bullshit." Amos jabbed his finger at his chest. "I was there."

Frank studied the anger on Amos' face. He had seen it other times on the faces of police officers, black and white, who had been passed over for promotion.

Frank set his glass down saying, "With all due respect, Amos, I thought there was an old military slogan that said, *There are no bigots in foxholes.*"

"Maybe now things are a little better. Maybe now there aren't segregated units. But back then? You didn't know if your enemy was in front of you or in your foxhole."

"Grandpa?" Latoya appeared in the doorway. "Can I go to the mall with Amy?"

Amos checked his watch. "What time are you going to be back?" He studied her bare midriff and short shorts.

"Two-ish. I left your lunch in the refrigerator. Tuna salad."

Amos leaned toward Frank. "Her momma says I should cut down on my fat. But when Latoya wants something, she makes my favorite sandwich, high in fat."

"All right. But you either cover your stomach or wear

longer shorts. You ain't goin' out there with all that skin showing."

She sighed, walked over and gave him a kiss. "Okay, Gramps."

After Latoya left, Frank asked, "What did you mean?"

"About the foxhole? You had to watch your back, boy. If whitey didn't like you, whitey shot you. If some young eighteen-year-old who had never been out of his town before sees his best friend scattered over a twenty-foot area and runs scared, they shoot him in the back."

"You are kidding...aren't you?"

"No sirree. I ain't never told this to anyone since the war. Not even my son. But I saw it. I saw it with my own eyes."

"Why not tell someone?"

"Who? My commanding officer who looked the other way? The White House who would just as soon cover it up and keep its lily white hands clean?"

"What about black leaders? What about Martin Luther King?"

Amos lit another cigarette. "You saw what they did to him. You think he woulda' stirred up a hornet's nest with an allegation of murder in the military? It's been so many years now, who'd believe us?"

Frank closed his notepad and put it back in his pocket. He eyed the proud man in front of him. Amos was still sharp, seemed of sound mind. "Amos, do you really believe there was a cover-up?"

Amos took a long drag from his cigarette and let the smoke trail out slowly from his nostrils. "I'd stake my life on it."

49

Sam looked up from the large volumes of back issues of the *Chasen Heights Post Tribune*. Jake was standing in the doorway of the conference room at the Chasen Heights Public Library.

"How did you know where to find me?" Sam asked.

"It's what I would have done. Your father was a reporter. Hap had a story to tell. There might be a clue in the papers," Jake pushed several volumes to the opposite side of the conference table. "How did you sleep?"

"All I saw were the lightning bolt shapes. I missed Abby this morning. She must have left early. I wanted to ask her about my father's car accident."

"So you slept through the alarm?"

"What alarm?"

"There was someone in the yard last night right after Abby and Alex came home. Alex and I searched the yard but we didn't come up with anything."

Sam shrugged. "Probably a deer."

"What have you found so far?"

"I actually started in January of 1977. It was a one-year project rebuilding that overpass. My father started getting involved in the political campaigns in February.

They skimmed the pages in silence searching for any bylines with Samuel Casey's name. "I need a break." Sam pushed herself away from the table, stood up and stretched. She walked slowly around the room trying to get the circulation going in her legs.

For the next twenty minutes, Jake worked his way backwards through the pages from August, July, June. Then he came across an obituary in June. "Sam," he called out.

She walked over and leaned on the table. The obituary was on Samuel and Melinda Casey. It was very complimentary, listing all of Melinda's charitable work and Samuel's literary awards. It mentioned the only surviving relative as their five-year-old daughter, Samantha. No mention was made of the car accident. Only that they were pronounced dead at the scene.

Jake asked, "You've never seen this before, have you?"

"No." She sat down and read the obit again. It contained pictures of the happy couple, youthful and vibrant.

Jake placed his hand on top of hers and gave it a squeeze.

"You okay?"

She didn't look at him, couldn't take her eyes off the page. But she felt the electricity flowing from his hand to hers. She felt her hand squeeze back, hold on tightly. His skin was warm, almost hot. Her eyes moved from the page to his hand and he quickly removed it.

"I guess I expected it to say more about the accident," Sam said.

"Maybe it's in the Wednesday edition."

He turned the pages as he worked his way back through the hard bound volume. It wasn't in Wednesday's paper or the one prior to that. But it did make the headlines in the Monday edition.

Sam inhaled deeply, her breath coming in short gasps.

EXPLOSION KILLS AWARD WINNING
REPORTER AND HIS WIFE

50

Sam picked up a small, white box sitting on the island counter. Inside was her father's lightning bolt pin hanging from a fourteen-carat gold chain.

Walking up behind her, Jake said, "Don't say I never pay my own way."

"You did this?"

"Actually, Alex modified the pin to a pendant. The chain was mine. It was too tight for me." Sam unclasped the chain. "Here, I'll get that." Jake grabbed the necklace from her and reached around her neck.

That familiar pounding in Sam's ears was distracting. She was close enough to see the yellow speckles in his soft brown eyes.

"Perfect fit," he said as he pulled away.

They heard a beep from the computer and walked to the study. "Great," Sam said. "Tim found Cain." She waited for the sheet to come off the printer. "Instead of focusing on Dallas, he focused on any repeat traveler who flew into Chicago, then Dallas, and back to Chicago. He used the name Al Morgan."

The one page gave a post office box number in Brooklyn. "Clever," Jake pointed out. "He never paid by charge card and even changed the post office box several times. It will be hard to prove anything. Let me handle this one." Jake took the page from her, folded it up and slipped it under his keys on the bar.

Abby and Alex entered through the patio door carrying bags of groceries.

"Abby," Jake said, "we really need to talk to you." He pulled out a stool for her at the counter. Sam took a seat next to her.

Alex placed the bag of groceries on the counter saying in an indignant voice, "And Abby needs to talk to you, Sam. Using your gift to have those mourning doves do such a disgraceful act." He rested his gaze on Jake as if he were the one who instigated it. "Bad influences."

"Another time, Alex." Abby turned to Jake. "What did you want to ask me?"

"What happened the day Sam's father died?" He recapped the Hap Wilson case, informing her of the pins, the death of George Abbott, Preston Hilliard's possible involvement, Elvis's efforts to find someone from Korea who might have known Hap.

Sam showed Abby a picture of Hap Wilson and the pin hanging from the chain around her neck.

"You found this in your father's jewelry box?" Abby touched the pin.

"Yes," Sam replied.

Abby sighed. "Are you sure you want to hear this? It's been so long." When Sam nodded, Abby started. "I am not aware of what story he had been working on but it was something big. After receiving a disturbing phone call, he made arrangements to go out of town. He was going to fly Melinda to Connecticut to stay with friends and wanted me to take Samantha to the reservation. He asked me to bring Samantha to the office to say good-bye. Samuel and Melinda then climbed into their car. He turned the key in the ignition and," Abby stopped and took a deep breath.

"And we know what happened next," Jake said.

Abby nodded. "It was a horrible sight." She looked

into Sam's eyes, touched the back of her hand to Sam's face. "You watched it all from the window, Sweetheart."

"The newspaper said the police had ruled out a car bomb." Jake told Abby.

"Yes. Nothing indicated that it was anything other than a freak incident, a gas leak, a spark from somewhere. I didn't really understand the explanation."

Sam tried to visualize the scene, search her memory, to no avail. "Why don't I remember anything?"

"The last time you saw your father, you saw his head blown through the windshield and the rest of his body blown apart. Your mind has blocked out everything that happened that day. You were catatonic." She brushed a wisp of hair from Sam's face. "You didn't speak for two years. That's why I always thought it best not to ever tell you about that day."

Alex said, "Abby did what she thought was best for you, Sam. Back then, clinics believed in shock therapy and drugs to bring patients out of catatonic conditions. She took you where our medicine could do you the most good."

Abby reached across the counter and patted Alex's hand. To Sam she said, "Your mind still blocked out that day but at least you started talking again."

Sam hugged her mother. "I understand. It's all right."

"But you haven't seen the pin before?" Jake asked.

"No. And I don't remember ever meeting this Mr. Wilson."

Frank walked in from the patio. They gathered in the study where Jake told him about his conversation with Sheila Ames, the daughter of Leonard Ames, one of Preston's unit members who, two days before driving his car off a cliff, had drawn a shape of a lightning bolt on his calendar.

"Something occurred to me while talking to her,"

Jake said. "Sheila told me her father was a trial lawyer before his sudden death." He handed them a sheet of paper explaining, "Sheila faxed this article regarding a case her father had worked on that caught the national media."

"I vaguely remember this one," Frank said. "The Blalock wife who hired the hit man to kill her husband. The case was used in a law class I took. Ames defended her?"

Jake pointed to the date of the article. "What if Hap had been searching for Preston and his buddies all along, lying low?"

"And then he found Leonard Ames in 1976." Frank skimmed the article. "This gives the name of the law firm, the city."

Sam shook her head. "For the purpose of murdering him? I don't think so."

"I don't either," Jake agreed. "But maybe what he wanted from Ames was information on how to find the rest. Maybe getting one of the pins and finding out where Preston, Parker Smith, and George Abbott lived, he would have something substantial for an ace reporter like Samuel Casey to work with."

Sam's fingers instinctively ran up past her medicine bundle to the lightning bolt pendant. "Sounds probable."

"Damn probable," Frank echoed. He described his interesting visit with Amos Washington, the lively war veteran.

"And you don't think he was just being overly sensitive about prejudice?" Jake asked.

"No. I believe Amos. He's completely coherent. Still has a great memory. He's seen a lot in his seventy-five years and I think he was pretty fair and honest with me."

"Had he ever heard the term, *lightning strike*?" Sam asked.

Frank shook his head no. "And he wasn't assigned anywhere near Hap Wilson in Korea."

Frank's cellular phone rang. It was Janet. When he hung up he announced, "Maury located Parker Smith, the last of the guys from Preston's unit in Mushima Valley. He's in a nursing home in Elkhart, Indiana."

51

Carl walked over to the window and gazed out at the night skies. Lights on the break wall could be seen in the distance. Turning away from the window, Carl said, "You look tired."

Jake leaned back against the couch. "Didn't sleep much." Jake had stopped by Carl's suite on the way home. A lot had happened since he had talked to him last. He handed Carl the list of Cain's flights Tim Meisner had obtained.

"Cain Valenzio may look big and dumb but he knows how to cover his tracks. We're keeping an eye on him." Carl placed his briefcase on the coffee table and opened it.

"What I'm about to tell you has to be kept in the strictest of confidence." Carl smiled a sincere smile. "But I don't have to tell you that." He took a seat across from Jake. "I had to get clearance first."

"From?"

"Jackson Whittier."

"The President?" Jake took a long swallow of beer.

"He was chairman of the Senate Armed Services Committee in 1977. I called him to brief him on what we've discussed. I thought he might be able to shed a little light on the case." Carl placed his horn-rimmed glasses on his nose, pressing them tightly to the bridge. "When he was chairman, a reporter contacted him with information about some alleged murders that took place in Korea."

"That reporter didn't happen to be Samuel Casey, did it?" Jake watched Carl intently.

Carl nodded yes. "Those were volatile times back then. We had Minister Elijah mounting a march on D.C. for more jobs for blacks, better housing. He was promising blood in the streets if all his black brothers he felt were incarcerated in our prisons on trumped up charges weren't released."

"What does that have to do with a reporter reporting the news?"

"Timing, Jake. We would have had all-out race riots if the story leaked that white soldiers shot and killed black soldiers in Korea. It happened in a war that was already twenty-five years old at the time," Carl explained. "It wouldn't have served any purpose to dredge it up."

Jake's brow furrowed. "Except clear the name of a man accused of being a deserter."

"You have to believe me when I say Jackson wasn't proud of what he had to do," Carl said. "The President and I have always been close. We went to college together. Samuel Casey was well-known in the media. When he asked to speak confidentially with the chairman, Jackson made time for him. They arranged a meeting time and place. All Casey told him was that he had a source who would confirm that blacks were murdered in Korea by white soldiers. He was going to bring the witness with him to Washington."

Carl pulled several sheets of paper from his briefcase and passed them across the table to Jake. "These are the names of the other three men in Hap's unit."

"You knew their names all along?"

"No, Jackson knew their names. I can understand Jackson's reasoning. He's a fair man, Jake. He's very concerned about all this surfacing."

Jake studied the names on the list. "What about *lightning strike?*"

"It was a play on the term the North Koreans used. According to what little Samuel Casey would tell Jackson over the phone, a soldier made a strike if he shot a black man."

"And the Armed Services Committee chairman didn't launch a full-scale investigation?" Jake tossed the pages back across the table. "Sonafabitch. He could have proved it." Jake stalked over to the bar and popped open another beer.

"What would that have accomplished?" Carl snapped his briefcase shut. "Samuel Casey died and his witness disappeared off the face of the earth."

"Wasn't the chairman curious about Casey's untimely death?" Jake moved to the arm chair, tapped his fingers on the beer can, the tapping increasing as his anger increased.

"Samuel Casey had been working on a number of stories, one of which was the sale of arms to Middle East terrorists and the Sanchez drug cartel. The police didn't rule it a homicide, but if it had been, there were a lot of people who might have had reason to silence Casey."

"Casey never mentioned Preston Hilliard's name?"

"Never. He only said it was a high-ranking state official. With the death of Casey, the story, the leads, everything died."

"I'm sure Jackson Whittier was thrilled." Suddenly, the beer didn't taste that good. Jake carried the half-empty can to the bar sink and poured out the remaining contents.

"Thrilled to avert a race riot? Absolutely."

"And what is he trying to avert this time?"

52

In the cloak of darkness, Lincoln Thomas checked into the Hampton Inn in Lansing, Illinois, a suburb just south of Chasen Heights. He had spent the morning explaining to his daughter and son-in-law exactly what he was planning on doing.

They gave him their full support. Nina cried and said she was proud of him. Raymond said he and Nina would keep the agency running smoothly and that he should take as much time as he needed. He hoped he wouldn't need much.

Lincoln tossed the keys to his rental car on the table and peered through the curtains. There were a number of restaurants within walking distance. He needed a current local newspaper and could use something to eat. After he made a call to tell Nina he had arrived safely, Lincoln left his hotel room.

53

"I've never seen you stumped before, Sam." Tim sat on the floor in the study while Sam fingered the books on the bookshelf.

"I'm just going through cranial overload. I need a diversion."

"You never told me why they changed your precinct."

She saw a videotape leaning against one of the books and pulled it out. It was the tape Jake had brought after her visit to Preston's. She popped the tape into the recorder, saying, "This is why."

Tim joined her on the circular couch by the entertainment center. Pointing the remote at the VCR, Sam pressed the PLAY button.

"Wow." Tim's eyes widened. "Whose house did you break into this time?"

"State Representative Preston Hilliard," Sam said proudly.

"The chief found out about this?"

Sam stretched out on the couch and propped her head up on one elbow. "No, not this one. At least not yet." Her voice trailed off, not wanting to go into full detail. "He found out about another one and wanted to distance me from him so as not to jeopardize HIS promotion."

They watched the video of Sam hiding in the closet, Preston entering, talking on the phone, then pounding on his keyboard.

Slowly, Sam lifted herself to a sitting position, then moved to the floor so she could be closer to the screen. "Did you see that?"

"What?"

She hit the rewind button. When she played it back, she pressed the pause button. "There. Do you see that, Tim?"

Tim crawled closer to the television set.

She pointed to an area on the screen. "The reflection of the computer screen in the window behind Preston. If we could enlarge that, I bet we'd find out his password."

"I'll get right on it." Standing, Tim said, "By the way, did you notice the dark sedan that's been parked on the street by the entrance to your house? It left when I arrived but I could swear it's the third time I've seen it. It changes location each day, but it's the same one."

54

Jake rubbed the sleep from his eyes. He was getting used to sleeping in Sam's study. After his conversation with Carl the night before, he had an unsettling feeling that the closer Sam got to the truth, the more danger she was in. He was suspicious of the perimeter alarm that had been set off the other night.

Jake made his way toward the gazebo. It was eight in the morning and already eighty degrees. Wearing a pair of floral beach shorts and a short, cropped tee top, he looked as if he should be on an island somewhere. He was supposed to be on the road with Frank enroute to Elkhart, Indiana, but he told Frank to go on without him. There was something else Jake wanted to check out.

He walked up the two stairs to the screened-in gazebo, set his cup of coffee on the small rattan-framed, glass-topped table, and stretched out on the glider.

Closing his eyes, he replayed his conversation with Carl. Jake had a feeling President Whittier's main concern right now was re-elections. To bring out information of a government cover-up would point a finger toward Whittier since he had been chairman of the Senate Armed Services Committee back in 1977.

Jake didn't like being a party to the continuing cover-up. Because now it wasn't just the murders of three black men in Mushima Valley, it was the murder of Hap Wilson and the questionable death of an investigative reporter.

Carl had agreed with Jake that Sam was going to dig until she got to the truth. Carl wanted him to head her off at the pass, and Jake hated having to do it. He had told Carl he wanted the bodies of the three men in Hap's unit found. Carl said they were already trying to locate them. If they weren't deserters and had been murdered, the first place to start looking was Mushima Valley.

Jake pressed the palms of his hands against his eyes. He didn't hear Abby enter the gazebo and sit down in the chair across from him. She reached over and touched his arm.

"You are agonizing over something."

"Agony is my middle name." Jake swung his legs around and sat up. He studied her calm facade, her gentle, caring eyes. Everything in her world seemed to have meaning and order. "Why is it you were never able to tell..."

"That Samuel and Melinda were in danger?" She shook her head. "It was something I had a difficult time understanding. We can't select what we want to see or what we want revealed. We don't have the choice. For that reason alone I think our trip to the reservation after their death was as much for me as for Sam. I had to talk to my grandmother, get some answers."

"Did you?"

"She said there are some things we can't control. We may think we direct our future but fate controls our destiny. She told me to focus on my successes, not the failures."

Jake reached across and grabbed Abby's hand. It felt soft, yet strong. Sam had her strength. Each day he saw more of her in Sam.

"Why is it no man has dragged you off to the proverbial tipi with the picket fence?"

He saw a trace of sadness wash over her face.

"I was married once, briefly." Abby smiled wistfully.

"It was small and ceremonial."

"Just you two and the spirits?"

Abby laughed, crinkling the tiny lines around her eyes. "We had a few more people but basically that's all a couple needs. They just have to exchange a treasured possession, offer it to the four directions, and express their love."

"So what happened?" he finally asked.

The sadness crept across her face again, washing away her warm smile. She studied her hands for the longest time. "I had an alcoholic husband, an alcoholic father, and a dead baby. That's what happened."

Jake saw tears push into the corners of Abby's eyes. She inhaled deeply, lifted her head. The tears dried immediately. He was sorry he had brought up the subject. They lapsed into a comfortable silence, until Abby broke it.

"I believe our fathers were very much alike, Jacob."

Jake looked at her sharply. He had never spoken of his father.

"Alcohol clouded his judgment. He wasn't physically abusive, but he was easily manipulated by my husband. My father wandered around drunk one cold winter night and froze to death. He died the same way your father did." She stared deep into his eyes. This time it really did feel as if she knew his every thought and could see into his soul.

Jake slowly straightened, a look of shock inching across his face. "How did you...?" He knew better than to ask. He remembered the day she had touched his back and the look on her face, of the times she would hold his hand between hers and stare into his eyes as though they were windows into his darkest thoughts.

"You keep a life of solitude, Jacob, because you believe you will end up like your father."

"Like father, like son, the saying goes."

"If that were true, then I would be more like my father, wouldn't you say?"

Jake lit a cigarette and took a long drag. He studied her face, a slight grin turning up the corners of his mouth. "I hate it when you make sense."

Even after she patted his hand and returned to the house, Jake was still staring at the empty rattan chair where she had sat. She never fully explained about her marriage or how her child had died. She just managed to turn the conversation to Jake's father. How could she know about his father? No one knew, not even Frank. She had touched his scars. Was it true she could touch his soul?

55

The elderly man behind the counter looked like a tall Yoda complete with pointed ears and wrinkled forehead. He squinted at the handwriting on the form Jake handed him. Charlie Buckmeister had retired from the police force ten years ago but couldn't seem to keep himself busy at home. So he was hired on as a part-time records clerk.

"Nineteen-seventy-seven? You weren't even born then."

Jake laughed. "I assure you, Charlie, I was alive and driving my mother crazy."

The Records Department archives were in the basement at Headquarters near Central Stores. The smell of paper dust mingled with subtle exhaust fumes filtering from the door to the underground garage.

Headquarters, Precinct One, was Sam's old precinct and home to Chief Connelley. Being a weekend, there would be a skeleton crew upstairs but Jake had no plans on browsing the halls.

"They've been trying to get all the records on those new-fangled computers but they've only gotten as far back as, I think, about 1982." He scribbled the name on a piece of paper. "Casey, Samuel. Okay, let me lookie-see what I've got."

Jake watched Charlie shuffle off to the filing cabinets. A half-empty cup of coffee sat next to a chocolate donut with two bites out of it.

"Have to try the back room," Charlie called out, having checked the dates on the cabinets in the front room. Several minutes later, Charlie returned. "Here you go. Need to sign out the file or do you just want a copy of something?"

"I'll let you know." Jake skimmed through the incident report on Samuel Casey's death. Reading Abby's comments made him conjure up a picture of a cute five-year-old girl, clutching a doll, waving to her father through the window.

The case was only investigated for three days. It seemed to have been thorough. Even the arson and explosive experts found nothing to point to a homicide. Jake wondered if the technology they had today would have come to the same conclusion. If he had been the detective on the case, he would have spent more than three days investigating it.

"Do you remember this case, Charlie?" Jake asked.

"That specific case, no. But I remember the date. June 6. That was the day before that letter bomb went off at City Hall. Injured three people. Killed the mailman."

"Nice diversion," Jake whispered.

"What?"

"Nothing." Jake pointed to a signature at the bottom of the report. "Do you recognize these initials?"

Charlie squinted again, studying the curly letters that looked like an ampersand with a line through it.

"Naw. Can't say that I do. He would have been the supervisor on the case."

"Why does it say *revise* on the top page?" He flipped through the back pages. "Where's the original?"

"Should be in there."

Jake checked the file again. Only the revised report was there. "What about the two men who investigated the incident?"

"Simms and Beransky?" Charlie rubbed his dimpled chin. "Simms I believe was killed in a high speed chase several years after that. Beransky quit the force not too soon after. Beransky had been driving the squad car."

"Could you make two copies of this sheet for me?" Jake handed the file back to Charlie with the page to be copied on top. He wanted one of the copies for Carl.

56

"You're lucky you came today, Sam," Benny said as he opened the door to the smaller examining room. "We're shipping the body to his sister in D.C. this afternoon."

"So soon?"

"I've delayed it for too long as it is." Benny looked through the glass window to his office where an assistant stood with a stack of papers for him to sign. "You have fun. Let me know when you're through."

Once Benny left, Sam took her necklace off and looked down at the mummified remains that now lay on a metal gurney. Hap probably had been filled with a lot of hope when he had spoken with her father. If that truck driver hadn't hit the overpass, Hap's body might never have been found.

She pushed the necklace into Hap's hand, the one that had held Hap's pin. Immediately a sea of lightning bolt shapes floated in her mind. All shapes and sizes. She sensed fear. Hap's fear. Then bodies, falling in succession. She heard footsteps running, ragged panting. She saw the smiling face in the picture, Hap's face. She saw a man's hands, lifting her onto his lap. She saw the shapes again, and this time, a hand drawing them. A small hand. A child's hand. Her hand.

57

"I wish you had called first, Detective." Mrs. Leland led Frank down the tiled hallway to Parker Smith's room. Her uniform fit snugly over her robust figure. Frank could hear the sound of her nylons rubbing together as her inner thigh's collided.

"I did call. The front desk told me Parker Smith was a resident here at Shady Pine Nursing Home."

She made a face that said *likely story*. "If you had asked his condition, we would have told you Mr. Smith had a stroke three years ago. He hasn't spoken a word. I don't know how you plan to question him."

They stepped into the sterile room. A poor attempt had been made to give the room some semblance of home ...floral paintings, potted plants, a quilt thrown over a rocker. Nurse Leland walked over to the picture window and turned the wand on the mini-blinds to let in more sunlight.

"I don't know why the nurse's aide closes these blinds. Sunlight rejuvenates a person." She motioned with her arms as though pumping iron. "Now, Mr. Smith. How are you doing today?" Her voice had increased in volume when she spoke. Walking over to the frail figure lying on the bed, she said, "You have color in your cheeks. Yes, you do." She plumped up his pillow, cranked his bed to where he was more upright. "You have a visitor." She motioned toward Frank.

Parker Smith showed no response. His glassy eyes stared straight ahead. The thin blanket covering him rose and fell with each breath.

"He's not on a respirator?" Frank asked. He saw the wires leading to a machine that registered his heart rate and blood pressure.

"He eats, breathes. We've had a therapist work with him on speech, but, no luck. He does have some movement in his right hand. Recognizes his daughter... some days." Looking down at Parker, Nurse Leland said, "I'm going to leave you with Detective Travis for a little bit." She patted Parker's arm and left the room.

Frank studied the man in front of him. The skin lay in folds where his muscles used to fill out his form. His gray hair was cut short. Pale blue eyes seemed bright against his pallid face.

Frank pulled up a chair and introduced himself. He watched for telltale reaction as he mentioned Hap Wilson's name and Mushima Valley. There wasn't a twitch, no flicker behind his vacant stare, no hint that Parker was understanding, much less hearing, what Frank was saying.

A cart rolled along the corridor stopping in front of the room. Visitors talked quietly as they passed, some pushing relatives in wheelchairs.

Frank stood up and pulled Hap's pin out of his pocket. He held it up in front of Parker's eyes, let the sunlight glisten off the shiny metal.

"Have you ever seen this pin, Mr. Smith?"

He thought he saw Parker's right finger twitch. The monitor on the cart next to the bed showed an increase in Parker's heart rate.

Second's later, Nurse Leland came running in. "Is everything okay in here?"

Frank slipped the pin back into his pocket. "Sure. I

did notice a change in his heart rate."

"You betcha. The damn machine lit up like a Christmas tree." She watched the monitor. "I don't like the way his blood pressure is rising, though. I think you better leave now. This is a little too much excitement for one day."

Moments after Frank left, Nurse Leland watched in awe as Parker started to cry uncontrollably. He emitted no sounds. His good arm shook, his hand clenched the side of the bed. His heart rate reached one hundred and ten. She made a frantic call to Doctor Chan, who prescribed a mild sedative.

An hour later when Nurse Leland checked on Parker Smith, she noticed he had pulled a pen off the nightstand and scrawled a simple note on his bed sheet. It said,

CALL NOLAND

58

"Shhh, don't say a word. Promise?"

The long cedar-colored tail whipped across the front seat. The Irish Setter cocked its head at Jake and padded restlessly across the front seat of Jake's Buick Riviera. Strands of copper hair clung to the burgundy and gray cloth seats.

"Thanks," Jake said picking up some of the hairs and flinging them out the window. "Now you'll force me to clean my car."

Jake snapped the leash on the dog and led it from the car. From the trunk, Jake hefted a bag of dog food. The Irish Setter sniffed along the driveway and the walkway toward the patio.

The sun was setting behind the tall willow trees. In the distance, Jake saw Alex kneeling in the grass fixing the brick edging around the birdbath. The dog spotted Alex at the same time and started pulling on the leash.

"You promised to remain quiet." Jake unsnapped the leash. The dog took off.

"Hey, Poco." Alex fell back on his rear as the dog jumped on him. "Where did you come from?"

Jake dropped the twenty-five pound bag of dog food on the ground. "She's my thank you for doctoring my head."

Alex looked toward the house. "Does Sam know?"

"It will probably be a week before she even discovers

the dog."

Alex rubbed the back of Poco's neck as her tail whipped the air furiously. He looked up at Jake's head, the gash that was starting to scab over.

"It is healing nicely." Alex looked at Poco, then Jake. Jake detected a grunt as Alex turned to leave. Alex mumbled something about "now I get to clean up all the crap in the yard. Lucky me." But it didn't stop Alex from reaching down to pat Poco on the head as they walked away.

Jake smiled. Alex wasn't exactly showering him with accolades or glowing in brotherly love. But it was a start.

59

Sam paced the length of the dining room table. Time on her hands, too much time. Tim was still working on the password. Frank hadn't called from Elkhart and it was close to seven o'clock in the evening. She had no idea where Jake was, and Hap Wilson's body was on its way back to D.C.

Hap—she had met Hap when she was younger. She had been the one tracing the pin at her father's desk. Hap had been at her father's office. Sam stopped pacing. No, Hap had been here, in her father's house.

She rushed down the stairs by the kitchen. The basement ran the entire length of the house with a ten-foot high ceiling. It was as tidy as the upstairs, decorated with the furnishings discarded from the redecorating Abby had done several years before. The patterned linoleum floor was dotted with a variety of area rugs.

Sam dodged the pool table and bookcase, stopping at the far end of the basement where a large mahogany desk sat. She heard a door upstairs close, then Jake's voice.

"DOWN HERE!" Sam yelled. When she heard his footsteps on the stairs, she said, "Help me move this."

He stared at the four-foot by six-foot red mahogany desk. "It's built like a Sherman tank."

"It was my father's. I remember now. Hap came over to the house, not the office. Maybe he left some notes."

She pulled out the heavy wooden chair and sat down.

Almost immediately the drawings of lightning bolts flashed before her eyes. She smiled and said, "I knew it. I knew there was something right under my nose."

"Don't you think Abby would have found whatever your father might have left?"

"Maybe, maybe not." Sam pushed the chair away from the desk and started opening drawers.

"What are we looking for?"

"I don't know. Something, anything."

"Let's see if we can move it away from the wall." Jake grabbed one end while Sam grabbed the other. It wouldn't budge. "Like I said, it's built like a tank." He looked around the room. "Do you have a flashlight down here?"

She disappeared into a closet under the stairs and came back with a flashlight. He flashed it behind and under the desk.

"Nothing," Jake said. They proceeded to take out the drawers and turn each of them over. Taped to the underside of the bottom right-hand drawer was a small, brown envelope.

Once upstairs, seated at the dining room table, Sam still couldn't bring herself to open it. "Here." She handed the envelope to Jake. "You do it." Jake ripped the envelope open and spilled the contents on the table. A long, silver key clinked against the tabletop. "What is it?" Sam picked up the key and clenched it in her hand. Nothing. No visions, no sounds or scents.

Jake took it from her and looked at the number. "I think it's a safety deposit key, Sam." He checked his watch. "Banks are closed. I'll check into getting a court order."

Frank called to fill them in on his visit with Parker Smith in Elkhart. The nurse had informed him of the name Parker had written—Noland. Noland was Parker's attorney.

After Jake hung up with Frank, he said, "I'm going to stop by the *Chasen Heights Post Tribune* office."

"I'll call the family attorney," Sam offered.

Instead, Jake headed over to the Suisse Hotel to brainstorm with Carl.

60

Ling Toy busied himself tying together makeshift cots to carry the wounded. But he never took his eyes off of the white soldiers. Hap and his friends were covered in dirt and dried blood. But the white soldiers had clean, sleeveless tee shirts, and looked as if they were catching a few rays while waiting to be picked up.

The shade from the scrub pines didn't hide the arrogance in P.K.'s face. George lowered his tall frame onto a felled tree trunk, pulled out his knife, and slowly ran it across the back of his hand. Smitty's bony fingers played with the dog tags around his neck. Len's brooding, dark eyes peered out from under hooded brows. They eyed Hap and his unit like hyenas waiting for the weaker one to drop.

Hap tossed his cigarette butt aside, grabbed his stomach, and told Booker, "I gotta go find me some bushes."

P.K. yelled at Ling Toy, "What are you looking at?" Ling Toy turned away quickly. He tried not to hear what they

were talking about. All he knew was that
Base had instructed Booker, Hap,
Bubba, and Shadow to bring the injured
in. But the white sergeant, P.K., wanted
them to take a look at what was over the
hill.

   Rays from the setting sun bounced off
the weapons drawn by the white soldiers.
Gunfire rang out.

Lincoln Thomas woke with a start.

"Whoa, didn't mean to startle you," Sergeant Scofield said. "Here's your tea." Too nervous to eat, Lincoln had skipped breakfast this morning. He pulled out his handkerchief and wiped his forehead.

"You okay?" Scofield asked.

"I am fine. Do you know when Detective Mitchell will return?"

"Sorry. He hasn't answered his beeper yet."

"And Sergeant Casey? Are you sure I can't have her phone number or home address?"

Ed shook his head no. "If you can't wait, I can have them call you."

"I will wait."

Lincoln unbuttoned his suit coat and, from his seat in the visitor's area, watched as detectives filled out reports at their desks, and others went from phone call to phone call. The desk sergeant himself was either logging in information or on the phone.

Lincoln moved an ashtray over to the table on the other side of the waiting room. The coffee table was littered with half-empty coffee cups and outdated newspapers. He picked up the coffee cups and emptied them in a nearby trash can. Gathering up the papers, he stacked them in one pile so he would have room to lay his paper down to read.

Voices pierced through the commotion in the outer office. Two figures emerged from the elevator. Hoping that they might be the detectives, Lincoln stood up.

He didn't know the well-dressed man the desk sergeant referred to as *Captain*. But the man with the captain, Lincoln would know in the dark. Even if he hadn't seen the cold eyes and arrogant smile, he would know the voice. It was loud, demanding, laced in cynicism. It was him. The man he hated. The man known as P.K.

Lincoln hid his face behind his newspaper and waited for the two men to disappear behind a door at the far end of the room.

Without a word to Ed Scofield, Lincoln left his cup of tea and newspaper and fled down the stairs.

61

Sam stood in front of one of the tall windows in the sitting room watching for Jake to return from the bank. He had discovered that the *Chasen Heights Post Tribune* had been paying on Samuel Casey's safety deposit box. It had been a little-known hideaway for their traveling reporters years ago that, somehow, slipped through the cracks in the Bookkeeping Department.

Abby stood in the living room watching her daughter. "Samantha, please come into the kitchen and eat your breakfast."

"Where is Jake? Why hasn't he called?" Sam reluctantly walked to the kitchen. She snatched a piece of crisp bacon as Abby pushed her onto a stool at the counter.

"The banks aren't open." Abby set a plate of toast on the counter.

"He had to get a subpoena but it shouldn't have taken that long."

Sam glanced out into the backyard. Alex was kneeling in the lawn repairing a sprinkler hose. Just as she was ready to turn away from the window, her eyes caught sight of something. "Is that a dog in our yard?"

Abby peered out of the windowbox over the sink, spatula in hand. "Yes, Dear, that's a dog."

Sam looked sharply at her mother. "That's not funny."

"That's Poco," Abby explained, smiling. "Jacob bought her for Alex."

"He did WHAT?"

"Alex has been admiring that dog for three weeks. He said she was going to be put to sleep. So Jacob bought her as a thank you gift for Alex fixing the cut on his head. That was very thoughtful of him, don't you think?" Abby didn't wait for Sam to reply. "She's very well-behaved, Dear. And she's going to be with Alex, not here."

"You're fawning, Mom."

"I'm what?"

"Fawning. You are fawning over Jake. All this time I keep waiting for the shoe to drop, expecting him to plop that videotape of me on Uncle Don's desk." Her hands moved in animation. Abby leaned against the sink, her arms folded in front of her as she watched her daughter rant. "But why does he have to? He has you cooking his meals, washing his clothes. He uses my house like a hotel with complete room service."

"I'm sorry, Samantha. I thought this was my house, too."

Closing her eyes, Sam bit back her irritation. She rubbed her temples, realizing how she must have sounded. "Of course. I'm sorry." She forced a smile. "I just...somewhere along the line I lost control. And it all started with that damn trip to Preston's."

"Yes, you do have a knack for complicating things."

"Sam?"

Sam turned toward the patio where Tim was standing, his face pressed close to the screen.

"Come in, please. I hope YOU have good news."

"Good and bad, I guess you could say." Tim gave a nod toward Abby.

"I found the second password," Tim explained. "It's GUVNER."

"That's the bad news?"

"No. The bad news is the program can only be accessed at the main terminal."

"Preston's? We have to go back to Preston's?" Sam's face twisted into a look of disbelief and sheer agony.

Sam walked him to the driveway where he had parked his bike. "Oh, by the way," Tim said as he climbed onto his bike. "I followed the dark sedan. The two men went to the Suisse Hotel. Suite 1411."

62

Jake drove up the driveway, resenting the fact that he had lied to Sam. He and Carl had obtained the contents of the safety deposit box last night. The bank president had personally driven over to open the doors.

Carl had made a copy of Hap's affidavit and even kept the last two pages. "Sergeant Casey doesn't need to see those two pages," Carl had said.

It was then that Jake knew Carl had seen the affidavit before. Carl hadn't even read what was in the safety deposit box. He had gone right to the last two pages.

Carl finally admitted it. "President Whitter received this report by courier from Samuel Casey AFTER Samuel Casey's death. He must have suspected that his life was in danger and wanted to make sure a copy got into the right hands. The President faxed me copies of it after I arrived in Chasen Heights. I'm as sick about this as you are, Jake."

Jake couldn't believe those bodies had been out there all this time, and no one had checked out the story. The families had been led to believe that their sons were deserters.

The coup de grace was, they had found the bodies, all three of Hap's friends. Question was: Did they die in battle? Or were they murdered?

Jake turned the ignition off, leaned his forehead against the steering wheel. Carl had to work on President

Whittier. An election seemed to be more important to the President. Carl's parting words were for Jake to make sure Sam didn't find out the truth.

63

Through the bay window Jake watched Alex tossing a ball to Poco. The sun was blinding, the air humid. The forecast said it would hit ninety degrees by noon.

Abby was cutting flowers in a rainbow of colors and placing them in a basket. She handled the flowers as gently as if they were made of fine porcelain china. *The flowers, trees, plants, and animals, they are all the children of nature*, he could almost hear her say.

Behind him, sitting at the dining room table, was Sam. Her head was lowered, eyes intense, dissecting every word on the pages found in her father's safety deposit box. Jake wished she wouldn't wear shorts. Her legs were too distracting. And he knew if he stared into her penetrating eyes, she would be able to read the guilt that was stamped all over his face.

Or maybe subconsciously he believed what Abby had told him. About why some people on the reservation avoided Sam for fear she could read their minds. Lucky for him Abby said Sam was only good with dead bodies. Jake smiled weakly. He was almost sounding as though he believed it. Abby saw him in the window and waved.

What was it Sam had said? Abby was a medicine woman and could see into his soul. The weak smile started to fade. Abby knew. If he believed Abby had the power, then he'd have to believe that Abby knew about him and Carl and the FBI. Of course, Abby did say they couldn't

pick what they knew and when. The question he now
pondered was, if she did know, why hadn't she told Sam?

Sam started with the signed affidavit by Hap Wilson
describing what had happened that August day in 1951.
He described the horrors they had found, how they had
pulled out the only survivors of the killing field. It had
been Hap, the three other black soldiers, and a young
Korean boy named Ling Toy, not Preston Hilliard and his
men, who had rescued the survivors.

"Listen to what Hap wrote," Sam said.

> *P.K. said he was taking over
> command and ordered us to go up the
> hill to see what the Koreans were up to.
> Sergeant Booker argued that our orders
> were to retreat. I was in the bushes
> about fifty feet away. But I could hear
> them real good. P.K. called us bug outs.
> It's a term used when a troop is
> abandoning its position because it is
> outnumbered or out-powered. When
> whitey speaks, it's synonymous with
> tactical maneuver or repositioning. But
> whenever it's used in relation to
> blacks, it's implied as cowardice. This
> was a Base-ordered retreat. And I was
> hell-bent on seeing that that was how it
> was reported.*

Sam read the rest in silence. "My, god. They just shot
them as they walked away. And Preston handed out the
lightning bolt pins as if they had won Oscars."

"I know, Sam. I read it."

"Hap was shot running for his life. They left him for dead floating in a filthy river. Did you read what *lightning strike* meant? How Preston called it out before they killed them?"

"Hap doesn't mention Preston Hilliard by name, Sam. Only as P.K."

"It shouldn't be hard to prove that P.K. is Preston, should it?"

"Preston Kellogg Hilliard was in Mushima Valley. What I'm afraid of is Preston will say it's Hap's word against his."

"Then how are we going to prove it?" She turned back to the rest of the pages. "I can't believe Hap had to hide out in Korea, then change his identity, and move to Hawaii. He spent his life in hiding. He didn't even want to chance contacting his family."

She returned to her father's notes, which described when Hap saw Preston for the first time since Mushima Valley. Hap HAD tracked Leonard Ames down through the article on the Blalock trial. He had told Ames he would go to the media and tell them the truth. Hap had even managed to steal Ames' two lightning bolt pins. Obviously, Mushima Valley wasn't the first place Ames had earned his medal of *dishonor*. Hap hadn't felt one ounce of remorse when he read about Ames' suicide.

It was on his way to Chicago to look up Parker Smith that Hap had seen the picture of Preston Hilliard, victorious from his first election to office. On the same front page, Hap had read a series segment on the exposure of corruption in the Cook County courts. It involved six high court judges and four high profile attorneys from the states attorney's office. The reporter was Samuel Casey. Hap was impressed by Casey's honesty and tenacity. So he had sought him out, told him what had happened and asked for his help in exposing Preston Hilliard, Parker

Smith, George Abbott and Leonard Ames.

"Hap wanted to confront Preston," Sam pointed out as she turned over the last sheet. "According to my father's notes, he made two copies. My father must have had the original and a copy on him when he died." Sam looked up at Jake who was watching Abby in the backyard. "Jake?"

Jake turned toward her. "I'm listening." He pulled out a chair and sat across from her. "Now we know how your father happened to get one of the pins. Hap probably gave him one of Ames' pins."

Sam flipped through the pages checking to make sure she didn't miss one word. "Hap probably confronted Preston with one of the pins. Preston felt threatened and that's when he must have killed Hap. And because my father was going to go to the Senate Armed Services Committee to expose him, Preston had him killed, too." Her voice trailed off as she thought again of the article reporting her father's death. "I wonder who was the head of the Senate Armed Services Committee back then?"

"Sam." Jake reached across the table and grabbed her hand. "We have no proof that your father was murdered. To keep focusing on Preston ..."

"Speaking of Preston," Sam started.

"No." Jake pushed away from the table and checked his beeper.

"Just listen for a minute." She told him how Tim had to use Preston's computer to access the lock and key icon.

Jake pulled his cellular phone from his pocket and dialed Janet. "Did he say what he wanted?...And no one saw him leave?" He covered the mouthpiece and asked Sam, "Did you receive a call or a message today from a Lincoln Thomas?" Sam shook her head no. He returned to Janet and asked, "Did he at least leave a number?... No, that's okay. I'll be in shortly. If he comes back, make sure he waits."

"Who is Lincoln Thomas?"

Jake shrugged. "He said he saw Hap's picture in the Korean newspaper. It's a pity he couldn't stick around."

64

"Where's he at?" Sam whispered, as she and Tim crept in through the back door by the kitchen.

"Upstairs getting ready," Jackie replied.

They were in Preston's house. The staff had been given the night off. Jackie had conveniently run into Preston earlier and made arrangements to stop by tonight.

"Wow." Tim's eyes took in Jackie's tight black skirt and gold sequined top that was stretched over her massive chest.

"Down, boy," Jackie laughed.

Sam stared at her reflection in the mirror above the sink—long, curly hair ratted for even more fullness, the sides punked out to display her cheekbones, cobalt blue eye shadow, lipstick thick and glossy, and large rhinestone earrings. Her royal blue spaghetti-strap dress looked as if it had been painted on.

Sam was thankful that Jake had been at the office most of the afternoon so she didn't have to explain what she and Jackie were up to.

"Are we ready?" Jackie asked. Looking down at Sam's feet, Jackie said, "And, *pulleeze* take care of my shoes."

"I know. They cost you a hundred and fifty dollars."

* * *

"That's what I hate about getting a call fifteen minutes before quitting time." Frank pounded the keyboard, pressed the PAGE UP key. "By the time we're done talking to the stiff's family and witnesses and writing up the report, half the night is over. Frank tugged on his tie. He pulled it off and tossed it on top of the IN box on his desk. "It's so goddam hot in here."

Window air conditioners were working overtime but did little to cool the central room. Ceiling fans droned overhead. Attempts were made to give desk clutter some resemblance of order by use of paperweights on haphazard stacks of papers or by placing everything from the top of the desks to the IN boxes.

Jake leaned over Frank's shoulder reading the report as Frank typed. Jerry Sauder, the night duty desk sergeant, lumbered over to Frank's desk. His jaws worked overtime on a piece of gum and he walked as if his feet were always in position one of ballet — pointed out, looking painfully awkward.

"Frank, call on one," Jerry barked between chews.

"Who is this Noland guy?" Jake asked when Frank had hung up the phone.

"Parker Smith's attorney. Parker Smith's daughter won't release a letter Parker wrote until she's had a chance to read it. It seems Parker gave it to Noland years ago and told him to hold onto it and not to release it until his death."

"I guess the sight of that pin literally scared the old guy to death."

When Jerry put another call through, Jake punched the speaker phone. "Mitchell here."

"Detective Mitchell?" The voice had a foreign accent, Asian, Jake guessed.

"Mr. Lincoln. I understand you came by earlier."

"I don't trust the phone, Detective."

Frank looked up from the report he was signing.

"Trust me, they are fine."

"No. Nothing is fine, Detective. And I really don't want to come back to your office. Not if he's going to be there."

"He, who?"

"Please, I need to meet you away from the office."

"All right." Jake checked his watch. It was almost eight-thirty. "You aren't familiar with the city so why don't you tell us where you are staying and we'll meet you there."

"I don't want to give my location over the phone."

Paranoid, Frank mouthed at Jake as he shook his head.

"You leave now. I saw your picture in the paper. I know what you look like. I will follow you."

"What do you make of that?" Jake asked after he hung up.

"Someone who is scared for his life."

65

"How are we going to get Parker Smith's daughter to let us have a peek at that letter he wrote?" Frank asked, sliding into a wide booth in the back of Izzy's, a restaurant/bar known for its jumbo-sized burgers, fried chicken, and bottomless pitchers of beer.

"She'll give it up once Carl exercises his authority."

Gloria Estefan was warning that *The Rhythm is Gonna Get You* over the jukebox, while a bar filled with men in baseball jerseys tried to talk over the game on the television set. The eating area and bar were separated by a plaque-filled wall.

The bar should be safe enough for Lincoln Thomas, they figured. Everyone in it was a cop, including Rover, the hog-jowled owner/bartender, who had retired from the force three years before.

Two minutes later, a well-dressed Asian man of average height, walked through the front door. Jake slid out of the booth and stood up so Lincoln would see him in the back room.

He saw Jake immediately, walked over and slid into the booth across from the two men. Jake introduced himself and Frank. A waitress came over to take their orders.

"Have you eaten?" Frank asked Lincoln.

"I'm fine. Just hot tea for me."

The two detectives ordered beer.

"You have a good memory," Jake said, referring to Lincoln's ability to pick Jake out of a crowd after seeing his picture.

"Yes, I believe I do."

The back door opened and a young couple walked down the short aisle into the restaurant. Lincoln gave them a quick glance.

"Is it true what the papers say? Have you closed the Hap Wilson case?"

Karen, their waitress, set the tray on the table and distributed the drinks. "Anything to eat?"

Jake and Frank ordered burgers with the works. Clamping the empty tray under her arm, Karen hustled off to the kitchen.

"That's the department's official stand," Jake replied, "but not ours."

"And Sergeant Casey? I thought she would be here."

"We tried reaching her but she wasn't home and she hasn't responded to her beeper," Jake explained.

Reaching into his pocket, Frank said, "Let me try again." After a few minutes, Frank reported, "Still no answer at home and her beeper isn't on."

Lincoln quickly checked the faces of the patrons at the tables and booths around them.

"You're safe here," Jake assured him. "All cops."

Emptying a packet of sugar into his cup, Lincoln said, "Even your precinct wasn't safe today." Jake and Frank peered inquisitively at him over the rim of their beer glasses. "Allow me to introduce myself. Lincoln Thomas is my American name. My Korean name is Ling Toy."

66

Tim followed Sam into Preston's study. On the other side of the wall, in the master bedroom, Jackie was keeping Preston busy.

Tim's eyes swept down the length of Sam's legs. "I can't get over how short that dress is."

"The computer, Tim." Sam pointed toward the desk. "And make it quick."

Bony knees protruded below Tim's wide-legged shorts. His high-top sneakers scraped along the carpet. Turning the computer on, he waited for the menu to appear.

Sam checked the surveillance camera. It was off. Jackie had seen to it when she arrived earlier. Sam walked over to the door that opened into the bedroom and pressed her ear against it. The sexy throbbing of an Enigma tune radiated through the door.

The gold sequined top slithered slowly down Jackie's body. She stepped out of it and kicked it to one side. Leaning forward, she exposed her ample cleavage toward Preston. His glass was almost empty and his eyelids were growing heavy. He moved around in the chair, shook his head, widened his eyes as the effects of the sleeping powder took hold.

There was a footstool by a makeup table. Jackie

swayed over to the stool and propped up one leg. She eyed Preston playfully as she slowly rolled the nylon stocking down one leg. After stepping out of her shoes, she peeled the nylons off and tossed them aside.

She eyed a silk scarf on the dressing table and picked it up, held it out with both hands, draped it around her shoulders, pulled it down across her breasts.

Preston's head was starting to bob. Jackie let one strap of her teddy slide down her arm as she moved closer to Preston. She lifted the empty glass from his hand and set it on the nightstand. She stepped back, dropped the front of her teddy to her waist, and shook her massive breasts. When Preston didn't react, Jackie said, "I do believe, Sugar, you are either dead or asleep."

"Jezzus, Sam. What is this?" Tim stared at the pictures on the screen. He had used Preston's password and accessed the lock-and-key file.

"Oh my god," Sam gasped. "No wonder he only needed one set of those pictures. He scanned them into the computer." She placed a hand on Tim's shoulder. "Do me a favor and forget what you just saw," Sam pleaded. "What did he program this computer to do? Can you tell?"

Tim's fingers flew over the keyboard. A list appeared on the screen. "It's programmed to send a full set of what's in this file to every major newspaper, television station, and..."

"He planned on sending the pictures to every rag sheet, too." Sam pulled Hap Wilson's affidavit from her purse along with her father's summary. She had planned to leave them on Preston's desk for him to find in the morning but thought of a more devilish plan. She pointed to the piece of equipment on the two-drawer filing cabinet next to the desk. "What does this thing do?"

"That's the scanner. You place the sheets in there and it scans it into the computer."

Sam smiled. "And you can delete what he currently has in there?" When Tim nodded, Sam said, "Wonderful."

She heard two raps on the door to the bedroom.

Poking her head around the door, Jackie announced, "All ready for you."

The two women struggled with the dead weight of a sleeping Preston Hilliard. They got the top half of him into the bed, then swung his legs up and over.

Jackie positioned Preston, removing enough of his robe to prove he had nothing on underneath while still leaving vital parts covered. Sam slipped out of the blue dress, revealing a royal blue teddy.

"Have the camera?" Sam asked as she crawled into bed next to Preston.

"All set, girlfriend. This is going to be soooo much fun."

Preston was propped up by three satin-covered pillows. Wrapping one of his arms around her shoulder, Sam leaned her head back, positioned the necklace so the lightning bolt pendant was in full view, then moved Preston's right hand to her upper thigh.

Jackie snapped pictures as she giggled. Sam moved Preston's head to her chest, pressed his head in close, and repositioned the necklace so it wasn't covered.

"Now lean your head back and close your eyes like you are in complete ecstasy," Jackie suggested.

"Oh, please. I'm going to puke." But Sam did it anyway. "You are taking two sets of everything, right?"

"That's right. One set for you. And one set that we are going to leave right here on his dresser."

The women dressed quickly, covered Preston with the bedspread, left one set of pictures on the dresser, and returned to the study.

"All done?" Sam asked.

Tim grinned. "This is some of my best work ever."

67

"Yeh, baby. I'll be home shortly. Abby's packin' us a late snack." Frank winked at Abby as he spoke with Claudia on his cellular phone. "Did you tell Justin I'll read him two stories tomorrow since I missed out tonight?...Okay, Sweetheart. See you soon." He hung up the phone and joined Jake at the counter.

Jake stirred his coffee with deliberation. He and Frank had deposited Lincoln Thomas and his luggage in Carl's suite. Lincoln's signed affidavit confirmed what Hap Wilson had written about Mushima Valley. Carl needed time to figure out his next step. Until then, he had instructed Jake to still not share any information with Sam.

"Did Sam say when she'd be home?" Frank asked Abby.

"She said she was going to see a friend of hers— Jackie."

They heard voices at the back door, laughing, school-girl giggling.

"You should keep the dress, Sam. You never know when you and Preston might have another date," Jackie said.

When they reached the doorway to the kitchen, the two women stopped. Frank, Jake, and Abby stared in amazement.

"Jackie," Abby said suddenly, her eyes taking in the

short length of Sam's dress. "I don't believe you've met
Jake Mitchell and Frank Travis."

"My, my." Jackie stretched her long talons toward
them. "Hello, boys. Why didn't they have guys like you
when the cops busted me in my youth?"

Frank smiled broadly, finding it hard to peel his
eyes from Jackie's well-endowed figure, Donna
Summer hair, and appealing smile.

"What's this about Preston?" Jake asked abruptly.

"Preston. I almost forgot." Jackie reached into her
purse and pulled out the pictures.

"NO!" Sam said quickly, but she was too late. Jake
grabbed the pictures.

"WOW! Frank yelled from over Jake's shoulder.
Abby leaned over the counter to have a look, then turned
away, a smile spreading over her face.

The necklace was in plain sight in all of the
pictures. It was difficult for anyone to tell that Preston
was not in control of his faculties.

Jake threw the pictures on the counter yelling,
"SHIT!" He leaped to his feet. "You better tell me this is
the only set."

"Uh, oh." Jackie took one step backward. "I think this
is my cue." She pointed at Sam's feet. "My two-hundred-
dollar shoes, girlfriend."

"Three hours ago they were worth one hundred and
fifty," Sam argued, stepping out of the royal blue heels.

"Inflation, baby." Jackie gave a wave of her hand to
the guys saying, "Nice meeting you." To Abby she said,
"Nice seeing you again."

Frank raised a finger as if a light bulb switched on in
his head. He looked at Jackie and asked, "Do you deal
blackjack by any chance?"

"Uhhh..." Jackie glanced sharply at Sam, then said,
"Gotta go."

"She was at Preston's, wasn't she?" Frank asked Sam after Jackie left.

Jake's eyes narrowed. "Tell me you weren't dealing blackjack, that night, too." Sam didn't reply.

Feeling another argument brewing, Frank slapped Jake on the back saying, "Uh, later." He picked up the container of cake, thanked Abby, and left.

Sam had never been on the receiving end of Jake's interrogative scowl before. His face was such a mask of contradiction—one minute grinning, mischievous, ruggedly good looking; the next minute menacing, frightening, threatening.

She felt the air move as Abby slipped past her and disappeared down the hallway. The sound of an owl hooting drifted in through the patio screen. Sam folded her arms in front of her and waited.

"What were you trying to do? Blackmail Preston into admitting he killed Hap Wilson?"

"I don't need to." She noticed Jake was wearing her father's arrowhead necklace and leather wristband but before she could say anything, he lifted up one of the pictures, his tight grip crimping one of the corners.

"Just look. You know he's going to see the pin."

"That's the plan."

He slapped the pictures on the counter again. "You are dealing with a dangerous man. If Preston is involved in Hap's and your father's deaths, he went through a lot of trouble to cover his tracks. He's not above making sure his secret stays dead. I think that intruder who tripped the perimeter alarm the other night was Preston's handyman."

"You're getting paranoid." Sam turned and headed toward the study.

"Don't walk away from me." Jake followed her.

"Who gave you the right to give me orders in my house?"

Jake glared at Sam's punked hair, her bright eye shadow, the thick lipstick. "Go wash that shit off your face."

Her mouth gaped. "Excuse me? I thought my father passed away."

"I thought his daughter grew up."

Sam bolted up the stairs to her bedroom, noticing that Abby's bedroom door was conveniently closed. Where was she when Jake was at his worst? She took a hot shower and washed her hair.

Dressed in sweat shorts and a sweat suit top, she ambled back downstairs. The lights were off in the dining room. She stretched out on the window seat and gazed up at the night sky. She felt bad about her argument with Jake. Part of her wanted to say it was none of his business where she was tonight. A larger part was flattered that he was concerned for her safety. She cursed herself for giving him such a hard time. Something was tugging at her heart. She found herself wanting to know all the secrets about his scars that Abby wouldn't tell her. At what point had she started caring what he thought? She wasn't sure. All she knew was that she did.

Her fingers played with the lightning bolt pendant. Memories of her father flooded back, like how he used to cuddle on the window seat with her. He had died needlessly. And she had been too young to properly mourn him. She thought of the little girl she had no memory of, waving at her father, and watching him destroyed trying to uphold what he truly believed in—the truth.

Tears fell freely. She didn't hear Jake enter the room. Nor did she feel his presence when he sat down next to her. But she felt his arms wrap around her and pull her against his chest.

"I don't need to be held," she sobbed.

He buried his face in her hair and whispered, "I do."

68

Preston slammed the pictures on the bar. Cain picked them up and studied them. He had no reaction, no smile, no sneer. He never had much reaction to anything. He was like a mindless robot. Cain's enormous biceps protruded from his short-sleeved knit shirt. He folded his arms like a palace guard waiting for orders.

"I was set up last night, goddammit." Preston had awakened with a dull headache and a vague memory of Jackie's voluptuous body. But not much more. He had stumbled from the shower, opened the drapes and blinked back the bright sunlight. It was when he was fumbling through his underwear drawer that he saw the pictures on the dresser. Four pictures of him in bed with an attractive woman, sand-colored hair, wearing an electric blue teddy cut high enough to make her legs look as long as the state of Florida. Him, a state representative, nuzzling his nose against her ear, nibbling at her breast through the teddy.

"I should have had you take care of Sergeant Casey weeks ago." Preston paced like a caged animal. "What the hell is she up to?" He balled up his right hand and pounded it into his left palm. "Nobody blackmails Preston Hilliard."

"When you told me she was working on the Hap Wilson case, I followed her, found out where she lives. But her place is guarded too well. Too many people there."

"Jezzus, Cain. What were you thinking?" Preston wrapped a hand around Cain's thick forearm and squeezed. "You only act when I tell you to act."

"Sorry." Cain picked up one of the pictures and studied it. He brought it closer, then said, "Did you see what this woman is wearing?"

"What?" Preston barked. He pulled the picture from Cain and studied it. He walked over to a table drawer, pulled out a magnifying glass and held it over the picture. "This better not be what I think it is." He looked at the enlarged necklace, the lightning bolt shape. "Goddam, sonofabitch."

"What about the black woman who was here last night? Do you want me to look her up? Apply a little pressure?"

Preston waved his hand. "No, no. I need to think about this. We need to proceed carefully." Preston cocked his head in thought. "Sergeant Casey was here with Monique the night of my reception, I'm sure of it. Must have been wearing a red wig. Shit," he muttered. "What if Governor Meacham hired them?" He rushed upstairs to his study with Cain close behind. He opened the wall safe and pulled out papers.

"What are you looking for?"

"Good, they're still here." He clutched the envelope marked A.M. in his hand. As he started to put it back, he hesitated. Curious, he checked the contents of the envelope and found the baseball cards.

69

"What do you mean she went to Preston's last night?" Carl demanded.

"That was my reaction, too." Jake looked at the two agents who stood at attention while Carl interrogated them.

"She must have been in disguise," the older of the agents explained. The two looked like the Blues Brothers, one short, one tall, dressed in dark suits.

"It might have been the car with the youth," the younger agent added.

"Youth?" Jake questioned him. "What youth?"

The older agent shrugged. "A youth showed up on a bike and then left in a car driven by the African American woman."

"Glasses? Nerdy looking?" Jake asked. The agents nodded.

"We didn't think..." the young agent started.

Carl held up a hand to silence the agent. Then swung his hand around to point at the door. "You inform the two idiots who are on duty right now to keep their eyes peeled on Casey's entrance. And if I catch anyone napping again, they'll be assigned to a cow pasture in Hebron, Indiana."

After the two agents sulked out, Carl exhaled, shook his head.

"What on earth was Tim doing there?" Jake rubbed the back of his neck.

"I don't know why I post anyone at that house. From what I hear, you spend almost every night there." Carl cast a suspicious glance toward Jake.

"That night I injured my head, Abby insisted I spend the night so she could monitor my condition. I just got into the habit. Besides, she's a great cook, a great woman. What can I say? I love her."

"Are we talking about the mother? Or the daughter?"

Jake ignored the comment, saying, "I wouldn't bother posting a surveillance on Sam. Tim already alerted her that she's being watched."

"Wonderful." Carl lead him down a carpeted hallway, past the kitchen, around the corner into the library where Frank was pouring himself a cup of coffee. They convened around an ornate, cherry wood conference table. Reference books and encyclopedias lined the wall-sized book case.

Carl snapped open his briefcase and pulled out a report. "I was faxed the autopsy results on the three bodies found in Mushima Valley. As you know, they were positively identified as Booker J. Jones, Calvin "Bubba" Leeds, and Shamus "Shadow" Lewis, Jr. Jones and Leeds were shot in the back. Lewis took one shot in the back and two to the back of the head. All bullets retrieved were U.S. Army-issued forty-five caliber."

Jake shook his head in disgust as he read the copy. "Have you convinced President Whittier to go public?"

Carl bent his head to where he peered over the top of his glasses. "You have to understand, this is a very sensitive..."

Frank slapped the autopsy report on the table. His words were slow, forced, his mouth forming each syllable. "Three black men were shot in the back by U.S.-military issued guns. The killers are identified both in this affidavit and in Hap's. Everyone thinks these kids are deserters. And here they are, victims of a racially-motivated assassination. For godsake!"

"I know." Carl looked to Jake for assistance.

"It's out of Carl's hands, Frank."

Frank's head swiveled, his eyes sweeping the ceiling as if looking for written answers or inspiration. "What about Hap's sister, Mr. Underer? She's counting on you to clear her brother's name. And Lincoln. He went out of his way to make sure the guilty parties are punished. How are you going to reward him for his efforts?"

"You're a friend of Jake's, Frank, and it was on his word that I'm sharing any information at all with you. But nothing," he raised a warning finger at Frank, "goes out of this room." Carl let his comment sink in before continuing.

Jake stood up, peeled off his navy sportscoat and walked over to the window. He peered down at the traffic heading toward the Bishop Ford Freeway—rush-hour traffic heading north to the Loop or east toward the Indiana steel mills and office buildings.

He was having a hard time concentrating. He kept seeing satin sheets and royal blue teddies. His instincts were in overdrive and something told him Sam was unstoppable.

"If I had it in my power to change things," Carl continued, "I would. I call every day to try to convince President Whittier that releasing this information is his only option. But you're detectives. Let's face it. What have we got? Lincoln's word against a highly powerful senior state representative whose distinguished war record has been documented in history books. Do you know what the press would do with this? They'll question whether Preston's opponent put Lincoln up to it. They can write it to sound like Lincoln is the one who aided and abetted the deserters. We need a signed confession. And I doubt we're going to get it from Preston."

"Well, maybe someone will have to force him to do the right thing." Frank began naming black congressmen and church leaders. "Don't fuckin' sweep this under the rug."

"The President is worried about race riots," Carl explained.

"Race riots, hell. He's worried about the election."

"Jake, give me a hand here," Carl pleaded.

Jake turned back from the window, studied the worry lines creasing Carl's forehead. Carl was intelligent, fair. Hated the bureaucracy of the job. Jake had no doubt that Carl was tormented by a choice of following orders and doing what was morally and ethically right.

Jake pointed to a copy of Samuel Casey's report saying, "Did you notice the reference to Samuel giving a copy of all of this to a trusted friend just in case something happened?"

"Wait, now." Frank touched the corner of Samuel's report. "If the original went to Whittier, a copy was in the safety deposit box, where's the copy that went to the trusted friend?"

"Better question is—who is the trusted friend?" Jake asked. They pondered that question for several minutes. "While we're here trying to strategize about keeping the lid on this," Jake warned, "Sam is up to no good. I can feel it. When she and Tim have their heads together, god only knows what havoc they can wreak." He clamped a hand on Frank's shoulder and patted it reassuringly. He looked across the table at Carl and said, "I believe the President should spend less time trying to stifle this issue and more time planning damage control. Because the truth IS going to come out. It's just a matter of when."

70

Sam whipped her Jeep around a corner and down Lake Drive to the hotel. She had entertained the thought of stopping by Preston's house but decided it was best to let him sweat for a while. The fact that he hadn't placed a call to her this morning told her he was already sweating profusely.

The dark sedan Tim had allegedly seen in the past had been replaced by a white van. After convincing herself that Tim's imagination was on overdrive, she finally had seen the suspiciously parked floral van for a floral shop that didn't exist.

She lost the van on the last turn down an alley on Wentworth. She was going to put a stop to this. Against her better judgment, she let Tim use his computer to access the guest list at the Suisse Hotel. The FBI had spent so little time with Benny, Sam had never suspected they would still be in town.

The elevator doors opened and deposited Sam on the fourteenth floor. She looked around for agents, body guards. No one. The hallway was deserted. Matter of fact, Director Underer had the entire top floor. Suite 1411 was the only room.

She pressed the doorbell twice. The door was pulled open by a tall, distinguished-looking man in horn-rimmed glasses. Carl Underer wore his navy suit like a uniform. She could envision his closet filled with twenty identical suits.

"Director Underer?" She stretched out a hand to him. "Sergeant Sam Casey."

He clasped her hand and after a faltering moment said, "Of course." Carl closed the door slowly. "To what do I owe this visit, Sergeant?"

"Please, call me Sam." She walked around the conference table eyeing the serving tray of coffee and hot water, the laptop computer, telephone, file folders, a black briefcase. She made herself a cup of hot tea. "Why are there two goons following my every move? Watching my driveway?"

She assessed his living quarters with its dark mahogany wood, floral wallpaper, Queen Anne furniture, and wet bar. Hallways branched out like expressway intersections.

"I wasn't aware you were being watched but I'll definitely check into it." Carl motioned toward the conference table. "Please, sit." Carl stole a brief glance toward Sam's lightning bolt pendant.

"If you are still in town because of the Hap Wilson case, I might be able to help." Sam watched for his reaction. He was as stone-faced as the statues at the entrance to the hotel.

A door at the far end of the room by the fireplace opened and an Asian man of medium height and slight build emerged. "I'm sorry. I didn't know you had company," the man said. The air was thick with tension. Carl made no attempt at introductions.

"You aren't interrupting," Sam said.

"I'm just going to leave these here for the cleaning lady." The man placed a stack of newspapers on the couch.

Sam saw the heading *Korean Today*. She moved to the couch and glanced at the address label.

"Wait." She looked up at the retreating man. "You're

Lincoln Thomas?"

"Yes."

Carl swiveled in his seat. "There's no need to..."

"Sam Casey." Sam reached for his hand.

"Yes." Lincoln's face brightened. "I stopped by to see you the other day." His eyes dropped down to her necklace. "Where did you get this?"

Suddenly, Hap's written words popped into Sam's head, the report her father had written, the account of Mushima valley. All the names, places, events.

She took a step back, assessed his age. Could it be?

"My, god," she gasped. "You're Ling Toy!"

71

Carl leaned back in his chair, his elbow propped up on the arm rest, a fist pressed wearily under his chin. Sam was reading Lincoln's signed affidavit as she paced the floor.

Carl said, "A copy of everything will be given to the Pentagon, Sam. So, we have just about wrapped up everything here."

"Wrapped up?" Sam pivoted on her heel. "Did I miss something here? Or did you? What about Hap's killer? My father's killer? You can't just let Preston walk. What are you going to do? File a report that those three men died in Mushima Valley of friendly fire and leave it at that?" She glanced at Lincoln who had remained silent. "Did you threaten Lincoln with deportation if he goes to the press?"

Carl held out his hand to retrieve the affidavit. "No one is threatening anyone here, Sam." Carl's phone rang. He walked over to the far end of the table and picked it up.

While he spoke, Sam opened a file folder by his briefcase. Her eyes scanned the handwriting, the paper yellowed with age. It was Hap's writing. He told of the men in his unit, how he believed they were buried in Mushima Valley.

"Things are getting out of control," Carl said into the phone. He took four long strides over to where Sam was sitting and pulled the folder out of her hands.

The pages flashed in front of Sam's eyes like a teleprompter. They had a copy of everything that had been in her father's safety deposit box.

"You knew! You knew all along." Sam could tell by the surprised look on Lincoln's face that he, too, had been kept in the dark.

"She found the report," Carl said into the phone. "With all due respect, there was a better way to handle the situation."

Sam lowered herself into the chair. Her father's papers, Hap's affidavit. Her father had called the Chairman of the Armed Services Committee who at the time was Jackson Whittier. Whittier knew and did nothing. Sam felt numb. Anger and shock overwhelmed her.

"They knew," she mumbled, "and they never bothered to look for them, to confirm what Hap had told my father."

Lincoln blinked rapidly. "All this time? I came here for nothing?"

Carl dropped the phone to his chest then held it out to Sam. "President Whittier would like to speak with you."

72

With a dampened paper towel, Sam slowly erased the writing on the white plexiboard. The names of Hap, Bubba, Shadow, and Booker disappeared one by one. Next was Preston, George Abbott, Leonard Ames, and Parker Smith. Their names reduced to faded images before one last wipe erased all evidence of their existence. It took longer to erase her father's name. It was like losing him a second time, as if his existing on a plexiboard somehow brought him back to life.

With the board completely cleaned off, she gathered the papers from the study and the dining room table and carried them to the living room. She pressed the igniter and brought the gas fireplace to life.

From the hearth in front of the see-through fireplace, Sam stared wistfully at the window seat in the dining room. She thought back to last night and the way Jake's arms felt wrapped around her, and the look of longing in his eyes, or maybe she had imagined it. Maybe it had been the longing in her eyes.

She struggled to bring her mind back to her encounter with Carl and her conversation with the President. Whittier admitted he had received her father's package of information. Carl denied having seen it until just recently. But he also had the pages from her father's safety deposit box. And there was only one person who could have given them to him.

The writing had been on the wall. She didn't know how she failed to see it. As she watched the flames flicker, she thought of the night Jake had appeared on her patio. The familiar way his eyes deciphered every movement, registered every detail, his serious demeanor. FBI.

Jake had been nothing more than another watchdog for Carl. His concern had been a lie, the key he finagled out of Abby, his staying here all these nights. She inhaled long and deep, daring those tears to make an appearance. She heard a key in the front door but didn't look up.

Jake walked down the steps to the dining room. The table was cleared of all the notes, papers. The sandblasted grapevine tree trunk was back in the center of the table with all its greenery, fake cactus, and flowers.

"It isn't hot enough outside for you?"

Sam tore sheets of paper into halves, then quarters, and slowly fed them to the fire. Out of the corner of her eye she watched him walk over, toss his sportscoat on the couch.

"You're destroying evidence."

She looked up at him, gave a resigned sigh and tossed another handful of scraps into the flames, watching the edges curl up and turn to ashes.

"I sold my soul to the devil today," she started. "I gave President Whittier an offer he couldn't refuse."

"President Whittier?" His eyes questioned her as he took a seat on the arm of the couch.

"Yes." She closed the door to the fireplace and brushed the dirt from her hands. She turned her attention to him, tried to look at him as her nemesis, not the man whose strong arms had protected her in the fall from Preston's fence. Focus. That had always been her strong point. She just had to force herself to focus.

"In exchange for not revealing that the Chairman of the Armed Services Committee was aware over twenty

years ago that the bodies of missing GIs were buried at
Mushima Valley, Whittier is going to appoint Abby to
the Bureau of Indian Affairs and grant a few other odds
and ends." A tense laugh escaped her throat. "I can almost
get used to this deal-making."

Jake's face became as stony as Carl's had been
earlier.

"The President, on the other hand," Sam continued,
"will make the murders and Preston's involvement public.
We can finally get the bastard behind bars and reinstate
Hap and his unit to their proper, honorable status."

"He agreed to that?"

He said it cautiously. Sam saw no hint of exposure
behind his eyes, those soft brown eyes. *Focus. All a lie.
Set up.* She had to keep saying the words like a mantra.
Meanwhile, her chest felt as if a four-hundred-pound
sumu wrestler were sitting on it.

"Oh, he blubbered on and on about how he couldn't
give the Black Hills back to the Sioux." She thought back
to the folder Carl had, wondered if Jake might have been
behind one of those doors all the time she was there. She
felt her face flush, felt tears welling up. Again, she forced
them back. "And I agreed to report that my father's papers
were just recently discovered without any hint that the
President was ever aware of their existence. He'll be a
hero in the black community. That should be great for
votes."

Sam glared at Jake. "Would you believe, there were
two more pages to my father's report? It mentioned the
names of the guys in Hap's unit and where Hap suspected
their bodies had been buried." She thought she saw a light
turn on behind those stolid eyes. She gave him time to
digest the information before asking, "How long were
you with the Bureau?" She wiped the tears away as soon
as they dared to show up.

Jake reached over to help wipe them but Sam pulled away and moved over to the love seat.

"I was going to tell you, Sam."

"When, Jake? After Preston received a pat on the hand?" She watched him move from the arm of the couch to the couch. The coffee table between them could just as easily been the Grand Canyon.

"I talked to Carl until I was blue in the face. Frank and I both did."

"Frank?" She was beginning to feel like the punch line of a bad joke. "You trusted Frank enough with the truth but not me?"

"It was what Carl wanted. And as far as Carl changing the President's mind, Carl's hands were tied, Sam. We both want nothing more than to see the reputation of Hap and the others cleared. And I DO want Preston to be tried for murder."

He reached across that canyon for her hand. For a brief moment he touched her. It unleashed her flood of tears again. She pulled her hand away and leaned back. Her eyes were penetrating, accusing, the same piercing coolness she had exhibited the first time she met him at Preston's.

"You had the videotape of me at Preston's but you never used it." Her voice was barely above a whisper. "Now I know why. You needed to be Carl's eyes and ears. He needed to know how close I was getting to the truth, how much I uncovered."

"That may have been true in the beginning."

She saw pain behind those brown eyes, but told herself he was a good actor. Where was Abby when it came to witnessing the true Jake Mitchell, the man she seemed to trust and mother ad nauseam? Abby's powers picked a bad time to go on shutdown.

The grandmother clock in the corner of the dining

room clanged, echoing off the walls, filling the cold silence. Sam leaned an elbow on the back rest of the loveseat. Her fingers tugged on her hair, winding and unwinding the strands around her index finger.

She despised the fact that Jake had broken through her shell, that he had made her vulnerable. More important, she hated the fact that he made her feel emotions that were foreign to her.

"You discovered Lincoln Thomas was Ling Toy and whisked him right off to Carl."

Jake leaned forward, elbows on his knees. He studied his hands as if answers were written in the deep creases. "There's nothing I can say that will make you understand why I had to do what..."

Her head turned sharply. "You're right." She was beaten. She didn't have one more ounce of fight in her. Her emotions had zapped it all out. Rising slowly from the couch she said, "I want you out of here." As she passed him she ordered, "NOW."

She opened the front door and stood waiting. Jake placed his hand on the door, leaned close to her. *Distance.* She needed to distance herself from him before she weakened.

"Sam." His voice was a whisper. "Don't do this to..."

She turned away. "Call first before you stop by to pick up your things. Make sure I'm not here."

Quietly, he left. She closed the door, started climbing the stairs to her room but dropped down on the third stair, too emotionally drained to move. She drew her knees up close and wept.

All this time she had never been able to find a way to get rid of him. She never knew it could be so easy, or so painful.

73

"You hardly touched your meal," Alex said.

Abby pulled her shawl up around her shoulders and leaned back against the bench outside of Flanigan's. The restaurant was across the street from the Three Oaks Shopping Center, a huge, renovated, enclosed center with aqua-colored spires at its entranceways.

Abby looked up toward the sky. The bright lights from the center and Flanigan's parking lot hindered any view of the stars on this clear night.

"I just have this uneasy feeling."

A young couple walked past, the mother holding the hand of a young girl. Abby smiled at the girl whose wide eyes stared back. The mother and daughter took a seat on the bench next to them while the father walked off to the parking lot.

The little girl, dressed in a pale yellow shorts outfit which matched her corn-silk hair, walked over to them.

Holding out her doll to Abby, the girl said, "See my dollie?"

"Your dollie is beautiful."

"Josie." The young mother gathered up her daughter. "Let's not bother the nice people." She led Josie back to the bench.

"You should not let your grandmotherly hormones take over your emotions, Abby. Maybe it wasn't such a good idea to go out tonight. We should have stayed home." Alex rose from the bench, positioning his hat on his head.

"I only wanted to give Sam and Jake some time alone."

A large bird was circling the parking lot. Seagulls scurried from their feasts of food scraps. Patrons emerging from the restaurant looked up as the bird with its forty-inch wing span descended on a nearby light pole.

The hawk turned its head, its beady eyes trained on Abby. It let out a rambling diatribe, a screeching that drowned out the noise from the traffic and the hungry seagulls.

Alex studied the bird and asked Abby, "What does the hawk say?"

Abby sighed heavily and hung her head. The hawk's report on Abby's home front was not good.

"Come." Alex helped Abby up from the bench. "Why don't we go take in a good blood and guts war movie?" He wrapped a consoling arm around her shoulder. "Definitely no romance movie."

As they walked toward the truck, Abby patted his hand and asked mournfully, "Dear Alex, is there really a difference?"

74

Two hours had passed since Jake left. Sam rose slowly from the staircase and walked through the study to the bathroom. She splashed cold water on her face and brushed her teeth.

Her last meal had been eons ago. Lunch maybe? But she wasn't hungry. The pain she felt was new to her. It felt as though a large hand had reached into her chest and pulled her heart out. It was a pain she never wanted to feel again.

She lowered herself onto the couch in the darkened study and pulled her feet up under her. Why wasn't Abby home? She needed a shoulder to cry on. Her emotions betrayed her as the phone rang sending a glimmer of hope through her veins. No matter how much she wanted to, she refused to talk to Jake.

She listened to the voice on the recorder. It was vaguely familiar. When he said his name was Cain, she rushed to the phone.

"Yes, this is Sergeant Casey."

"I...I have some information I think you might be interested in, Sergeant."

The hair on her arms rose. "About?" She carried the portable phone upstairs to her bedroom where she stripped out of her shorts and top.

"Your father's death. I can't talk now."

"Then when?"

"Meet me at 1600 Cornell at ten o'clock tonight. And come alone, Sergeant."

As she listened to the dial tone, bells and whistles went off in her head. A tingling sensation washed over her body. She had pushed Preston's back to the wall. Maybe Cain was going to turn Preston in. Maybe he had a falling out with his boss. Maybe encompassed a lot of options. But she couldn't back out now.

75

A vacant four-block stretch of industrial sites stood dark and quiet. Litter from what seemed like the entire city appeared to have been sucked into this isolated part of town.

It had flourished years ago. A steel container corporation, roto gravure printing company, steel tubing company. All either gave way to new technology or were the victims of cheap, overseas labor.

She had heard the property was being rezoned for a golf course community. Anything would be better than the haven it had been for the homeless, drug addicts, and four-legged creatures. The homeless had moved on. The drug addicts had been cleared out. But the creatures, four-legged and furry, big and small, were in abundance.

Shadows moved along the edges of the building as Sam inched her Jeep to the end of the block. Every nerve ending in her body was dancing a jig. A voice in her head told her to turn the Jeep around and drive out of there. She checked the address again on the side of the warehouse. It stood dark and abandoned, windows broken, weeds snaking up the sides of the building. Pressing the button on her pen light, she checked the address on her notes, then checked her watch. It was ten o'clock.

She pulled around to the side of the building. A patrol car sat in the middle of the parking lot. She breathed a sigh of relief. After backing her Jeep up to a freight door, Sam checked her Glock 26 9mm and shoved it into the pocket of her jump suit.

The tightness in her chest from her encounter with Jake had ceased with Cain's phone call. It had now been replaced with a persistent pounding. Walking cautiously along the concrete drive, she looked for movement in or near the squad car. Her black clothing helped her blend into the shadows. One dim bulb on a building across the street did little to help her view of the dark lot.

Pulling her gun from her pocket, she carefully took the safety off. Staying in the shadows, she made her way around the back of the building. Darkness stared back at her from the scum-and-soot-covered windows. She pressed her back against the building and listened for several minutes. A kite, caught in the burned-out bulb of a street light, flapped softly in the breeze. Birds flitted in and out of the windows of the steel container corporation across the street. The thought crossed her mind that birds don't fly at night, or do they? Or were those bats she was seeing?

A cold chill shot up her spine. Her eyes finally adjusted to the dark. Slipping her gun hand into her pocket, she slowly approached the patrol car. The driver's side window was rolled down. A notepad and clipboard lay on the passenger side. The radio, a cop's lifeline to headquarters, was turned off. Her eyes scanned the top floors of the warehouse. Suddenly, she felt like an ideal target, out in the open with only the car to shield her.

"Anyone here?" she called out. Slowly she walked around the back of the car, her eyes scanning the dark, the buildings across the street. When her foot touched something by the passenger side, the adrenaline rushed through her body. Tiny pulses of electricity raced up her spine, lifting the hair off the back of her neck. *Run*, a voice in her head screamed.

The body of the police officer was lying face down on the gravel-pitted pavement. She felt his neck for a pulse. Nothing. Sam reached through the opened window for the radio. *Ping*. She ducked as a bullet shattered the front windshield.

"Don't even think of calling for backup," a voice in the darkness called out.

Sam peered over the side mirror, her eyes searching the building for shadows, the upper story of the warehouse for movement. "I thought you wanted to talk, Cain?" Tightening the grip on her gun, she moved forward, toward the front of the car only to be met with another barrage of gunfire. To remain here was suicide.

Think before you act. Jake's words nagged inside her head and she hated the fact that he was right. She had held a faint hope that Cain really did want to give up Preston on a silver platter. Maybe had proof that Preston was the mastermind behind Hap's and her father's deaths. Maybe that Cain wanted to testify against Preston in exchange for a lesser charge.

"I AM talking," the cottony voice yelled back. It was followed by more bullets riddling the front of the car, flattening the tires.

He's aiming for the gas tank, Sam told herself. *The damn car is going to blow up.*

Suddenly, the air was filled with the odor of oil and gasoline. A small stream was etching its way across the pavement. A maniacal laugh sliced through the air. She couldn't chance returning gunfire. Instead, she bolted, away from the car, away from the warehouse. A spray of bullets stalked her retreat, followed by an explosion. A blast of hot air picked her up and tossed her to the ground like a match stick. Her gun, which she had thought was gripped firmly, popped out of her hand on impact.

As she rolled her body away from the car, she made a mental assessment of bodily damage. She could still breathe—no broken ribs. Her brain didn't register any excruciating pains.

As soon as she tumbled to the safety of the corner of the building, she jumped to her feet in time to see a second explosion lift the back of the patrol car. Her hand slapped against her chest, feeling the bulk of her medicine bundle beneath her jump suit.

Once she reached the safety of her Jeep, she didn't feel very safe. Panic gripped her like a winter deep-freeze. Her hand shook as she turned the keys in the ignition.

As she drove off she heard the faint sounds of sirens in the distance. She reached across the seat for her cellular phone but it wasn't there. Leaning over, she patted the floor on the passenger side, then under her seat.

The thought that Cain took it, that he had been in her Jeep became apparent. A new sensation overcame her fear. It wasn't just the panic that gripped her. This was different, and it was over-powering. She felt the overwhelming sensation of impending doom...death.

Cain stood and watched the inferno with immense satisfaction. He smiled as Sam's tail lights faded in the distance. There were so many innovative ways to make a bomb these days. Not like the dynamite he had used on Samuel Casey's car. Today there was plastique. It was efficient, clean. And by setting a heat sensor on the thermostat, his victim's Jeep would be miles away before it blew up.

Walking toward the burning police car, he picked up Sam's gun with a gloved hand. The heat from the explosion was intense. The officer's uniform was smoldering but the sounds of the sirens told Cain that the fire would be put out soon.

"Just can't trust these cops nowadays." With a smile, he pointed Sam's gun at the officer's back and fired three times.

76

"I've made several copies. Study his face carefully." Preston passed Cain's picture to the three security guards, copies of the picture Sam had left with him. "You can check with Chief Murphy if you want. This man is suspected in the possible murder of a Korean War veteran in Dallas and the MIA whose body was found recently in a concrete overpass. He's been seen in Chasen Heights and I could be his next target."

The three guards were former mercenaries who had trained with the Secret Service. Preston had used them in Springfield when he had received numerous death threats after introducing a bill to end welfare as we know it. On the surface, his argument for the bill had basis. There were almost ten thousand alcoholics and drug addicts receiving Social Security benefits. Preston had argued that all they did was take their checks to the nearest bar or drug dealer.

But Preston actually was targeting the black inner cities. He had made a statement to a close friend that welfare to the blacks was nothing more than a way for them to receive monetary restitution for years of slavery suffered by their ancestors. He hadn't realized the cameras were rolling.

The guards were well-trained and heavily armed with Ruger police carbines, Stealth C-1000 9mm handguns, laser sightings, and night vision glasses. They would spend the night patrolling the grounds.

Two of the guards referred to the taller one as, "Sergeant." Sergeant Cowles passed out walkie-talkies to his men instructing them what channel to use. They were dressed in dark jumpsuits and combat boots.

"This man is armed and dangerous," Preston continued. It was unfortunate, but Preston couldn't leave any witnesses behind. The only other person who had seen Cain in the house was Juanita. This morning he sent her back to Mexico on a one-month vacation. In a week, he would send her a telegram informing her that her services were no longer needed.

"How do you want us to handle it, Sir," Sergeant Cowles asked.

Preston tilted his head up in a condescending posture and replied, "Do whatever needs to be done."

Having left his fortress under the protection of Cowles and his men, Preston retreated to his study. He flipped the master switch on his computer just as the phone rang.

"Avery, it's about time you returned my call." Preston said. "The baseball cards were a nice touch, but really. Couldn't you have tossed in a Babe Ruth?"

"I don't believe you have any more than one set of those pictures, Preston. I will not resign nor will I ever endorse you. So don't try to..."

"Shut up. I don't give a damn what you believe." The cursor on the computer ran down the menu to the lock and key icon. Preston clicked the mouse. "I do have to admit, though, I didn't think you'd have the balls to hire someone to steal them. Now, I want you to listen carefully."

A rectangular box appeared on the screen with one question, *Do you wish to execute program? Yes - No.*

Preston placed the cursor on *Yes* and clicked it once. *Executing*, the screen flashed. A time clock appeared in the lower right hand side. At the press of a button it would begin a countdown preset by Preston. He had given it a relcase time of seven in the morning. Enough time for the press to review it before his speech. Once released, the time could not be altered or canceled.

"Did you hear that, Avery?" Preston leaned back, a triumphant smile turning up the corners of his mouth. "That's the sound of your career crashing and burning."

77

Jake stood with one foot on the patio and one in his living room. The hot shower and a cigarette hadn't done much to remove the emptiness he felt. Except for a green banker's light on the desk, the apartment was dark. He wasn't sure how long he had been standing there, barefoot, clad only in a pair of jeans, but he knew he was on his fourth cigarette.

He watched his neighbor, Cyrus, pulling his poodle, Jellybean, by a leash. Jellybean wanted to stop and smell every blade of grass but Cyrus was up way past his bedtime. Jake flicked the cigarette butt over the railing.

Carl had finally reached Jake to tell him about Sam's visit. A little too late, Jake had thought. At least if Jake had had some forewarning...but it still didn't change anything. The what ifs, and only ifs, weren't going to make Sam understand. Maybe if he had told her he loved her. Maybe if he could have pulled those unfamiliar words from his mouth. They were there, on the tip of his tongue, unused during his entire thirty-four years. Sam was the only woman who tried his patience. She was so stubborn sometimes he could shake her. But she had Abby's strength, beauty, loyalty. And he wanted her so bad sometimes he couldn't think straight.

If it were any other woman, he would have shrugged it off. He had never lost his head or heart to a woman before. He had never wanted to fight for anything in his life before. Not his job with the Bureau, not for the salvation of his family life as a youth. He wouldn't even fight for his badge. If Murphy wanted it, he could have it. Sam was that lone exception. All he could do now was let her cool down, maybe talk to Abby in the morning. Have her intercede on his behalf.

First, Carl needed his help in the morning. Even Carl had found it difficult to explain how Sam derived all that she did by merely touching the file folder. But it was enough to convince President Whittier that Sam could do some major damage to his political career.

Preston's speech was going to take an exciting twist tomorrow, thanks to Sam and Tim. Without going into too much detail, Sam had explained to Carl what Tim had replaced in Preston's computer program. Carl wanted Jake and Frank to join him at the Jenkins Art Center.

Sam raced her Jeep down a residential street. She didn't know why she took this turn. It was another ten minutes to her house. Her thoughts kept racing back to Cain and Preston. The sense of impending doom was so strong, it overpowered the scent of burning fuel that had filled her nostrils back at the warehouse.

Chills racked her body. She felt something else maneuvering the Jeep, some force steering the vehicle to a safe place. She pulled up in front of an apartment complex and looked up at the three-story building. The address was familiar although she had never been there before. It was Jake's apartment building.

When Jake opened the door, Sam's heart crept up into her throat. He looked good, damn good. All the old feelings resurfaced. She vaguely remembered that they had argued, but she couldn't remember why, wasn't sure if it was something more significant than the feeling of death.

A rush of tears filled her eyes as the sensation that she would never see him again overwhelmed her. Her life was hanging in the balance and she hadn't made proper arrangements for Abby.

She stumbled through the doorway pleading, "Promise me, Jake. If anything happens to me, promise me you'll take care of Abby."

But he didn't answer. He pulled her into the room and slammed the door shut. His hands plunged into her hair snapping off the banana clip. Covering her mouth with his, his fingers found the zipper of her jumpsuit. She returned his kiss in desperation, her hands helping to strip his clothes away.

Their passion was fueled by the erotic images that had plagued their dreams. Sam needed to feel his touch, feel their bodies entwined.

"Sam," Jake whispered.

"Don't talk," she whispered back. "Just make the first one quick."

Jake lowered her onto the rug right in front of the door amid discarded clothing. There were no apologies for what had happened earlier, no discussions or explanations. Feelings dominated. It was lust, passion, and love knowing no boundaries.

Through the opened patio door, among the drone of cars on the street and Jellybean yapping, the sound of a hawk could be heard screeching in the night.

Jake's breathing was slow and deep as he lay behind Sam in bed, his arms wrapped around her tightly. Sam reached up with her right arm and ran her hand up to his shoulder. Every cell in her body still ached for him.

The feeling of impending doom had passed, eclipsed by the love and safety she felt in Jake's arms. She pressed her cheek against his warm skin, his body heat radiating. She wished she could stay just like this forever, in Jake's arms.

She looked at the leather and turquoise bracelet Jake had slipped on her wrist. She in return had given him her medicine bundle. They had exchanged possessions after offering them to the four directions. It was tradition.

There was one more custom Jake didn't know. When two people are married, if one of the spouses dies, it's up to the other to take care of the in-laws.

She drew his arms around her even tighter and whispered, "Now you HAVE to take care of Abby."

78

Cain pulled into the back parking lot of an all-night restaurant just a block from Preston's house. He never parked on Preston's premises, always walked around to the side of the estate and through the opening in the fence used by the landscapers.

He was puzzled that he hadn't heard on his police scanner about the car bomb. The thermostat on the Jeep should have reached the required temperature in fifteen minutes. But the delay might work to his advantage.

For a large man, he moved silently through the shadows. In the distance, he saw lights on in Preston's bedroom. Cain would pick up his money and go back to his motel room. As far as he knew, his job here in Chasen Heights was complete.

As Cain crossed the parking lot, he saw movement in the trees. He stopped to watch and listen. The movement stopped. Maybe it was Jasper walking the dogs, but he would have heard the dogs bark by now. About fifty yards south of the first movement, he saw a second one.

Slowly, he pulled out his .357 Magnum from his hip holster and moved deeper into the shadows. The full moon slid behind a large cloud. In the distance, he could hear the bubbling of the fountain in the flower garden.

Cain moved from one tree to the next, stopping to listen, his eyes darting from shadow to shadow. The moon made an appearance from behind a cloud. When a figure darted out of the light, Cain made his move.

"STOP WHERE YOU ARE! a voice yelled.

Cain was bathed in spotlight. He aimed and fired.

It took four shots to bring Cain down. Cowles and his men approached the fallen man carefully. Cowles felt for a pulse, looked at his men and said, "Good job."

Upstairs in his bedroom, Preston sat up in bed re-reading his speech for tomorrow morning. When he heard the gunshots, he snatched his reading glasses off and smiled broadly. He picked up the phone and made a call. But this call wasn't to Captain Murphy.

"I told you to keep her in line. Now it's too late." Preston hung up before he could hear a response. Then he unplugged the phone, laid his glasses and speech on the nightstand, reached up and turned off the lamp.

79

Sam checked her watch. Five-thirty. Sunlight was struggling to break through the room darkening shades. It had succeeded with the vertical blinds in the living room.

She glanced down at Jake, lying on his side, the sheet pulled up to his waist. She was afraid to kiss him for fear of waking him. If she woke him, she'd have to do all the talking she had avoided last night, like how she had met Cain on her own, how she lost her gun. And she didn't want to listen to lectures.

Last night at the warehouse was a blur. There had been an officer down and she hadn't called it in. The feeling of doom and death were gone. She dismissed it as the shots that had been fired at her. Nothing more.

Right now, she needed to get home before Abby woke up, and then get to the precinct as soon as possible. If anyone questioned her whereabouts last night, she was sure Abby would cover for her.

Slowly she bent down until she was within eye level of Jake's broad, strong shoulders. She resisted the urge to climb back into bed. Her eyes traced the map of scars on his back. Softly, she kissed one of the scars.

The moment Sam climbed into her Jeep and turned the key, that feeling of impending doom reared its ugly head. With each block she drove, the feeling intensified, gripping her with a fear she had never experienced before. She told herself to fight it, concentrate. If she could figure out the source of the fear, she could eliminate it. Abby would help.

She chose whichever streets were the least crowded, not exactly sure how to get to a main street, but needing to get home as quickly as possible. She avoided a city street cleaner on Superior Avenue only to be delayed at a railroad crossing while an Amtrak train rumbled by.

Her thoughts turned to Cain, Preston, the warehouse, the dead cop. Doom hung over her like a black umbrella. The realization that Cain was nearby struck her full force. He was going to try something in broad daylight.

She found herself searching the faces in the vehicles around her...the pickup truck driver with the black Stetson; the yuppie with the starched white shirt and wide floral tie driving a red Beemer; the elderly man in tattered clothing bending over a wire trash can looking for aluminum cans. Cain was around somewhere. She could feel his presence.

Someone familiar ran over to her Jeep. It was Chief Connelley.

"Uncle Don, what are you doing here?"

"Slide over, Sam." He gave her no choice but to climb over the console to the passenger seat. "I tried reaching you all night. I've tried your portable phone, your house. I pulled my car over as soon as I saw you." Chief Connelley's tie was loosened, his hair disheveled. Beads of perspiration formed on his forehead.

The train passed and traffic started moving again, people heading to the train station, others toward the expressway. He stole a quick glance in the rear view mirror as he turned the corner.

"I lost my portable. I left early for a jog and was just headed home to shower."

"I want you and Abby to go out of town for a while, maybe the reservation."

"We already went over that."

"Your life is in danger." He stole a quick glance toward her. "You have to trust me on this." Connelley's fingers and knuckles were white from gripping the steering wheel. His breathing came in short, asthmatic bursts.

Sam stared at his hands. Her eyes were drawn to his cuffs which protruded from his suit coat. A scene played over in her mind—Hap lifting her up on his lap to trace the lightning bolt pin. But something never seemed right. Now she knew it couldn't have been Hap. The skin wasn't dark. The skin was light. And the person holding her had cuff links shaped like bullets.

"Oh, my god," Sam whispered. "It was you!"

"Listen to me," Connelley yelled. He had to apply the brakes quickly as a traffic light turned red. "He is going to kill you if you don't get out of town."

Sam wasn't listening. She was too busy remembering. "YOU were the one who lifted me on your lap to draw the pictures of the lightning bolt pins. My father told you about Hap Wilson. You KNEW! YOU were the friend who he entrusted with his copy of Hap's affidavit.

"Honey..." Connelley reached for her, grabbed her hand. "Let me explain."

Sam pulled away and reached for the door handle. Every instinct in her body told her to get out of the Jeep —*NOW!*

80

Jake stretched and reached his arm across the bed. It touched sheet, not Sam. He swiveled his head toward the bathroom. The door was opened. He called out Sam's name. Silence.

Maybe last night was just a figment of his imagination, like the night he was in the whirlpool. After all, he hadn't even buzzed Sam upstairs last night. She simply appeared at his door, just as she had appeared floating through the whirlpool.

He pulled a pillow over and pressed it to his face. The subtle scent of Sam's perfume still clung to the fibers. He shoved the pillow behind his head and glanced over at the wing-backed chair sitting in the corner. Last night he had sat on that chair wrapped only in a towel. He remembered Sam coming out of the bathroom in one of his shirts, unbuttoned, but she held it together with all of her refreshing naiveté.

If it was all a dream, it was one of the most fantastic dreams he had ever experienced. Sam straddled him, his towel fell open. She pulled some yin-yang thing on him that she said she had read about in a magazine. Told him to stare into her left eye, to inhale when she exhaled and vice versa. And to not move. They stayed that way, inhaling, exhaling.

For the first time in his life he cried out. When they wrapped their arms around each other she had whispered in his ear, "Strong, silent type my ass."

Dream? He refused to believe it had all been his imagination. Propping himself up on one elbow, he felt something solid hit his chest. He looked down and saw Sam's medicine bundle.

The buzzer rang just as Jake stepped out of the shower. Jake pressed the buzzer to let Frank in, then quickly slipped into a blue dress shirt and navy blue pants, official clothes for arresting a state representative. He had told Carl he would meet him at his hotel and they would go together to the Jenkins Art Center.

"Jake." Frank was breathless from running up three flights of stairs. "Did you hear about Stu Richards?"

"Who?" Jake closed the door behind him. Frank followed him into the bedroom.

"He's only been on the force one month. He was killed last night while patrolling that industrial site on Cornell."

"Gang shooting?" Jake pulled a blue tweed sportscoat from his closet and tossed it on the bed.

"Have you talked to Sam this morning?" Frank trailed Jake from the bedroom to the kitchen.

Jake turned from the counter and studied Frank's face. "Why? What's going on?"

Frank looked at the phone and answering machine on the counter sitting next to the toaster. He lifted up the cord which had been unplugged from the wall.

Jake did not remember doing it. "I must have knocked it out when I cleaned off the counter last night." He took the cord from Frank and plugged it back in.

"Guess you've really been out of touch. You probably don't know about Cain Valenzio either."

Jake blinked, his eyes drawn back to the telephone as

if trying to remember if he or Sam had unplugged it.

"Cain was shot and killed." Frank slapped Jake on the forearm. "Hey, stay with me here, buddy. Did you hear me?"

Jake leaned back against the kitchen sink. He had never asked Sam where she had been last night. They had gone from the living room to the shower, where the lingering smell of smoke in her hair was washed out before he had a chance to ask her about it.

"Preston's security guards shot and killed Cain last night."

Picking up the phone, Jake asked, "Have you tried calling Sam?"

Frank placed his hand on top of Jake's.

"The cops haven't been able to reach her at home. There's no answer and Abby hasn't seen her."

Jake wasn't sure what time Sam had left. When his alarm had gone off at six, she wasn't there. But she should have been home by now.

Frank moved his hand to Jake's shoulder, saying, "Word from Ballistics is the bullet that killed Stu Richards came from Sam's gun."

81

While Frank drove them both to the Suisse Hotel, Jake
again tried to reach Sam's cellular phone. Then he called
Abby who said she hadn't seen Sam this morning. Abby
was tactful enough not to say that she hadn't seen Sam all
night. It was while Jake was talking to Abby that the call
came in about Sam's Jeep.

They could see the flames and smoke from blocks away.
Frank couldn't drive fast enough to suit Jake. The words
Sam spoke last night came back to haunt him.
   If anything happens to me, she had said.
   Wooden horses were set up around the perimeter to
keep traffic and bystanders as far away as possible. It was
a busy intersection with strip malls lining the street, a
Burger King, lumber company, and mom-and-pop stores.
As though frightened by the explosion and debris, the sun
had slipped behind a large dark cloud.
   Jake ran around the barricades toward the Jeep, but
the heat from the explosion was too intense. Frank caught
up with him and pulled on his arm. "Jake, it's too late."
   A blue door lay fifty feet from the flaming wreckage.
There was so much smoke, it was difficult to tell how
much of the Jeep was still intact. Grief-stricken, Jake
turned away and leaned against the side of a brick
storefront. He felt Frank's hand on his shoulder. His

senses were numb. Reality wasn't quite setting in. He felt something flutter under his shirt and realized it was Sam's medicine bundle, the one thing that was to protect her from harm. In his anguish, he slammed his fist into the building.

Refusing Frank's suggestion that he have his hand X-rayed, Jake slipped around the back of a two-story renovated courthouse where he found a shaky fire escape leading up to the roof. His gnarled right hand hung limp, sending searing stabs of pain up his right arm. He didn't even wince. The pain was nothing compared to the grief.

He couldn't handle the press right now much less listen to eyewitnesses recount details about the explosion and the victim caught inside. Reaching the four-foot ledge, Jake stopped and peered down. He saw Russo directing Civil Defense cars around the wooden horses and Frank writing down names of eyewitnesses. Clusters of curious bystanders pressed against the barricades

Slowly Jake turned, sliding his body down the brick wall until he was crouched in a catcher's position. Holding his left hand out to catch some of the ashes, he remembered Sam's smooth skin, the feel of her body under his. How synchronized were their movements, as though in a previous life they had been lovers and knew every curve of each other's body.

The last time Jake cried he was ten years old. His earliest recollection of his father's fury was at age three when he had dumped a glass of milk on the floor. His father had picked him up by the back of his corduroy bib overalls and held him over the mess making him wipe it up with a paper towel.

His father never showed affection, never played ball, never took him to Cub Scouts like other kids' dads. All he knew was how to hit. His mother told him it was the liquor that made his father mean, that made him want to strike out. *He doesn't mean it, Dear. He really does love you,* she would say.

At age ten, Jake decided he wouldn't give Evan Mitchell the satisfaction of seeing him cry. Evan Mitchell, who played poker with the boys in the back room of the Frolick Club, who played Santa for the kids at Mercy Hospital. There were two sides to Evan Mitchell. Gradually, the drinking cost him his friends, his job. It reduced his two-hundred-pound bulk to one hundred and sixty. But Ann Mitchell stuck by her man.

She would comfort Jake after his beatings. She would argue with Evan not to hit the boy. Then Evan would hit her. Jake tried to protect her, tried to fight him off. He realized too late how weak his mother really was. Too weak to stand up for herself much less her son. Jake hated her for that weakness.

When he was fifteen, Jake suddenly sprouted up and filled out. It seemed to happen overnight, something Evan hadn't counted on. When Evan smashed a hammer against Jake's head and split his forehead open, Jake hauled off and punched him, sending his father flying down the back stairs of their rented town house. Rather than tending to Jake's bleeding skull, Ann ran down the stairs and cradled her husband's head in her lap.

Jake didn't cry at his father's funeral one year later. Nor did he cry when his mother passed away three years after that. He hadn't thought about his childhood since his mother's funeral, as though burying the last of his parents also buried his past.

Each year of his life from age ten on, Jake added another brick to the wall around him until it was so high even he couldn't see over it. He vowed that nothing would ever get through that emotional barrier. Until Sam. Now he could feel that wall building up again, brick by brick. He had opened up, only to feel pain.

Jake stared at the ashes accumulating in his palm. He closed his fingers around those ashes as if they were the last remnants of Sam he would ever touch. Pressing his fist to his forehead, he wept.

82

Jake stood on the bottom step of the patio. The sun was shining brightly, too brightly. He expected the skies to be crying, mourning his loss.

He had sent Frank to the Suisse Hotel, saying he would meet up with them at the Jenkins Art Center. Anger and revenge had propelled Jake down those grated stairs, off the rooftop. He had thought briefly of driving over to Preston's house and placing his Colt 9mm to the back of the politician's head, execution style. But there was something more pressing he had to do. Someone had to tell Abby and he wanted her to hear it from him.

How damn clever Preston was. Smarter than Jake gave him credit for. In his statement to the press, Preston had shown them the picture of Cain Sam had given him. Told them she had warned him he might be Cain's next target. Preston's hands were lily white—in Cain's death, Hap's, Samuel Casey's, and now Sam's.

Jake stood by the patio table and thought back to the first time he had stood in this same spot. So smugly he had clung to that videotape, congratulating himself for out-maneuvering the clever Sergeant Casey.

But he was the one who had been blind-sided. When he saw her with that mass of long, spiraling hair daring to be touched, the trace of wine clinging to her lips, that defiant glare in those blue eyes, he felt that first brick fall. And in succession they fell like squares of dominos.

"Jacob." Abby's face brightened as she stepped out of the house. Her gaze dropped down to his swollen hand. "What happened?" Gently she cradled his injured hand. Jake winced. He wrapped his good arm around her and held her close.

"I promised you I'd watch over her," he whispered. "I'm sorry I let you down."

Abby pulled away from him. She frowned when she saw the anguish in his eyes. She turned her attention back to his hand. "You should really have this looked at, Jacob. Come, sit down." They sat at the patio table. Abby turned away from him and looked out toward the flowering garden. A soft spray from the underground sprinkling system misted the flower beds. "I'll have to show you Alex's roses. They are finally opening up."

Jake pulled her to him, kissed the back of her head. She turned toward him, placed his left hand between hers and squeezed tightly. And waited.

"There was a car bomb." Jake could barely get the words out. All he knew was that three hours ago Sam was alive. For seven hours last night they had lived and loved for a lifetime. He wondered now if that had been Sam's idea all along. Sensing her impending death, she wanted to experience it all.

"Sam?" Abby searched his face.

He expected her to get hysterical, be emotionally overwrought. He didn't expect her cool detachment. She straightened up and lifted her face as though listening. Her eyes closed briefly. When she opened them, she spoke in a calm, confident voice.

"When I lost my first daughter, I knew the moment I awakened that she was dead. I could feel that her spirit was no longer of this earth." She cupped his face, stared so deeply into his soul that he almost felt her hopefulness, her certainty. "Not this time, Jacob. I can feel her spirit. My Samantha is still alive."

83

Preston glanced over his speech as he stood backstage at the Jenkins Art Center. Already an hour late, he moved as if he had all the time in the world. The waiting area was small but lavishly decorated with burgundy velvet upholstered chairs and solid oak flooring which was carried through to the stage.

"Mr. Hilliard." A man in full military regalia greeted Preston at the door. Ivan Lambert was a World War II veteran. He offered a pale, veiny hand to Preston. It looked as if a strong wind could blow his frail body from here to Chicago.

"Sorry, I was up late last night giving a statement to the police." Preston peered behind the curtains at the sea of veterans, most in uniform. The first two rows were filled with reporters and cameramen. "Nice crowd."

"About four thousand, Sir."

Preston looked toward the exit door and saw a dark-suited man wearing sunglasses, his hair cut short. A cord snaked around the side of his neck to his left ear. A man dressed identically was positioned at the doorway to the auditorium. Preston assumed they were there for his protection.

"What the hell is going on, Preston?" Gordon Sudecky snapped. The seam of Gordon's auburn hairpiece shifted slightly as he moved his head. "I've been trying to call you all morning."

Preston's raised eyebrow prompted his stout press secretary to take two steps back. "I had an attempt on my life last night," Preston explained, "or haven't you heard."

Gordon stuck an arm toward the stage. "Have you seen the press release? You have to..."

Dismissing him with a wave, Preston said, "After my speech. I know it's a terrible revelation and I'm sure the reporters have a lot of questions."

A man in his fifties wearing fatigues rushed in from behind the curtain. "Any time you're ready, Mr. Hilliard."

Preston checked his hair in the mirror and straightened his navy pin-striped tie. The news about Sergeant Casey's death had made his morning. Things couldn't be better.

Turning back to his press secretary, Preston said, "Just go out there and tell them to make the introduction." Preston smiled, imagining how the media must have reacted this morning when they received the photos of Governor Meacham.

84

Jake took the stairs up to his apartment two at a time. Abby had placed makeshift splinters and wrapped an Ace bandage around his hand. Alex thought he had at least three broken bones, possibly more. But Jake didn't have time to go to the hospital. He had time for three aspirins.

Abby told him that after Sam witnessed her father's death, she had run home. The police had found her in Abby's bedroom, in a corner by the closet, her small body rolled up into a tight ball of fear and confusion, shaking so hard the police couldn't budge her. So Abby suggested that Jake look where Sam had felt the safest. She and Alex would check the house. Jake knew if Sam would go anywhere, it would be his apartment.

The door to his apartment was unlocked. Whatever mental state Sam was in, she was still able to pick a lock. He entered slowly, the door closing softly behind him. He was stunned and exhilarated at the same time. It had been hard after seeing the wreckage to believe Abby especially after Benny's call that on preliminary investigation they had found human remains in the Jeep.

But there she was, curled up on the couch, her back to him, still dressed in the black jumpsuit she had worn last night. He wanted to gather her up in his arms, never let her go. Abby had warned him to approach her cautiously.

Sam's arms, wrapped tightly around her legs, shook

violently. Jake saw sections of her hair singed, her jumpsuit ripped and burned. Her eyes stared vacantly, hinting that she could still be in shock...or worse. But she was alive. That's all that mattered.

Slowly, he lowered himself onto the couch next to her. "Sam?" he whispered.

Her eyes brimmed and tears fell like silent rivers. Reaching out, he carefully wiped the tears with his handkerchief, moved strands of singed hair from her soot-smudged face. He took a visible check of her clothing, arms, legs, looking for breaks, burns, blood. All he could see were a few abrasions.

"Sam? I'm here. You're safe." He choked back tears. Sitting in front of him was a dazed five-year-old girl inside a twenty-six-year-old woman's body.

He held his arms out to her. "Come here, Sweetheart." Haltingly, her blue eyes shifted toward him. Her brows curled up in confusion. She saw his arms. It took what seemed like a lifetime for her to finally reach out to him. Once she did, he gathered her up and held her close. Her arms encircled his neck, her fingers grabbing fistfuls of his shirt.

He thought of the condition of her Jeep and wondered how on earth she ever got out. More importantly, whose body was it that burned beyond recognition?

85

"So, she's okay?" Carl asked Jake.

"Physically. She's with Abby now." Jake offered his left hand to Lincoln who seemed more at ease than Jake had ever seen him.

The lobby of the Jenkins Art Center was lined in chrome and glass with a large crystal chandelier hanging over the entrance. Floral carpeting led up the stairs, through the lobby, disappearing into the entranceways to the theatre.

An aging veteran in Army fatigues exited one of those entrances, spilling Preston's arrogant voice into the lobby.

"She wasn't able to tell you what happened last night?" Frank asked.

Jake shook his head. "She hasn't spoken at all."

Frank eyed Jake's swollen hand. "You should have gone to the hospital."

Jake winced as he tucked his arm back inside the makeshift sling. "There's time for that. I could have broken every bone in my body and it wouldn't have kept me from this moment." He showed them a fax Chief Connelley had sent to Sam's house last night. Jake pointed to the bottom of the page. "Look at the initials." He explained the supervisor's initials on Samuel Casey's accident investigation. "Connelley was the supervisor who closed the case. It was under Connelley's authority that no further examination was made of the evidence gathered from the scene of Samuel Casey's accident. Connelley was Casey's closest friend. And six months after Casey's death, Don Connelley was promoted to chief of police."

Frank shook his head in disbelief. "So Connelley was pressured by Preston to drop the investigation."

"That would be my guess," Jake replied. "Preston has probably been holding it over his head all this time. Since Benny confirmed that the body in the Jeep was Chief Connelley, all the answers we need went up in smoke. The only one who might have heard Connelley's explanation is Sam."

Frank asked, "So how does Murphy figure in all this? Are his hands lily white?"

"Far as we can tell," Carl explained, "he's only guilty of keeping a local politician apprised of community matters. Murphy had no idea Hilliard was involved in anything other than politics as usual, one hand washing the other sort of thing. Contrary to our hopes, he passed a polygraph." Carl pressed his hand to his ear piece. "We better get in there."

They gathered in the back of the auditorium—Carl, Jake, Frank, and Lincoln Thomas. A sea of uniforms from all branches of the armed forces sat in silence and with some admiration for the speaker as he told of his war experiences and his efforts to pass bills for increased health care and disability benefits for veterans. The press was moving around distractingly in the first two rows. Preston talked over their heads, addressing only the audience, gazing up at those in the balcony, across the long rows on the main level.

Carl handed Jake an envelope.

"What's this?"

Several heads turned toward them. One matronly

woman in dress blues placed a finger to her lips and gave them an annoyed "shhhhhhhh."

They found a small secluded alcove by the door where they could whisper. "David Noland, Parker Smith's attorney, sent this by courier," Carl said. "It was Parker's instructions that it not be opened until after his death. This is the nail in Preston's coffin."

Jake unfolded the letter and while Frank held a small flashlight, read the confession signed by Parker Smith admitting his involvement in the 1951 killings in Mushima Valley, and accusing Preston of not only ordering the executions but also personally shooting one of the victims twice in the back of the head.

"What about Hap and Sam's father?" Jake asked.

"Cain was our only proof that could link Preston to the murders of Hap and Samuel Casey," Frank whispered. "And there are no witnesses that Preston knew Cain now or twenty years ago. The butler never met him and Preston's housekeeper has left the country."

"But, Carl, your men have photos of Cain entering and leaving Preston's house," Jake reminded him.

"True, but no photos with Cain and Preston together. Preston can always say Cain was casing the place out."

Jake handed the letter back to Carl. "At least Hap's affidavit proves he was going to confront Preston."

Folding the letter back into the envelope, Carl said, "My men did find the pin in Preston's safe. Maybe we can find Cain's prints in the house. Maybe we can find Cain's prints on the bomb in Sam's Jeep. My money says Cain killed the officer last night but he wore gloves so only Sam's prints were on the gun."

"Take a look at this." Frank handed Jake a copy of the press release. "Looks like Tim's programming worked like a charm."

Jake smiled when he saw Hap's and Samuel Casey's

reports. "I'm sure Preston thinks the press is looking at embarrassing photos of Meacham."

Something Preston said rewarded him with thunderous applause. He held up his hands to silence the crowd, some of who stood up to cheer. Preston had just announced that he planned to run for governor.

"Mr. Hilliard, Mr. Hilliard." A wiry reporter with a resonant voice started to speak.

"Questions, later, if you don't mind," Preston pleaded.

"But what about the press release we received this morning?" another voice asked.

Preston had prepared a quick speech regarding the unfortunate incident involving Governor Meacham but another reporter cut him off before he had a chance to speak.

A smartly dressed woman from Channel Seven News stood up. "What about these allegations concerning Korea?"

Preston blinked. *Korea?* "What?" he stammered. "What are you talking about?"

Six reporters tried speaking at once. Ivan Lambert was handed several sheets of paper. He teetered over to the podium and handed them to Preston. Expecting to see the pictures he had sent on Meacham, he was horrified to see a written affidavit by Hap Wilson and Samuel Casey.

"What on earth? This is preposterous!" Preston's face twisted into an expression of startled horror. The flood gate of questioning opened up.

"Is there any truth?"

"Did you murder those boys?"

"How many did you kill?"

"Did you have anything to do with Hap Wilson's death?"

"What about Samuel Casey?"

They fired questions at him from all directions. The murmur from the audience grew louder as shock and realization settled in. Those that had been standing for the round of applause, sat back down.

Preston held up his hands and yelled, "ENOUGH." A hush fell over the crowd. "This is an election year. For someone to circulate this kind of blasphemy is an outrage." He pounded the podium sending pages of his speech floating to the floor. "I am a decorated hero. How can anyone believe accusations surfacing now about something allegedly happening over forty years ago. My fellow veterans ..." He stretched his opened arms toward them. "How can anyone believe the ramblings of a war deserter?"

"What about one of your men who you ordered to participate in the killings?" Carl shouted as he walked down the aisle toward the stage. Heads, cameras, and microphones turned his way. He held up Parker Smith's envelope saying, "Carl Underer, FBI Director."

Cameras started flashing. Gasps and comments could be heard as he passed the rows of spectators.

"Name, names, Mr. Director," Preston challenged. "I've nothing to hide."

"I have a signed confession from Parker Smith." A portable microphone was shoved into Carl's hand as he read Smith's account of Mushima Valley and how the true heroes had been Hap and his unit and how they had been needlessly eliminated.

Preston laughed. "Parker Smith had been delusional since he was released from the Army on a physical disability. What we had seen in that valley had a traumatic effect on him. On all of us. And if he did sign anything, someone put him up to it. No." Preston waved a finger back and forth as though scolding him. "You are going to have to do better than that."

"All right. How about an eyewitness?" Carl turned toward the back of the auditorium. Heads swiveled again. Cameramen jockeyed for unobstructed views. "Do you remember a young house boy named Ling Toy?"

Lincoln walked proudly down the ramp. His eyes glared at Preston. Soft murmurs rumbled through the crowd. Lincoln looked into the faces of the veterans he passed. Shock replaced the skepticism Preston had tried to plant in their minds. Disgust and revulsion replaced the admiration.

Preston's world was disintegrating before his eyes. He moved away from the podium, his exit blocked by two FBI agents.

Epilogue

Jake watched Abby and Sam from behind a glass door. The nurse had told him he could go in but he wasn't sure he could handle the rejection again, that vacant stare in Sam's eyes of complete lack of recognition.

After spending two days being evaluated by department shrinks and private psychiatrists, Sam had been officially suspended by Captain Murphy pending her testimony on the death of Stu Richards. She had not uttered a word since Jake found her in his apartment.

Alex frowned as he observed Abby with Sam. He played with his hat, running the brim through his fingers as if it were a coil of rope. "Abby should have never brought Sam home years ago. They should have stayed on the reservation. That's where she belongs."

Jake wasn't in the mood to go another round with Alex. Alex must have had a glimmer of regret because he clamped a hand on Jake's shoulder and added, "The doctor says she is already getting better." Alex turned and mumbled something about going to get the car.

Jake lifted his right arm to give a wave, but winced. A cast ran up close to Jake's elbow, leaving only the tip of his right thumb exposed. X-rays had revealed seven broken bones and a fractured radius. He was having a hard time getting used to this unwanted attachment to his body.

He watched Alex cross the spacious lobby with its

marble floors and ornate archways. The Sara Binyons Retreat was located about two hours south of Chicago in a small town near Terre Haute, Indiana. It was out in the country on two hundred acres of peaceful streams and wooded meadows.

It was not a place for the criminally insane or patients with serious mental problems. Some prominent politicians and Hollywood-types were known to frequent Sara Binyons when they wanted to get away from their hectic lives.

On a wide-screen TV in the lobby Jake could see a re-broadcast of a ceremony held earlier at Arlington National Cemetery. President Whittier had awarded the Distinguished Service Cross, Congressional Medal of Honor, and Purple Heart posthumously to Sergeant Booker J. Jones, Calvin Leeds, Shamus Lewis, and Harvey Wilson.

The crowd of politicians, family, war veterans, and press, applauded President Whittier's remarkable gesture. The screen showed Carl standing with his arm around a black-veiled Matilda Banks, Hap's sister, who clutched the folded American flag.

The broadcast cut away to the Korean War Veterans Memorial at the west end of the mall near the Lincoln Memorial. Workmen had just finished engraving the four names of the honored recipients in the granite wall. The camera panned the mural of sand-blasted images of medics, chaplains, and support troops. Near an image of the Korean peninsula were the words, *Freedom is Not Free.*

The TV reporter made a closing statement, "More than fifty-four thousand Americans died in the Korean War. That number has just increased by four."

"It was still a wonderful gesture on the president's part," Abby remarked as she appeared in the doorway, a picture of tranquillity wrapped in festive cotton and a sunshine smile.

"His arm is probably still sore from Sam twisting it." Jake looked past Abby's shoulder at Sam. A stocky, red-haired nurse with a cherub face was coaxing Sam off the couch.

Jake leaned against the door jamb finding it hard to restrain the impulse to run in there and carry Sam out of this place. The last time he had seen her hair loose and carefree, she had been lying in his bed. He looked away again.

Abby tapped his arm. "Let's go."

Nurse Petree placed her hands on Sam's shoulders. "It's time to go back to your room, Dear." Mrs. Petree's fingers touched Sam's necklace. "Oh, my. I'm sorry, Miss Casey. Jewelry is not allowed." She fumbled with the clasp. "Let me give this to your mother before she leaves."

Sam watched as the sunlight bounced off the lightning bolt pendant. The way the nurse held the necklace reminded her of another time it was held in front of her, with the pendant swinging, someone's muscular arms reaching around her neck to fasten it. Sam inhaled the scent of a woodsy aftershave. She remembered a man's rugged, handsome face.

Reaching out, she grabbed the necklace from Mrs. Petree's fingers. For a brief moment, other memories flooded back. That same man, holding her tightly in a darkened room. She could see his chiseled features, the sharp angle of his chin. Her head turned quickly toward the door.

"Miss Casey, wait!" Mrs. Petree hurried after Sam.

Sam rushed past the potted calla lilies resting on the sill of the tall, narrow windows lining the wide hallway. When they heard the commotion, Abby and Jake turned around. Cautiously, Sam approached Jake. Her eyes moved from his face to the pendant. Slowly, she reached up and fastened it around his neck.

Jake gathered her in his arms and held her tightly, inhaling the smell of her hair. He could feel her body tremble but she didn't push away. He whispered, "Just remember, I love you."

She didn't pull away when he kissed her on the mouth. Her face was masked in confusion as she backed away from him. As Mrs. Petree led her back down the hallway, Sam stole several glances over her shoulder at Jake.

Jake and Abby walked along the brick circular driveway to a sidewalk framed in low shrubs. Tall oak trees near the curb loomed overhead, shading them from the late morning sun.

"You will move in with us, Jacob. You are family now. It will make the waiting less painful."

"Listen, Abby, I know it's customary for you to choose your daughter's husband."

Abby hugged him and laughed. "But Jacob, you WERE my choice."

Puzzled, he thought back to the strange visions he had of Sam when he was in the whirlpool, the all-consuming love that seemed to mushroom overnight.

"You mean that my feelings for Sam aren't real?"

"Of course they are. But there was so much animosity between the two of you at first that I didn't think you'd ever get to know each other. So I just had you see each other through my eyes, to see the good points. The spirits took over from there."

"I just wish Sam and I had been able to talk. We left a lot of things unsaid. When she remembers the last argument we had..." Jake gave a hopeless shrug. "I don't know if she's going to be very happy with this arrangement."

"She has no choice in the matter."

"Everyone has a choice, Abby. Besides, she's very headstrong."

"Ahh, yes." Abby entwined her arm through his as they continued their walk to the curb. "But who do you think she got it from?"

Abby knew fate always wins out. When she had touched Jake's scars that day, she saw more than just his pained childhood. She saw children, all blond-haired. Some with blue eyes so bright they seemed to glow. And some with soft brown, the color of doeskin.

END

BIBLIOGRAPHY

Keith, Sidney. *English-Lakota Dictionary,* Black Hills State University, 1989.

Lake-Thom, Bobby. *Spirits of the Earth. A Guide to Native American Nature Symbols, Stories, and Ceremonies*, Penguin Books USA Inc., 1997.

Nylander, August. *Survival of a Noble Race,* Argus Printers, 1987.

Powers, William K. Yuwipi, *Vision & Experience in Oglala Ritual*, University of Nebraska Press, 1984.

Wall, Steve. *Wisdom's Daughters, Conversations With Women Elders of Native America*, HarperCollins, 1993.

Wall, Steve and Arden, Harvey. *Wisdomkeepers, Meetings With Native American Spiritual Elders,* Beyond Words Publishing, Inc. 1990.

Walker, James R. *Lakota Myth,* University of Nebraska Press, 1989.

Zeilinger, Ron. *Sacred Ground, Reflections of Lakota Spirituality and the Gospel,* Tipi Press.

Zeilinger, Ron and Charging Eagle, Tom. *Black Hills: Sacred Hills*, Tipi Press 1987.

••••••••••••••••••••••

Bussey, Lt. Col. Charles M. USA (Ret). *Firefight at Yechon - Courage and Racism in the Korean War*, Brassey's, Inc. A Division of MacMillan, Inc., 1991.

Rice, Earle Jr. *The Inchon Invasion*, Lucent Books, 1996.

Stokesbury, James L. *A Short History of the Korean War,* Morrow, 1988.

Sullivan, John A. *Toy Soldiers - Memoir of a Combat Platoon Leader in Korea*, McFarland & Co., Inc., 1991.

DATE DUE